Praise for the work of

Girl Squad

Intrigue, romance, and girl power: Hoover's debut novel delivers that and more with small-town Texas charm. In this story set during the 1970s in Dumas, Texas, readers meet Cal on the day she learns to her great distress that her parents are getting separated. But distraction arrives in the form of the new girl, Jane, who recently relocated to the area with her wealthy family after living in big cities. When 15-year-old Cal and her best friend, freckle-faced Rachel, get to know Jane at church camp, Cal develops feelings for Jane, and they soon pursue a romantic relationship. However, Cal is worried about her mother's relationship with a strange man. When her mom goes missing, the trio's amateur sleuthing leads them into trouble. Worried that her mom's involvement with an organized crime leader may have led to her being kidnapped, the girls continue to snoop until they are caught in the center of the action. The drama unfolds at an even pace between the new couple struggling to come to terms with their feelings and social expectations while solving the mysterious affair between Cal's mom and the criminal mastermind. Ultimately Cal comes to understand the complexities both of her mother's situation and her own identity. Major characters are assumed white; Native American characters are referred to generically without recognition of their nations. A mystery/thriller wrapped in a hopeful coming-of-age and coming-out tale.

-Kirkus Reviews

I loved how fun and original the story was. I had no idea how it would end. It was a satisfying ending with a satisfying story and great characters.

-The Lesbian Review

(Un)finished

Kim Hoover

Other Bella Books by Kim Hoover

Girl Squad

About the Author

Kim Hoover is a lawyer by training, a real estate entrepreneur by experience and a writer by nature. Raised in Texas, she spent three decades in Washington, DC, where she built her career and her family. She and her wife of twenty-five years raised two daughters there and now split their time between Miami and New York City. In her spare time, Kim is most likely curled up with a cup of coffee and her latest political advocacy project or philanthropic endeavor. She is a board member of Voices for Progress, Advocates for Youth, and the Affordable Housing Advisory Board of Miami-Dade County, Florida.

(Un)finished

Kim Hoover

BELLA
BOOKS
2023

Bella Books, Inc.
P.O. Box 10543
Tallahassee, FL 32302

Printed in the United States of America on acid-free paper.

First Edition - 2023

Editor: Kay Grey
Cover Designer: Heather Honeywell

ISBN: 978-1-64247-466-4

Dedication

To my wife, Lynn, and my daughters, Stephanie and Lauren, for their steadfast love and support. I love you all, always and forever.

CHAPTER ONE

May, 2016

I got the call early on a Sunday morning—too early. Six a.m. At least she had politely waited for the sun to rise on the West Coast. I was already awake, up and stretching in the driveway of our Victorian row house, prepping for my daily run.

"Wait," I said, walking back inside, but speaking softly so as not to disturb my sleeping wife. "Alex, slow down. I can't understand what you're saying."

"He's dead! I said Dave's dead!"

She sobbed into the phone.

"What? Oh my god," I said. "What happened?"

"He shot himself," she said, her voice hoarse and deep. "He blew his fucking head off."

"Oh my god, oh my god, oh shit," I said, pushing at my brow as I slowly started to comprehend my sister's words.

"You have to come home," she said, sobbing again. "I'm losing it. Mom won't understand what's happening and I can't handle all this shit by myself. I can't believe he did this to me."

"I'm so sorry, Alex. I'll get there as soon as I can."

I walked back to my bedroom slowly, entering the room, watching Mary sleep for a moment or two before nudging her awake.

"Alex just called," I said, an edge in my voice.

"What's wrong?"

"It's Dave. He—" My voice broke.

"He what? What is it?"

She sat up, alert, reaching for my hand.

"He killed himself. With a gun."

"Oh, no. Oh, god. Poor Alex."

"Yeah, it's bad."

"How did she seem?"

"Fucked up," I said. "Pissed at him."

"So selfish," Mary said, trying to pull me down next to her. I resisted.

"There's so much to deal with. The kids. His business. And meanwhile, there's Mom."

"Are you leaving right away?"

"I have to," I said.

"I guess that's right, but…" She turned away. "We need to talk."

"Maybe this is"—I hesitated—"a good time for us to take a break."

She threw the covers off and stood up.

"Jen," she said, "don't push me away."

"Don't let someone else in our bed!"

"Stop it!"

She slammed her fist into a pillow.

"One time. One fucking time," she said, raising her voice almost to the point of a shout. Then lowered it. "When you hadn't been home in a month."

"Oh, is that the test? I'm busting my ass on a road show and you can't keep yourself busy enough to dodge some teenager coming at you?"

"She was not a teenager."

"Whatever. I have to get to Dallas."

"I don't want to lose you," she said, reaching for me.

"I just can't do this right now, Mary. I'll call you when I get there."

"What about Eli and Claire? We should let them know about Dave."

"Please call them. And tell Claire she doesn't need to come. She needs to stay focused on school."

"Okay. Will Alex do a service?"

"I don't know, but as soon as I have details, I'll let everyone know."

"Let me hug you," she said.

I stood stiff while she hugged me and unresponsive when she kissed me. But I agreed to let her drive me to the airport. We rode along in silence. She tried to hold my hand, but I couldn't bear it. I could still see it in my imagination, so vividly I felt I'd been there. Some kid, twenty-something, had tasted my wife's sweet sex in our own home. Had sweated in my bed. Had pissed in my toilet. I retched thinking about it.

"Sweetie, please. Talk to me," she said, pleading for my attention. "I love you. You're everything to me. Please say something."

"Clearly I'm not everything to you."

I stared out the window, the fog burning off the hills as we sped down the road to SFO.

"And don't be so selfish," I said. "Alex is going through hell. Worse than hell. Think about her for a change."

"Let me come with you. I can help with your mom. She loves me."

"I need some time, Mary. I don't know if I can get past this."

She pulled the car off on the shoulder and slid to a stop, erupting into tears, heaving with deep belly sobs. I softened, so quickly won over by her raw, unselfconscious pain. I drew her to me, holding her while she soaked my blouse in her regret.

"I can't bear the thought of life without you," she said, looking at me through disheveled strands of hair. "Please don't leave me. Please forgive me."

I kissed her forehead, smoothed her hair away from her face.

"We need to get going or I'll miss my plane. I'll drive."

I got out at the terminal and kissed her goodbye lightly, resisting when she tried to go deeper.

"Call me when you land," she said, her eyes damp again.

On the plane I kept going back to what had happened the month before. For the first time in twenty years, I questioned how I felt about my wife. Her betrayal had done more than hurt me; it had changed my basic assumptions about myself. Since the day I knew I was in love with her, I had never once considered life without her. I hadn't seen it coming. The tryst with the girl. Now what I questioned wasn't so much my marriage, but my own awareness. What about Mary had I misunderstood so profoundly? Was I somehow to blame? Why had she thought that she could keep her relationship with me intact while indulging in an affair with a young woman not much older than our own children? By the time I landed in Dallas, I had so thoroughly relived every detail of that painful incident that I was almost in tears. I hoped it wasn't over for good, but I couldn't guess at the end of the story. Not yet.

* * *

"There you are!"

Alex ran to me as I came through the doorway of her suburban McMansion north of Dallas. She crushed me with a bear hug, knocking me off balance.

"I'm so sorry, Al. I can't imagine…"

"The cowardly son of a bitch," she said. "He's fucked me good this time."

"Jesus. I know. What do we need to do right away?"

"Oh, god, Jen. I don't know where to start."

She settled me into a bedroom upstairs and we ended up in her kitchen, the size of a small restaurant, filled with people she knew bringing food and trying to be helpful. Her two teenage boys, Ben (sixteen) and Harry (thirteen), wandered the room, looking haunted and threatening at the same time. They asked permission to go to their friends' houses and Alex let them go.

"Can you believe he did this to them?"

The house cleared eventually and it was just the two of us.

"What kind of service will you do?"

"The most minimal I can do. He didn't have any friends left. He'd alienated everyone. I want to get it behind me so I can start sorting out the mess he made of his company."

"It's tragic, Al. How did it come to this?"

She slumped into a chair, pushed her glasses on top of her head, into her mousey brown shoulder-length hair.

"One bad gamble after another. Always swinging for the fences. Sure the next big idea would bail him out of all the failed ones. In debt up to here. Lawsuits. Bankruptcy looming."

"I didn't realize it had gotten to that point."

"He was always the best bullshit artist we knew, right?" She smiled at this, looking far away.

"Yeah, that's Dave all right."

We sat quietly for a moment or two, lost in memories of so many years of his antics.

"We need to talk about Mom," Alex said, breaking the reverie.

"How is she?"

"How long has it been?"

I felt my cheeks burning. "I'm sorry. I know—"

"That's not what I'm getting at. I just don't remember when you were here last."

"I think it's been about six months. Too long."

"She's a little worse. Can't remember anything new. But she's still basically fine on her own, except she eats like a homeless person. She keeps the house. Remembers who everyone is."

"At least there's some good news."

"The problem is, I can't let her drive. She's mad at me about that, so I haven't actually sold the car, just confiscated her keys. With all this crap going on, I need you to stay over there. Cook now and then. Take her where she needs to go."

"Of course. No problem. I'll go over in the morning."

"Thanks, Jenny. I'm so glad you're here," she said, hugging me tight.

"Could I give you some files to look over?" Alex asked me the next morning as I walked back into the house after my run. I was prepping for my first marathon later in the year and couldn't let any distraction, even my brother-in-law's death, get in the way.

"Sure. What files?"

"Dave's stuff. You're a lawyer. Maybe it will make more sense to you than it does to me."

"Okay, but remember, I haven't actually practiced in years."

"I know, but you're my super smart big sister. Just see what you think."

I smirked, then frowned as she brought out several large overflowing bankers boxes full of files.

"Holy shit," I said.

"I know. I told you it's a mess."

I loaded it all into my rental car and drove the short distance to Mom's house.

"Mom!" I said, opening the door to her bungalow, downsized in retirement from their much larger home, in a neighborhood not far from Alex.

"There's my baby girl! Home from California!"

"Hi, Mom. You look great!"

"Thank you, sweetie. Are you still in San Diego?"

"San Francisco, Mom. I've been in San Francisco for more than twenty years."

"Oh, rats. That's right. I don't know why I always think it's San Diego. Same difference anyway."

I frowned, but resisted responding to that. She always tried to push my buttons on my decision to move to San Francisco from Dallas years before.

"What did you have for breakfast?" I asked her.

"Don't listen to Alex. I'm just fine. I had some toast. How's your girlfriend? What's her name again?"

She knew very well it was Mary.

"I'm not playing that game with you, Mom."

"Now, you haven't been here five minutes and you're already picking a fight with me."

"I am not. I just hate it when you act like you can't remember Mary's name. And she's my wife, not my girlfriend."

"I don't know where you get the idea you can have a wife. You know I don't condone all that. I should never have let you go off to California."

"I'm not going to argue with you, Mom. This is a dead issue. Thanks to the Supreme Court. So let's just drop it. And, by the way, it's not California's fault that I'm gay."

"What do you want to watch?" she asked, moving into her study where she spent most of her time in front of the television. "I like Mary. Where is she?"

We sat in the well-worn lounge chairs that dated back to when my father was still alive, some ten years before. Mom was a pro at taping movies and TV shows, and they were almost the only stimulation she had these days.

"Mary is at home. She's busy with work. Doctors can't work remotely, you know, especially when they're surgeons."

"Oh, that's right. I forget. You know, my mind's not what it used to be. How about *Dancing with the Stars*?"

I brought the boxes of files into the study and sat on the floor going through them while Mom fixated on the competition unfolding on the television. When an ad for Hillary Clinton's primary campaign came on, Mom perked up.

"Don't you have something to do with her?"

"Hillary? Yes, I'm one of the California Finance Committee chairs for her campaign."

"That sounds like a big job."

"Lots of fundraising," I said, prepared to go on, but Mom was quickly back to her dance competition.

Before long, I discovered that Dave's company had been forced into involuntary bankruptcy and, as far as I could tell, he hadn't hired an attorney. I would need to fix that right away. I sat back, suddenly flushed, my heart pumping adrenaline into my chest, memories of Laura Peters crashing in on me without warning. I had followed her career from afar and knew she was one of the best bankruptcy attorneys in all the United States. But

I hadn't spoken with her since… I couldn't bring myself to think about it. Not even after all these years. So much had happened since then, but, sitting there on the floor in my mother's house, the wound was throbbing again, like an almost-healed gash torn open anew.

"Don't you want to watch?" Mom asked, jolting me back to the present. "What's all this paper everywhere?"

"I'm helping Alex with some legal issues. I'll clean it up."

"That husband of hers. He's always in trouble. I'll never understand why she stays with him."

Alex had warned me she wouldn't remember, so I didn't bother to correct her.

"I need to make a phone call, Mom. I'll be back in a little while."

CHAPTER TWO

Summer, 1996

"I'm Laura Peters," said a good-looking young woman, her shoulder-length hair pulled back and clipped with a simple barrette. She held her hand out to me in the conference room where, as new associates, we had been instructed to report.

Her grip was strong, but her hands were soft. I noticed because she cupped mine in both of hers as she drew me closer and whispered, "So glad to see another girl."

"Woman!" I scolded.

"Of course," she said, smiling at me. "Time to grow up."

"All right, ladies and gentlemen," said the partner in charge of orienting us. "For the next six weeks, we'll pay you to study for the bar exam. Just report to work every morning for a few hours of billables. Then study in the afternoon. And pass the bar!"

As we got into the groove of work/gym/study/class, a camaraderie developed across new lawyers from all over town. On the weekends, a large group of us would go out and drink. A lot. And, of course, it being Texas, we drove.

I had an out-of-town boyfriend who would show up occasionally, but I discouraged him for the most part because I really didn't have the time for him. Laura also had a relationship, but she kept him scarce as well.

"Because of the bar exam," she said.

One Friday night, three weeks in, I got so drunk that even I knew I couldn't drive myself, and Laura volunteered to take me home with her. She staggered under my dead weight as she half-carried me up the stairs to her second-floor apartment. My head, suspended on the thread of my neck like a yo-yo, lolled to her shoulder and I surprised myself by breathing deeply into the scent of her skin. Endorphins flooded my brain and I held tighter to my rescuer to keep from tumbling down the stairs. In her bedroom, she handed me a T-shirt and, thanking her, I asked for socks, my tongue so thick it sounded as though I wanted chalk.

As I lay in Laura's bed that night, sobering up in that way that keeps you awake, I sat up on one side and stared at her sleeping soundly. Her camisole and panties matched in satiny taupe. Her strawberry-blond hair decorated her pillow in a swan-like pattern. Her tan skin stretched over an athlete's body. Observing her this way prompted a reprise of my admiration for her finish in an Ironman Triathlon that spring. Her dedication had inspired me to think about at least trying a triathlon, though I had only ever done a 10K and I couldn't swim more than a lap or two at a time. As I continued to gaze at her peaceful and sweetly sexy pose, I had the most overwhelming urge to touch her. The intensity of the desire jolted me, draining the blood from my brain and mimicking intoxication. I turned away from her, sure I would make a mistake if I kept looking. I fell hard asleep at that point and woke the next morning feeling ashamed, as though I'd followed through.

"You closed the place down last night, you know?" she said, smiling. "I'm impressed."

"I feel like there's a little dude in my head with a hammer and he's hanging shelving or something," I said, barely able to open my eyes. "Oh my god."

"There's Advil in the bathroom cabinet."

"Thanks for rescuing me. I don't usually get that crazy."

"I'm sure you'd do the same for me. Maybe next weekend!" She laughed. "Hey, wanna get some breakfast? We can walk to a little diner a couple of blocks from here."

"Sounds good. Let me wash my face."

In the bathroom, I tried deep breathing to get my heartbeat down in a normal range. Something about her and this situation wouldn't stop suggesting outlandish ideas to my otherwise boringly hetero inclination. Wasn't there a vibe from her? Weren't my crazy visions of pushing her onto the bed and taking her clothes off coming from somewhere besides nowhere? I thought about it. Imagined what it might feel like to touch her. My heart raced again.

"Forget it," I said to myself as I slapped water onto my face and dressed quickly, doing my best to block out thoughts of sex with her.

One last look in the mirror revealed my untamable shock of brown hair. My solution was to grab a UT cap off her shelf on the way out.

"Hope you don't mind. I'll wash it and get it back to you," I said.

"Keep it. It looks good on you." She smiled.

As we walked to the diner, I sipped the coffee she had handed me on the way out the door, grateful for the caffeine that revived me with every step. Along the way, she narrated the story of her neighborhood.

"There's an amazing flea market that happens over there in that field on Sundays. You would not believe the stuff that people buy. I like to wander through just for entertainment. Oh, and look at that. That body shop has been here since the twenties. The guy who owns it worked for his dad, who worked for his dad, who founded it."

I grunted a response now and then, but mostly I enjoyed the sound of her voice. She spoke with authority, and with a confidence that I found magnetic.

At the diner, we ordered eggs and bacon and biscuits. I ordered mine over medium. She ordered hers sunny side up. I watched, weirdly enchanted, as she sopped up the egg yolk with her biscuit and sucked on the bread before biting into it.

"What are you doing after the bar exam?" she asked, as we sat satiated from the food and the coffee.

"I was thinking Europe. I've never been there. I don't have exact plans, but there are plenty of people from school who'll be over there, so I guess I'll hook up with whoever."

"What about your boyfriend?" she asked.

"I don't know. He can't get that kind of time off. He might come over for a week. Or not. We'll see. What about you?"

"Europe for sure. Maybe you and I could hook up? We'd make a great wing woman team." She winked.

"No Mike?"

"Nah, I want to have fun, if you know what I mean."

"Of course," I said, eyeing her closely. "Let's talk about it. Like I said, I don't have any concrete plans yet."

"I was thinking we should start in London," she said, assuming the sale. "Some kids from my class are going there first. Then Paris, maybe Germany or Brussels. And Amsterdam for sure."

"How could I say no when you've got it all so well planned out?"

"That's what I wanted to hear."

She smiled at me in a way that drew me in, as though to a secret club made up of just us two, her eyes fixed on mine for a beat too long, like she wanted to say something more. Something dangerous, maybe.

"Okay," I said, pulling my eyes to my plate. "Let's take a look at some flights and train schedules and stuff like that next week, if you want."

"I can't wait," she said, back to business. "I'm so tired of this grind right now."

"The last mile."

"Speaking of miles, how about taking a run with me. First thing in the morning. Before it's too hot."

"Oh, I don't know. You're way out of my league. I don't run that fast."

"That's okay. I have to do a slow run tomorrow. Part of my training."

I hemmed and hawed a bit, but finally agreed, sorry almost immediately, as I considered how painful it would likely be.

"Hey, c'mon. I'll drop you at your car," she said, announcing the end of our sleepover.

She tugged at the bill of my cap as she got up from the table and lightning flew through me. I questioned her motives as I followed her out of the diner, fixated on her body, clad in tank top and running shorts. I wondered whether she was doing this on purpose. Flirting with me. Or was I simply hypnotized by the unselfconscious sexuality she exuded with every step.

Our Sunday run was, as I predicted, excruciating for me. We met up in Trinity Park at seven a.m. She wanted to do ten miles, but I negotiated her back to 10K. Her slow pace was a lung burner for me. I checked my heart rate monitor halfway in and, clocking a seven-minute mile, I was anaerobic.

We ended at the flea market in her neighborhood and I collapsed onto a bench, my head between my knees, happy to have made it.

"You can do a triathlon, girl," she said, sitting next to me, not even breathing hard. "You just need to train."

"No joke?"

"Yeah, assuming you know how to swim."

She grabbed my hand and pulled me to my feet, dragging me toward a taco stand. I swallowed hard, desire for her boiling up in me. The rest of the world faded away and all I could see was her, laughing and smiling at me as we walked hand in hand through the market.

CHAPTER THREE

"Alex," I said, keeping my voice low on the phone because Mom could hear a dog whistle. "Mom has no memory of what's happened to Dave."

"I told you. That's the kind of thing she can't retain. We'll have to explain it to her over and over."

"It sucks."

"It does."

"Hey, I've been over these files lightly. And this is way worse than I would have ever thought," I said.

"Is there a way out?"

"I don't know. Did he ever talk to you about any of this?"

"No. He stopped discussing business with me years ago. What is it you've found? I can tell it's not good."

I hesitated before plunging ahead with the bad news.

"It looks like he emptied the kids' college trust funds. Unfortunately, he was the trustee under his parents' will."

"Are you fucking kidding me?"

She started crying and I instantly regretted having the conversation over the phone.

"Oh my fucking god!"

I could hear her screaming and throwing things.

"Alex!"

A few more seconds went by. Then she picked up the phone, whimpering. My heart ached for her.

"What do I do now? When does this stop?"

"I understand how you feel, Alex. This is truly awful. And there's more, but I'm going to help you through this."

"What else have you found?"

"Well, this is very strange to me, but a rare bookstore in London filed a petition for involuntary bankruptcy against Dave's company. We have to meet with a lawyer as soon as possible."

"This just gets better and better. How am I supposed to pay for that?"

"Don't worry about that right now. Apparently, he hasn't done anything to respond to this filing. We need to get on it."

"Do you know someone?"

"Do you remember Laura Peters?"

"Oh, shit. Of course I remember her. How could I forget?"

"Well, she happens to be one of the top bankruptcy lawyers in the country now. So I think I should call her."

"You're kidding," she said soberly, her tears apparently dried in their tracks. "That's awkward."

"Yeah," I said, breathing a long sigh. "It will be extremely awkward. But I can't let that stand in the way of getting you the best possible help with this situation. It may take a miracle to salvage it for you and the kids."

"Oh, Jenny. How did this happen? How could I have been so stupid?"

"It's not your fault. No one saw this coming. Stop beating yourself up. You need to be strong for the kids."

"You're right, as usual. The kids are the only thing keeping me partially sane."

"I know you probably don't want to talk about this right now, but what about the funeral arrangements?"

"Yeah, we all need to get past that, so I've decided to cremate him and do the smallest possible service at the chapel. I'm trying to schedule it for the day after tomorrow. It doesn't make sense for your kids to come, but will Mary make it?"

"I, uh, I'm not sure. I'll have to check with her. She may be on call."

"Is something wrong? You sound like there's something wrong."

"Umm, oh, I don't know, it's, oh, god, it's a rough time for us right now."

"What's going on?"

"Do you mind if we don't talk about it yet? I can tell you she's desperate to be here. For you and for Mom. But, I don't know, there's just…something happened and I don't really want to see her right now."

"That's awful! I never thought anything would come between you and her."

"I know. Neither did I."

"Shit."

"Look, I don't want to be selfish about this. I guess I should ask her to come for the service."

"Well, honestly, I think it would help Mom, if nothing else."

* * *

"I'll catch the red eye tonight," Mary said when I called her. "I love you."

"Yeah," I said. "I'll pick you up at the curb."

I ended the call with Mary and Googled Laura Peters. Her firm profile came up, a glowing recitation of her accomplishments over the years. She was famous for working out the complicated and circuitous entanglements of high-rolling businesspeople in a way that allowed them to walk away with far more than any normal person would think was fair. But hey, that's the law and she's good at it. She was a partner at one of the largest firms in the state. She was married to a male lawyer in another firm, and they had two children. All neat and tidy.

My thumb hovered over the telephone number highlighted on the screen. My tongue lay heavy in my mouth, like a piece of felt. My heartbeat responded to the adrenaline surge. I couldn't make the call. Not yet.

I tossed and turned in bed that night, keyed up over the prospect of having to get in touch with Laura Peters. Finally, I gave up and went out to take a predawn run, the scene of my last encounter with her playing over and over in my mind. I considered the possibility of finding a different lawyer, but dismissed that thought as cowardly. Surely twenty-plus years of separation could temper the emotion around what happened between us.

I glanced at my watch and was shocked at how long I'd been out. I had to rush and didn't have time to change before heading to the airport to pick up my wife. As she came out of the terminal, looking around for my nondescript rental car, I caught my breath. Mary was still one of the most beautiful women I had ever seen. Even at this hour, after an overnight flight, she was stunning. Her beauty was casual, not enhanced by makeup or fashion. She wore ripped-up white jeans and a sleeveless black cotton shirt. Her sandals, with a one-inch heel, gave a sexy lift to her 5'7" frame. Her arm muscles were defined just enough to let you know she worked at it. Her sandy colored hair, highlighted with blond streaks, fell at her jaw line.

"Over here!" I said, stepping out of the car to get her attention.

She exploded into a bundle of emotion, running toward me, smiling and crying at the same time. She collided with me, planting her lips on mine and pinning me against the car. Her hands crept under the thin material of my running shorts, but I pushed her away.

"Okay, okay," I said. "Get in the car, please."

"How is Alex?" she said as we drove toward my mother's house.

"Just what you would expect. Like a soldier marching through the jungle, fighting off predators. Defending her troops."

"You've been going through Dave's business affairs?"

"I've just gotten started. It's worse than any of us thought. I'm not even close to the bottom of it yet."

"And your mom?"

"She has no idea what's going on. That's where you can really help us," I said, looking at her for the first time since she got in the car.

"You know I'll do whatever you need me to do."

She tried to hold my hand, but I pulled it back.

"I love you," she said. "I'm going to keep telling you that."

I took a deep breath and stared straight ahead.

"Just talk to her. Keep her company. We'll explain things to her as they happen. There's no point in doing it in advance because she doesn't remember anything new."

Mom was thrilled to see Mary. Despite her obligatory reminders that she could not condone my relationship with Mary, she loved her as much or more than she did me.

"I'm so glad you're here," she said, hugging Mary and offering her a cup of coffee. "Jen is my daughter, and I love her, but she's, well, she's a workaholic. All she does is sit on that computer or dig around through a bunch of paperwork."

"Well, Mom, what would you like to do?" Mary said, giving me a sidewise glance.

"Let's go watch the last episode of *So You Think You Can Dance*." She winked. "I just know that little boy from Oklahoma is going to win it!"

"I'll put your stuff in the study," I said to Mary.

"Why?" Mom asked. "I thought you were married?"

Mary started laughing and I had to smile a little, myself.

"She's got you there," Mary said to me pointedly.

"What's wrong with you two?" Mom asked. "You can't fool me."

"It's nothing, Mom."

"Lovers' quarrel. Well, you know what your father always said. 'Don't let the sun go down on your anger.' So work it out before bed tonight!"

Mary and I exchanged a fatalistic look.

"Hey, before I forget, that woman from Hillary Clinton's campaign, I can't remember her name, I ran into her at the grocery store yesterday. She wondered why you hadn't returned her calls, so I told her," Mary said.

"Thanks. Yeah, I have to get to work on a big event we have planned for this summer."

"I'm sorry I'm no help. I can't stand that stuff, as you know."

"Don't worry about it. I have to get over to Alex's. I promised to help her sort out some life insurance questions."

"Jen." Mary stopped me at the door.

"What is it?"

"Your mom is right, you know."

"I think this is a little more complicated than a lovers' quarrel and you know it."

"But the point is that it shouldn't languish unresolved."

"If you want a quick resolution, it's going to be a negative one."

She sighed with exasperation and left me standing at the door.

"Mary," I called to her and she turned expectantly.

"Yes, sweetie," she said without irony.

"Thank you for coming."

"There's no place I'd rather be."

CHAPTER FOUR

In the last two weeks before the bar exam, Laura and I started hanging out one-on-one, studying in her apartment or mine, or talking on the phone. We made plans for our post-bar exam trip.

"What do you think about this?" Laura asked as we sat on her couch combing through reams of pages she had printed from her computer. "We could take this nonstop to London and go by train to the other cities, end up in Amsterdam and fly back from there. All in the budget, as long as we stay in cheap hotels or hostels."

"Were you a travel agent in another life?"

I laughed and poked her shoulder.

"You know, it's amazing what you can do with modern technology. You've heard of the World Wide Web, right?"

"Okay, smart ass. But, yeah, that all sounds perfect. It's weird to think about traveling for thirty days."

"Oh my god, am I crazy? How can I possibly stand you for thirty days straight?"

She pushed me off the couch in a playful shove.

"Well, I guess I can get the BF to come over and relieve you, if necessary," I said. "I can tell you right off the bat one thing that's going to be a problem."

I picked up her tennis shoe, which sat next to me on the floor.

"Your feet stink!"

"What!" she screamed, jumping on top of me and pinning me down, wrestling style.

She held me there, her face close to mine, her breath heavy enough to move the strands of hair that drifted across my eyes. I lay still, ready to surrender to her if only she would take it further. But she didn't. She released her grip and sat next to me, breathing a little quicker than normal, our arms touching. Did she mean to be pressing against me? It seemed that way, but it was just subtle enough that I couldn't be sure. I waited, hoping for something more, and, at the same time, worried that I was completely off base.

"Hey," I said, breaking the silence. "We need to go over Civ Pro one more time. We want to actually pass this stupid test."

We finished the night over a bottle of wine, she insisting that I stay long past what I thought was polite. More than once, I caught her looking at me as a little smile played across her lips, but as my eyes met hers, she would look away. Finally, I insisted it was time for me to leave.

"Be careful driving home," she said. "I shouldn't have let you have that last glass."

"You're not my mom," I said. "See you at the office."

When she said good night and closed the door, I lingered on the stoop, staring at the peephole, half wondering if she was looking back at me. I wanted to go back in. I wanted to ask her what it meant to feel what I was feeling, to ask her if she felt it, too. I lifted my hand to knock, but, terrified by my own desire, let it drop and walked away.

The weekend before the exam, we took a break to do some shopping at a camping store, picking up some gear we needed for our trip.

"What does Mike think about you traipsing off to Europe without him for a month?" I asked.

"I think he's mainly fantasizing about the two of us in a threesome with him when he surprises us somewhere between Paris and Berlin."

I laughed.

"There is some appeal to that." I winked.

"Really? I didn't know he was your type."

"I didn't say anything about him."

She blushed crimson red and turned away quickly.

"Hey, I was just kidding," I said.

"Obviously!"

She took her things to the checkout and kept her back to me until we got to the car.

"Hey, Laura," I said, getting into the car. "It was a joke. Why are you acting so weird?"

"I'm not. Look, I'm sorry. I'm nervous about the test. It sucks that you spend years in school, working your ass off and doing really well, and then your whole career boils down to three days in a room with a timed test."

"It's almost over. And you'll be fine. You know this stuff cold."

She smiled, back to normal.

"Thank you," she said.

Laura and I threw a party the night after the exam. We took over a bar in Lower Greenville and invited everyone we knew. My boyfriend, Chris, came up from Houston. It was the first time he and Laura had met. Before long, I noticed he had her cornered. She looked uncomfortable.

"Hey," I said, taking his elbow, "what's up?"

"I was just getting to know your girlfriend," he said without humor, pushing his glasses up his nose and shifting his feet.

"Seems like Chris doesn't know much about our trip," Laura said, lifting her eyebrows at me.

"Yeah, well, we haven't had much of a chance to talk the last few weeks. I've been a little busy."

I nudged him and said, "Let's talk about this later, okay?"

"I can't believe you made all these plans and never said anything to me."

"I said let's talk about it later."

Laura pulled me aside.

"You didn't tell him you were going away for a month?"

I looked away. I drank the rest of my beer.

"We're not, I don't know, that serious. At least I'm not. I didn't want to get into it with him. I don't need his permission."

"Whatever you say," she said, ordering us both another beer.

I watched her with Mike, his arms around her as she leaned into him, comfortable. I had a strange, vacant feeling that I couldn't shake. Chris pulled me onto the dance floor on a slow song. He whispered as he held me close.

"I've missed you," he said. "It's been too long."

I didn't respond. I held my head against his chest, not looking up at him.

"Why don't I come over for part of your trip?"

I looked at him, pulling away a little.

"It's not that kind of trip."

"What do you mean?"

"It's not a girlfriend-boyfriend thing. I just want to get away with the kids who've been through the same thing I have. You understand."

He walked away, stood at the bar. He ordered shots for everyone and then someone else did. Before long, things got out of hand and the bouncer started pushing us to wrap it up. I tried to say good night to Laura, but Chris pulled me the other way, dragging me out of the bar and down the street toward his car.

"You're too drunk to drive," I said. I was sober enough, but I didn't want to take any chances. Not with the exam results still to come and my bar license yet to be granted. "Let's call a cab."

"It'll take forever. I'll be sober by the time a cab gets here," he said, swaying, his mouth hanging open.

"I'm not getting in the car with you," I said, walking back toward the bar.

"Hey," Laura said, "there you are. I was looking for you guys."

"Chris shouldn't be driving," I said.

"That's why I was looking for you. Mike's got a cab on the way. Come with us."

"Chris! Come on. We're going with them," I snapped at him.

"What about my car?" he complained as we joined Mike in front of the bar.

"Really, dude?" Mike said.

Laura pulled me into the cab in the back seat, next to her and Mike, while Chris was left with the front seat.

"Great party," she said, her arm around my shoulder. "We make a good team."

Her breath on my cheek, warm and moist, stirred an ache in my groin. I leaned my head toward hers, closed my eyes. She locked her foot around my leg and we sat in a near embrace for the rest of the ride. When we got to my apartment, I didn't want to let her go.

"Come in. It's not that late," I said.

"Look at them," she said, pointing to Mike and Chris, both of whom were passed out, their heads dangling like those bobble-headed car toys.

"Let's just get them up the stairs."

The cab driver, a burly guy from Louisiana, helped me with Chris, who weighed in at 190. We got him into my bedroom and he keeled over face-first onto my bed. Mike dozed on the couch. Laura and I poured whiskey and sat out on the balcony overlooking the pool. The July night was hot. A sheen of sweat glistened on Laura's skin, as one of the skinny straps of her silky top slipped halfway down her arm.

"Cheers," I said, "to a new era."

"Good times ahead," she said.

"Does it feel like this is it?" I said.

"What do you mean?"

"You know, like there's nothing more to look forward to. We made it. We're here. Now what?"

She laughed.

"Well, I don't know. I think it's just the beginning," she said. "I have a five-year plan."

"You do? Wow, hmm. Just getting to this point has been my plan forever. I guess I haven't thought about the next plan."

"You don't know where you want to be in five years?" she asked, giving me an astonished look.

"I guess, well, no, when you put it that way. I assume I'll be here. I don't have a reason to be anywhere else right now."

"Why did you go to law school?" Laura asked, swirling the whiskey in her glass.

I thought about that for a half second.

"I picked up a book in the library when I was about thirteen. *Paper Chase*. Remember that one? I thought it was such a great story. So romantic. I got interested in the experience of law school the way he describes it. I didn't really think beyond that too much. I don't have any lawyers in my family."

"That was it? One book?"

"Well, I read a bunch of other books about lawyers. Clarence Darrow. *To Kill a Mockingbird*. There was one called *The Lady and the Law*, or something like that. You know, pretty dramatic stuff. I think I sort of expected to be a hero. Mesmerizing the jury. Saving people from a grave injustice…" I laughed a little. "I had no idea what I was getting into."

"So what do you think now?"

"Uhhhh, well. I mean, working for these big firms, it feels a little boring. Robotic. Long stretches of tedium punctuated by the occasional onset of absolute terror."

"You could have gone to work for the public defender."

I smiled.

"Yes, that's true. I think the bigger issue is that practicing law is probably not my thing. I just have to figure out what is. But, enough about me. What about you?"

"I have an accounting degree and I passed the CPA test after college. But I worked at an accounting firm for a while and couldn't stand it. So law school seemed like a good option. I want to do securities or bankruptcy, corporate stuff, something where the accounting background is relevant."

"No do-gooders in this crowd," I said, leaning forward to clink her glass.

"We can do well and then do good," she said. "Nothing wrong with that."

I stood up to lean over the balcony ledge, yearning for a little breeze. Sweat ran down my back and trickled through my butt crack into my underwear. She got up to stand next to me, sighing as the wind picked up strands of her hair. She took a scrunchie off her wrist and pulled her hair up into a ponytail. Beads of moisture joined together to form a river down her cleavage and my eyes crossed as I followed its route.

"I dare you to skinny-dip with me," I said, nodding toward the pool in the courtyard.

She hesitated for a beat, then said, "You're on!"

We grabbed towels and ran down to the pool. The fence was locked since it was after hours, but I climbed over and opened it for her from the inside. We stripped and jumped in. I didn't try to get a look at her naked, but I could have sworn she looked at me. I treaded water in the middle of the pool. She swam a lap, doing an official turn at the wall, reminding me of her expertise as a swimmer, on top of everything else.

"Pretty slick," I said as she swam toward me, spewing water like a dolphin.

"This feels great. Good call, Jen-meister."

"Want to have a tea party?" I said, joking.

"What a silly idea," she said, but she held her nose and went under.

I joined her at the bottom of the pool. The night lights shone on our bodies as we pretended to sit and drink dainty cups of tea. What I wanted to do was wrap my legs around her and kiss her breasts and more. But what I did was come to the surface, bursting into the air to find Mike staring at me.

"Hey!" I said, greeting him.

"We need to go," he said to Laura as she popped to the surface. "I have to drive to San Antonio in the morning."

"Do you mind?" I said, feeling my nakedness as I swam toward the steps. "We'll be out in a minute."

He left and we scrambled for our towels and clothes.

"That was awesome," I said, wrapping my towel around me.

"Best bar exam party ever," Laura said, pulling her clothes back on over her damp body. "And a lovely tea party, too."

She looked at me, smiling, her eyes lingering a bit, then turned to leave.

"Next stop, London!" she said as she ran to the cab.

CHAPTER FIVE

Alex's house was an obstacle course of food and flowers and unopened mail and balls and cleats and rackets. I picked my way through it to get to her in the kitchen where she sat with stacks of paper piled around her. She looked at me through bloodshot eyes.

"Good morning," she said. "I guess Mary got in okay?"

"She's with Mom," I said. "What's all this?"

"Bank accounts, brokerage statements, the life insurance policy. I'm trying to sort out what I've got. Can you look at this policy? I can't figure out whether it's going to pay."

She handed it to me and I reached for the coffee pot to fill a mug. I cleared a spot on the counter and sat down to work.

"So, what happened with you and Mary?"

I hadn't talked to anyone about it. It would have humiliated me to talk to any of our friends. And, if there was any chance that I could get over it, put it behind us, I didn't want people to know that it had happened. Maybe it was pride, but it was also survival. With Alex, it was different. I wanted to confide in her.

"A few months ago, a new resident came to work at the hospital with Mary. She's a lesbian and she was very aggressive with Mary, flirting with her, wanting to spend time with her, coming to the house for dinner, just hanging around."

I took a few sips of coffee as I remembered the way it unfolded.

"I didn't think too much about it, even though my radar was up a little when she was around. She came on to me, too, but I took it as just, she's a puppy, she's impressed with our lifestyle. That kind of thing. And Mary has mentored these kids before, so it was all in a normal range, I thought."

Alex filled my coffee mug again and squeezed my shoulder as she sat down next to me.

"Then, a couple of months ago, my partners and I were ready to take one of our companies public and I headed out on a road show. I was gone for three or four weeks, but that's always the way it is. We started in New York and made our way west. Nothing out of the ordinary for what I do, right?"

"Of course," Alex said.

"My point is, Mary wants to use that as an excuse for what happened, but that's bullshit. She fucking indulged herself, that's what she did. And she thought she could keep it a secret, which is the worst part. She lied to me."

I couldn't hold back the tears any longer and they soaked my face, falling onto the counter.

"What happened, exactly, and how did you find out?"

Alex handed me some tissue and I wiped my face and blew my nose.

"This kid, her name is Alyssa, came over for dinner one night during my trip. I knew about it. Mary had told me." I paused. "Mary and I have a routine when I'm out of town like that. We talk every night before bed. But that night, she didn't answer her phone.

"I got really pissed that she wasn't answering, but it never occurred to me that anything was going on. I just thought she probably drank too much and fell asleep. I left her some pretty nasty text messages. I said some things I shouldn't have."

I took a deep breath and sipped some coffee.

"The next morning, I look at my phone and there's a long voice mail from Mary. I thought, okay, she's profusely apologizing. But no, it was a butt-dial. It was a recording of them having sex. It was obscene. I vomited from listening to it. I was out of my mind."

"Oh my god," Alex said. "Jesus."

"I was in Chicago when this happened. I had so many thoughts. I wanted to call her up and scream. I wanted to jump on a plane and go straight to the hospital and confront her in public. I wanted to drink myself into oblivion. I wanted to go out and find someone to have sex with."

I had to stop for a moment before I could go on, the memory choking off my voice. When I could speak again, it was almost a whisper.

"In the end, I just walked. I walked the entire length of the path around Lake Michigan from The Drake. I walked all day. I didn't take my phone. I didn't show up for the meetings we had that day. I decided that I wouldn't confront Mary just yet. I would carry on as if it didn't happen. I would finish the road show. I would act like I didn't know anything when I talked to her. I wanted to see what she would do."

"Oh, Jen, I can't believe this."

"I still had ten more days on the road. I talked to her every day. She acted completely normal. When I asked her about Alyssa, she didn't miss a beat. She was an amazing liar. I got angrier and angrier, but I kept it to myself."

I paused, becoming aware of obsessively twisting my wedding ring.

"She picked me up at the airport when I got home, which was unusual. She brought me flowers. Classic, right?"

"Dead giveaway," Alex said.

"I let her put on her show for a couple of hours and then I played her the voice mail."

"Oh my god, what did she do?"

"She turned as red as that apple. She started shaking. She collapsed on the floor, writhing and screaming. She begged me to forgive her. She wanted to explain, but I wouldn't have it. I said horrible things to her. Things I didn't mean. It was awful. We slept in separate bedrooms for a week, but I gave in after that. She swears it was just a stupid mistake. That it only happened that once and will never happen again."

Alex hugged me tight.

"Oh, sweetie," she said. "I feel so bad for y'all."

"It sucks and I'm still angry as hell. I have terrible thoughts, violent thoughts, but, I feel bad even talking about it right now. What you're dealing with, there's no comparison."

"Don't feel bad. This is not a competition. If you lose your partner, you lose your partner. I don't want to see you and Mary break up. You're such a beautiful couple. And your kids would be devastated."

"I know. I know. It's a powerful motivator, right? It's always in the back of my mind."

"What about counseling? You should see someone."

"That's what Mary keeps saying. But I'm just not ready. I couldn't stand sitting in some stuffy office recounting how humiliated I was by what she did."

"Well, for what it's worth, I think you should try as hard as you can to get past it because, as far as I can tell, even with this, she's the best thing that ever happened to you."

I contemplated this as Alex rinsed dishes and wiped down the counter.

"What about your kids?" Alex asked. "How are they doing? Do they know anything about this?"

"God, no. I couldn't bear it," I said. "They're both doing well. Eli loves Stanford. And Claire just started at Pomona. I know I'm biased, but they're both brilliant. I'm so proud of them. They both wanted to be here, by the way, but I told them it was too short a turnaround and you would understand."

"Oh, god, I wouldn't want them to have to go through it."

"How are the boys?"

"I sent them to Dave's parents' last night. I couldn't handle them. They've gone wild. They look at me like I must have done something to him. They blame me."

She sniffed and buried her head in her hands.

"I'm sure they don't!"

"It's just their way of dealing with it right now. Ben screamed at me last night. Called me a bitch. Said no wonder Dad killed himself. He couldn't take living with me."

"He doesn't mean it. He's scared. He's angry."

"They both know we're in trouble. That I'm scared. That I don't know what's going to happen to us. They feel it."

I felt helpless. My sister's husband had committed the most heinous act against his family. It was hard to see how it could all be put back together.

"Let's see if we can figure some of this stuff out," I said, pointing to the piles of paper. "Let me put together a spreadsheet of your assets, your cash, your payables. At least we can try to get a grip on that."

"I don't know what I would do without you," she said.

When I got back to Mom's, Mary was outside with her on the patio, sitting in the sunshine and drinking coffee. I watched them from the window as they laughed and talked. Mom looked ten years younger, and happier than before Mary arrived.

"Hey, what are you girls up to out here?" I asked, joining them on the patio.

"We were just telling stories about your dad," Mom said. "Mary has so many good ones!"

"He was larger than life," Mary said, reaching for Mom's hand.

"That's for sure," I said. "Have you thought about dinner?"

"I've been shopping," Mary said. "I bought things to cook out on the grill. It's such great weather right now. The perfect temperature."

It would be so easy for me to fall back into life with her. I watched her in the kitchen, chopping and prepping the meal, then running back and forth from the grill. I had not fallen out of love with her, and I didn't think I could. But would I trust her? With my heart? Would I ever again have that unshakable confidence in the idea of "us"? It seemed unlikely.

We set the table outside and ate under the dusky sky, the moon bright and close, hanging over us like a cradle. I had to interrupt the pleasant flow of conversation with the plans for the next day, Dave's memorial service. I knew we would have to repeat it all in the morning, but I still held on to the hope that some of what we said to her would stick and not be completely unfamiliar the next time around.

"Mom," I said, leaning forward and speaking gently. "There's a service tomorrow for Dave. He passed away a few days ago."

"Oh my lord!" she cried, tears forming at the rims of her eyes. "What happened?"

"He…he had an accident."

"Why didn't anyone tell me?"

I looked at Mary who gave me a sympathetic smile.

"Well, I think Alex didn't want to upset you. But I wanted to tell you and prepare you for tomorrow. We'll need to be ready by eleven."

"What will Alex do? She'll have to go back to work. Thank goodness she's a nurse. They always need nurses."

"That's true, Mom," Mary said. "Alex will be fine. She has Jen and she has you."

"Those poor boys. Without a father. What a shame."

"Yes. It is a terrible shame," I said.

We cleaned up and said good night and as Mom turned to walk to her bedroom, she said, "What are we doing tomorrow? Did you say we were going to the movies?"

"The memorial service, Mom."

"Oh, for heaven's sake. My mind is gone."

"Don't worry about it. We'll see you in the morning."

Mary and I headed to the guest room, and I asked if she minded me using the bathroom first to get ready for bed. I didn't want to undress in front of her, as I had not since the tryst. She nodded and turned away from me. When I came back into the bedroom, she had changed into very modest pajamas, not her usual slinky nighty. She slipped past me for the bathroom.

I sat in bed reading, waiting for her to come back, in a strange way feeling a sense of normalcy returning. We had slept in this bed so many times before. She got in next to me and turned toward me, running her hand along my arm.

"Your mom is really sweet. She's actually nicer now with the dementia."

"It's strange, isn't it? Is it always that way?"

"I don't think so. Sometimes people can get really mean. So we're lucky."

"You really care about her."

"Of course I do! I always have. You're lucky to still have her."

"You know, I would sleep on the couch if it wouldn't upset her."

She took a sharp breath.

"Jen, we need to go to counseling. We can't keep having this conversation between ourselves. It's going nowhere."

"What is there to talk about with a counselor? What was it about our relationship that made you think that what you did was okay?"

"I didn't think it was okay. It was a mistake. People make mistakes. I was lonely, yes, but I'm not blaming you."

"You were lonely?"

"This is why we need a counselor. I feel like you don't hear me. You don't listen to me."

"I don't hear you because what you're saying doesn't make any sense. How could you be lonely?"

"I need attention from you. It's not enough for you to be in the same room with me. I need you to be in the moment with me."

"So you were punishing me by sleeping with her?"

"No!"

"Because that's what it sounds like. I don't give you enough attention, so you have the right to get it from someone else?"

"Stop. That is not what I am saying. This is why we need to see someone. You keep twisting my words."

"Let's go to sleep. We have a hellish day tomorrow."

I clicked the light out and pulled the covers over my head, turning away from her. I could feel her still sitting up, looking at me, not giving in. Let her sit up all night if she wanted. I couldn't talk about it any more. I couldn't see a way to forgive her.

CHAPTER SIX

My sister, Alex, took Laura and me to the airport on the day we left for London. Alex had been curious about my relationship with Laura, I guess because I talked about her a little too much and with more enthusiasm than was probably appropriate for a garden-variety friendship. She gave me a knowing look as she saw us off at the gate.

Laura and I were kinetically excited. Neither one of us had left the country before. To save money, we had taken an itinerary that had us stopping and changing planes at JFK in New York. We both felt we were off on the adventure of a lifetime. We were stuck in the back of the plane, near the lavatory, on both flights. We flipped a coin for who would take the middle seat on the flight into London. She lost. She fell asleep easily and slumped onto my shoulder. I didn't mind. I liked it. I breathed in the smell of her hair, perfumed and sweaty at the same time. I dozed off, thinking about kissing the top of her head. That's weird. Why would I think that? But in my dream, I did that and more. And, in my dream, she wanted to do a lot more. She asked me if I wanted to fuck. That's what she said. "Do you want to fuck?" I woke up, a little scared, my heart pounding. I had fallen over onto her while I slept. She didn't wake up.

What the hell? It was so real. But where had it come from? What would she think if she knew I had dreamed about her that way? With her head on my shoulder, with her breath gently falling on my arm, I could almost believe that it had happened. Did I want it to happen? I knew I did want it and I felt terrified by that. Where was this coming from? Should I forbid myself ever to think it again? But I enjoyed the feeling. I enjoyed it so much, I closed my eyes and visualized her stirring and sneaking her hand under my shirt, turning her face to mine and kissing me hard, pushing her tongue into my mouth. I had to quash a cry of release as I had an orgasm right there in my seat with her still breathing softly into me. With that I fell asleep again and woke only when the flight attendants started the breakfast service.

We waited in the passport line for over an hour, each growing cranky toward the other.

"This sucks," Laura said, bending forward to stretch her back.

"I'm starving," I said.

"I can't believe I didn't ask them to fill my water bottle."

Something was wrong with the air-conditioning and we stood sweating and dying of thirst. When we finally got through to the baggage carousels, we couldn't find our luggage. After several minutes of helpless, confused searching, Laura found them set aside with others from our flight. At last, we got to the Tube station to catch the train that would take us into London. We had stopped along the way to buy water and bananas, which, once consumed, brought us instantly back to enthusiastic anticipation.

"The perfect food," Laura said, finishing hers. "C'mon. Here's our train."

We came up out of the station near our small hotel, but it was too early to check in. I noticed a beautiful church nearby and it was open. It was Sunday and there was an early Mass.

"Let's go inside. It might be fun. At least it's a place to sit for a while," I said.

The cathedral, bound by stained glass on all sides, with a magnificent carved stone alter and organ pipes soaring up to the heavens, felt ten degrees cooler than the outside. It felt good to rest and reflect with the few worshippers who were there. We watched as they took communion.

"I'm not Catholic," Laura whispered. "Are you?"

"No. Southern Baptist."

"Methodist," she said.

By the time the service had finished, we were ready to drop our bags, even if we couldn't check in yet. But to our surprise, our room was ready. The matronly proprietor took us up the narrow dark staircase two floors to a low-ceilinged hallway. She showed us the bathroom we shared with two other rooms. We had one bed, which was not quite as big as an American double.

"I hope you don't move around a lot in your sleep," Laura said, putting her bag down.

There was almost no room to walk with an armoire at the foot of the bed and a small table on either side, each with a lamp. One of us would have to crawl across the other to get in and out.

"Just get me drunk enough and you won't have to worry about it," I said.

"This is perfect. We don't want to spend time in the room anyway."

We decided to power through and get our body clocks turned around, so we headed over to Piccadilly to catch one of those double-decker tourist buses. We got off and on all day, catching all the must-see's like Big Ben, Buckingham Palace, the Tower of London, the Globe Theatre. By happy hour, we were ready to pass out.

"I'm dying," I said. "I have to take a nap."

"No! That's the worst thing you can do. You'll sleep for hours and you'll be wide awake at four a.m."

"Let's walk then. I don't think I can fall asleep if I'm walking."

We walked along the Thames and talked about what we would do the next day.

"I have some friends who are going to Bath tomorrow," I said. "Some kids from my class. We could meet up with them."

"Let's look at the train schedule," Laura said, pulling a book out of her backpack. "We could take this one at nine and come back on this one at seven. What do you think?"

"Good," I said. "I'll call my friends. There's a payphone over there."

Laura had a Frommer's that she had marked up and annotated with all kinds of underlines and stars. She had researched cheap but good places to eat and had one she wanted to try for dinner that night. As I sat across from her at an outdoor table at a café near our hotel, I had a flashback to my dreams on the plane. Instantly I felt awkward. She looked at me and I thought she must know what I was thinking. She held my eyes for a few seconds.

"You're exhausted," she said. "We'll go back right after dinner."

"You might have to carry me."

"Don't worry," she said, reaching across the table to touch my hand. "I'll take care of you."

Every drop of blood in my veins rushed to the center of my body, leaving me dizzy and out of breath. My hand tingled as though the spot she had touched had been electrified. Did she know what she was doing? Or was it me? Did I imagine that she meant something by it?

"Don't you believe me?" She smiled as I sat mute.

"Of course," I smiled. "I know I'm in good hands."

I managed to get through dinner, my sleep deprived brain leaving me devoid of thoughts fit for conversation. I don't really remember how we got back to the hotel.

The next morning, we rushed through breakfast and ran to the train station, making it just in time to buy our tickets to Bath. We found my friends on the platform and I introduced them to Laura. Tom was from New York and would be clerking for a judge in Washington, DC, when he got back from this trip. He was tall and skinny, with delicate features and pale green eyes. His light-brown hair curled around his ears and down to his collar. Elliott was from California. He had a job waiting in

LA. He was shorter and stocky, with very dark hair and a heavy beard that, no matter how often he shaved, always gave him a five o'clock shadow.

We sat in the café car and drank coffee as Tom smoked cigarettes.

"What's the political climate like in Dallas," Tom asked. "Must be pretty conservative. Is everybody Republican?"

"Pretty much," Laura said. "I'm not political, but everybody in my family is a Republican. Contract with America and all that. My cousin works for Gingrich's office. He went to law school at GW."

"Really?" I said.

"That's intense," Tom said. "So you're voting for Dole?"

"I don't know. Probably not. I like Clinton."

"I like the First Lady," I said. "She's kick-ass."

"Me too," Laura said. "Too bad she can't run."

"You never know," I said.

"It doesn't bother you?" Tom asked.

"What do you mean?" I asked.

"Living there. I never thought of you as, you know, someone who could live there. Texas."

"Well, I'm from there, as you know," I said, staring him down. "So, I've already lived there and I guess it was path of least resistance. For now."

"You think it's all that bad?" Laura looked at me.

"Things have gone so far right since I left for college. It's a little scary. Moral Majority and all that. The mega churches. It isn't really where my head is, you know?"

Laura got quiet and it felt a little uncomfortable.

"Hey, let's talk about religion now," Elliott said, laughing. "My tribe is well represented in your firm, I'm sure."

"Hey, lighten up, guys," I said. "How did we get on this?"

Laura got up and left the café car.

"Thanks a lot," I said. "Can we drop all this and have a good time?"

"Sorry," Tom said. "I just hate to see you end up all Christian-y. Married to some macho conservative dude who traps you in the suburbs and saps your brain with Bible verses."

"That's your vision of what's going to happen to me?"

"I worry about it."

"Don't worry," I said, increasingly more annoyed.

"Seriously. You need to get out of there. I don't think it's a healthy place for you."

"Can we just table this for now? And drop it in front of Laura. Let's have a good time today."

I got up abruptly and left the café car in search of her. I found her standing between the cars near the back of the train. She turned her back when she saw me.

"Hey," I said. "They're jerks, but they're really nice guys under all that East Coast, left coast, intellectual bullshit."

She didn't respond or move.

"Laura," I said, touching her shoulder. "Come back to the café. Can't we just forget about it?"

"Is that what you think of me?"

"What do you mean?"

"That I'm a brain-dead, Christian right, zealot?"

"No! Why would you even say that?"

"That's what your friends were saying, more or less."

"No, look, they like to push buttons, that's all. It's true they're very prejudiced against conservatives. But they think they can reason with them, win them over. It's just a thing they do."

"I want to know what you think."

What I thought at that moment was that I wanted to push her against the wall and kiss her and touch her all over. She did not take her eyes off mine, and I felt like maybe she was thinking the same thing, but I couldn't move.

"I think you're smart. I think you have good instincts. I trust you."

"Can we agree not to bring up politics for the rest of the day?" she asked.

"It's done. Will you come back with me?"

She walked past me, back toward the café car. I followed, my eyes riveted on her shoulders peeking out from her tank top, her sleek athlete's body slicing down the aisle.

CHAPTER SEVEN

Mary and I took Mom to Alex's so we could all ride together in a limo we had arranged to take us to the memorial service. She had decided to hold it at a chapel in the Baptist Church they had occasionally attended over the years. We kept having to remind Mom what we were doing and why.

"Mom! Please!" Alex said in exasperation at the question yet again as we arrived at the church.

"I'm sorry, sweetie," Mom said, tears brimming over her eyes and rolling down her cheeks. "My mind…"

"It's okay, Mom," Mary said, taking her hand. "She doesn't mean it. This is just a really hard day for her."

Mary and I took Mom on either side and helped her into the building. The dimly lit chapel enveloped us in a heavy, oppressive fog of grief. I wanted to ask them to turn the lights up, but Alex stopped me.

"I don't want to brighten this room. He doesn't deserve it."

"Alex! What about the boys?"

She collapsed into me, a torrent of tears and heaving convulsions, out of control for the first time since he died. I held her and the whole room joined us in hushed versions of the same release of pent-up emotion. When she recovered and was settled on the front pew, I had them raise the lights a bit. The pastor delivered a message full of irrelevant platitudes while those of us who knew him best suffered through the hypocrisy of it all.

Alex rocked back and forth on the pew, her sons looking on in palpable fear. Mary and I sat behind her with Mom. Mary nudged me and nodded to the boys as though I should do something. Reluctantly, I moved to their bench and sat between them, my arms around them in an attempt to comfort them. The older one resisted me, but the younger one buried his head in my chest, sniffling and rubbing his eyes.

The service was mercifully short and there was no graveside burial to endure. The meager crew of guests gathered at Alex's house to graze over the mountain of food that had been offered.

"Now comes the hard part," I said to Mary as I sipped a glass of wine and watched Alex talking quietly with friends.

"How much longer will you be down here?" Mary asked.

"I'm not sure. I have to organize things to deal with Dave's bankruptcy. And since I think she'll be going back to work, we'll have to figure something out for Mom."

"What can I do to help?"

"You need to get back to work."

"Yes, but maybe I can work on getting some help in for your mom. It's time. Would you let me do that?"

She took both my hands in hers and I didn't resist. In fact, I was overwhelmed with a desire to hold her, and I gave in. She melted into me and, if we had not been standing in a room full of people, I am sure I would have kissed her and more.

"Thank you," I whispered through her hair.

"I love you," she said. "I love you more than life."

I stood back and looked into her eyes. I felt how much she loved me and I wanted to forget the cheating. More than anything. But it was there, in the back of my mind, always.

Mary flew back to San Francisco the next day and I got to work in earnest on Alex's problems. I knew I had to call Laura

Peters. Sooner than later. So I gathered my summaries of the situation in front of me and keyed in her number. Her secretary answered. She was not available, but would I leave a message?

"Yes," I said. "Could you tell her that Jennifer Adair called. I have a case I would like to discuss with her."

I clicked off the line, trembling, breathing a sigh of relief that I hadn't actually reached her. A slight reprieve. I couldn't believe how much it affected me. Just the thought of speaking with her over the phone.

As I sat staring at the piles of files on the floor at my feet, I remembered I had some good news for Alex. I rang her.

"Dave's life insurance will pay," I said. "It's not enough to live on, but it will help smooth things over for a few months."

"Thank god," she said. "Something to hang on to at least."

"I finally called Laura Peters's office," I said. "I'm sure she'll get back to me."

"I know how hard that must be," Alex said.

"Yeah, it's weird. It's been years, but, when I think about it, it feels like yesterday."

"Did you ever tell Mary the whole story?"

"A sanitized version. She knows something happened with 'the straight girl' as she puts it. But when I met Mary, I was trying so hard to get over the whole thing that I didn't want to relive it. Then, after a while, there was no point in bringing it up."

"And you haven't spoken to or seen her in all these years?"

"Nothing."

"Wow."

"So," I said, "now you know how much I love you, sister."

"Are you sure you want to do this? Aren't there other lawyers we could use?"

"She's the best. If anyone can salvage this situation for you, it's her. I'll be fine."

Laura's office called that afternoon and offered me a time to come in and meet with her in person the next day. I spent the evening distracting myself as best I could with conversations with Mom about Dad and the good times we had on family vacations to New Mexico. I slept restlessly and got up early to get in a swim at the YMCA nearby. After that, I did a spin class, which was okay as a stopgap, but I would have to find a road bike if I was going to be away from home much longer. I was determined not to let my training slip.

Back at Mom's, I showered for the longest time, dragging out the inevitable coiffing for the meeting. I dressed carefully, putting far too much effort into how I would look when Laura saw me for the first time since our train wreck of a parting. I had brought one of my Armani suits, the ones I used for meetings in New York with Wall Street guys. It was sharp, but not severe. I had a pair of Gucci loafers, but I went with the Stuart Weitzman heels. Thank god I'd had a pedicure right before all this happened. It was a good day for my hair, so that was a big plus. I used a little bit of makeup. Just some mascara and a bit of foundation powder. Lipstick to finish it off.

I looked myself over in the full-length mirror, feeling a bit like I was girding for battle. I was satisfied with the results. I took my briefcase and kissed Mom goodbye. On the drive downtown, I pumped myself up with positive self-talk, the way I did for an investor pitch. But my mind sabotaged me with flashbacks to my twenty-five-year-old self, sapping my confidence and reducing me to an anxiety-stricken shell. I parked in the office building's garage and did a quick breathing exercise.

"C'mon!" I shouted to myself, channeling Serena Williams, as I stood tall waiting for the elevator.

I checked in with the receptionist and they put me into a conference room, offering me coffee and water, both of which I took. I walked to the window with a glass of water, looking out from the top floor over the Dallas skyline. I had been in conference rooms like this a million times. I felt at home and that helped me stay calm.

"Jen!" The familiar voice emanated from behind me.

I turned, doing my best to steady my voice before speaking.

"It's good to see you, Laura," I said, instantly captivated by the older version of her athletic beauty. She wore knit pants and a tight sweater, not much makeup, and loafers. Her strawberry-blond hair fell to her shoulders, pretty, like it had twenty-some years before.

"You look amazing," she said. "Oh my god, what a package!"

She came toward me and we exchanged somewhat formal greeting kisses.

"Stop," I said. "You're embarrassing me right off the bat."

My heart rate, which had accelerated on seeing her, would not return to normal. I sipped from my glass in hopes it would help.

"Sit down," she said. "I'm so glad you called. I can't believe it took so long."

"So long?"

I was taken off guard by her enthusiasm. I wasn't sure what I had expected, exactly, but it wasn't this warm welcome after so many years and after the way we left it then.

"What I mean is, I've wanted to get in touch with you but, just assumed you didn't want to hear from me. So…"

"I…that surprises me. I'll be honest."

"I've sort of stalked you on the Internet over the years. You've done really well for yourself. Your wife is gorgeous. And your kids!"

The look on my face must have given away my incredulity.

"I'm sorry. Is that creepy? I hope I haven't offended you."

"Oh, no, no. It's, these days, everybody keeps up with people that way, I guess. I just wouldn't have thought that I was someone you would follow."

"For years I've wanted to apologize. But I couldn't make myself get in touch. I was so ashamed of what happened. You have every right to hate me. I always thought if I approached you, you might get a restraining order!"

"Oh, for god's sake, Laura. Look, we were young. It was such a different world. I haven't held a grudge. It was, in some ways, the best thing that could have happened to me. It got me out of Texas and that was a good thing."

"So it seems," she said, a flicker of, what—sadness, regret?—playing across her face. "Okay, I know you have some important business to discuss with me, but will you promise me that you will make some time to get together socially while you're here?"

"Of course," I said, still dazed by this reception.

We discussed Dave's business and I briefed her on what I knew about the bankruptcy case. She took control immediately, calling the judge's clerk while we sat there. We made arrangements for a courier to come to Mom's house to retrieve the boxes of files. I signed a retainer agreement on the spot.

"I can't tell you how much I appreciate this, Laura," I said as I packed my briefcase. "Alex is…she so doesn't deserve this."

"I will do everything I possibly can to make this a good outcome for her," she said. "I'll keep you posted on every development. But, before you leave, can we compare calendars? I'd like to have you over for dinner, if you'll come."

We made a date for Friday night. I left the building feeling a mixture of relief and trepidation. I wasn't sure what I thought about rebuilding any kind of connection with Laura. Though I had been dismissive of her comments about what she had done to me, the truth was, it was one of the most painful memories of my life. Seeing her had stirred those old emotions, putting me back into the skin of my youth where I felt the wounds more keenly, the drama of a broken love affair looming ominously close.

CHAPTER EIGHT

When we got back from Bath that night, we went out drinking with the guys and met some other friends who had just gotten into town. One of them had always had a thing for me and he focused all his attention on me. I tried to escape, but he was persistent and dragged me onto the dance floor. His hard-on was stiff and he begged me to go into a corner of the hallway.

"I have a boyfriend, you know," I said.

"C'mon. We're in Europe. What happens here doesn't count. Please."

I gave in just to get rid of him. The whole thing only took me a minute or two. I left him in the hall and went back to find Laura and the others.

"Did you just do what I think you did?" Laura asked me.

"Are you judging me?"

She turned back to her beer sitting on the bar counter.

"I'm going back to the room," she said.

"I'll come with you."

She walked quickly, not waiting for me. I ran after her.

"Laura, what's the problem?"

"Stay. I don't need an escort."

"I don't want to stay."

She slowed down and we flagged a taxi. We didn't say anything on the ride home. I was dozing off anyway, without enough energy to prod her about her mood. When we got to the room, I stripped and fell into bed naked, in too much of an alcohol haze to remember she was sleeping next to me. At one point during the night, her hand brushed against my breast. It woke me up and I looked at her in the dark, but she seemed to be asleep. I grabbed a T-shirt from the floor.

"What are you doing?" she said.

"Sorry, I didn't mean to sleep naked."

"It's okay. I don't mind," she said. "Get back in bed."

I pulled the shirt on anyway, feeing exposed, vulnerable. She fell back asleep quickly, her hand resting on my arm. I couldn't sleep. I was so confused by her. I spent the rest of the night beating myself up for being such a coward, for not confronting her about her flirtations. Just before dawn, as the sun began to peek into the room, I fell into a heavy sleep. When I woke some time later, she was dressed, sitting across the room, gazing in my direction.

"Hey, good morning," I said.

"Nice of you to wake up, sleeping beauty."

I threw a pillow at her and got up quickly.

"I'm starving," she said. "Let's go."

Laura and I left London after four days, headed to Paris on the train. We had found a small hotel in the Latin Quarter that was within our budget. We dropped our bags and headed for a sidewalk café where we ordered wine and charcuterie for a snack.

"I feel like we should be smoking cigarettes," Laura said, looking around. "Just to be polite."

I laughed, flipping through the tour book in search of something fun.

"Let's do this river boat," I said. "The Bateaux Mouches."

The sun was bright and hot and beat down on us as we walked along the Seine to the river boat launch. I noticed the highlights in Laura's hair as the wind blew strands of it into her eyes. She tied it back and I thought, how beautiful she is. She spoke a little French and tried to communicate with the ticket vendor in his language, but she had trouble with the numbers and he, in frustration, took the money out of her hands and made the change for the price of the tickets.

"So much for that," she said.

"At least you tried. Numbers and menus. Those are two of the hardest things."

On board the boat, we asked another tourist to take our picture. We posed with Notre-Dame in the background and Laura, at the last minute, planted a big kiss on my cheek as he snapped the photo. She tossed my hair playfully, telling me she loved the color, which was an auburn closer to red, and turned to look over the bow of the boat.

"I'm so glad we decided to do this trip together. Do you wish Chris was coming over?"

"Not at all. I haven't even thought about him. I think it's over with him anyway. I'm so not into it. It's not fair to him."

"I struggle with that, too, with Mike. Life just seems more serious now that we're not in school anymore and I don't feel serious with him."

"Not in your five-year plan?" I poked at her, smiling.

"I do want to be married in the next five years. I'll be thirty and I want to have kids."

"Something tells me you'll get it done."

"You don't want kids?"

"Why do you say that?"

"I don't know. You don't seem focused on a relationship. You don't talk about it."

"I don't see myself married with kids. I don't know why, but the idea of being tied down to a man and his career and kids… it feels oppressive to me."

"I think if you meet the right person, that could change."

"I guess so. Right now, the only thing on my agenda is happy hour. Are you up for barhopping after this?"

"I already have it all planned out."

"I should have known," I said, smiling.

We headed to Pigalle where we hit several seedy bars and got pretty drunk, walking by the peep shows and hazy byways. Laura really wanted to go to the concert hall at Les Trois Baudets, so we bought tickets and went inside, finding a seat in the back. We happened to catch the French hip-hop phenom, MC Solaar. We danced and drank and danced some more. We went on from there to a gay bar on the Left Bank where we were approached by a couple of masculine lesbians who bought us drinks.

"Do you like that?" Laura whispered in my ear, nodding to the women in leather pants and boots and cropped, slicked back hair.

"I like you," I said and lingered with my lips near her neck.

By the time we headed home, it was five a.m. In the taxi, without warning, Laura leaned over, took my face in her hands and started kissing me, thrusting her tongue into my mouth and pulling at the buttons of my shirt.

"Wait," I said. "Not in the cab."

She stopped trying to get my shirt off, but didn't stop kissing me. When we got out of the taxi, she pulled me, running, into the hotel and up the stairs. She fumbled for the key to the room and, once we were inside, quickly unbuttoned my shirt.

"Laura, are you sure…this could be the booze talking. I don't know…"

She pressed her fingers against my lips to stop my protests and pulled off her own shirt. She kissed my neck and made her way down my body. I quivered as she pulled off my jeans and underpants and went down on me. I grabbed the railings of the headboard behind me and arched my back, pressing into her mouth and coming as hard as I ever remember.

Quickly, I unhooked her bra and pushed her down on the bed, taking control. Tracing her nipples, her navel, I unzipped her jeans and pushed my hand between her thighs. She gasped into my ear and climaxed right away. She looked at me through half-closed eyes, then passed out in my arms.

We stirred awake well after noon the next day. I had slipped into the second bed. She looked over at me through bleary eyes.

"Shit," she said. "I need coffee…or a bloody. What's better for the worst hangover you can imagine?"

"A cheeseburger," I said.

"Yes!"

We sat outside at a café eating cheeseburgers and french fries and drinking Cokes. I wanted to ask her about what had happened, but I didn't have the courage. It had been my first time and I couldn't believe how good it felt. How right. How much better. I wanted to talk about it, but I didn't dare.

"You're awfully quiet," she said. "What are you thinking?"

"I'm wondering…just wondering how you feel about what happened."

I looked at her over the rim of my glass, trying to read her expression. She stared at her plate, circled a french fry in ketchup. She stole a look at me from the corner of her eye.

"It was nice," she said quietly.

I waited, but she didn't go on.

"It was nice, but?" I said.

"No buts. Just no promises."

I nodded. She leaned forward.

"It's Paris. The City of Love, right?" she said.

"I guess I'll hope it blows over by the time we get to Berlin."

"Why?" she said.

"Because I think I really might be falling in love with you," I said, feeling my cheeks flush.

She sat back, looked off into the street.

"Are you happy?" she asked.

"Very," I said.

"Then let's just enjoy it for what it is. For now."

She reached across the table and took my hand.

CHAPTER NINE

I mentioned to Mary that I had met with Laura about the bankruptcy and that she had invited me to dinner with her family at their house on Friday night.

"Wait," she said. "Laura. Is this the same woman you went to Europe with after the bar?"

"It is."

"I'm not sure how I feel about that."

"I'm not sure you have a right to feel anything about it," I said. "And she's married, straight, kids, the whole nine yards."

"I thought you hadn't heard from her in twenty years. Why is she keen to make nice with you now?"

"Guilt, I would guess. Maybe she's in a twelve-step program that requires her to make amends."

"That's not funny, Jen."

"Look, I don't know. The world has made progress on the gay issue, even in Texas. It seems like she wants to make herself feel better about that."

"I just don't want you to be hurt by her again."

"The only person who's hurt me in a long time is you."

Mary was silent. While I knew I had the right to feel the way I did, I also realized my attacks were getting old.

"Mary?"

After a hefty sigh, she finally said, "The sniping, Jen, it's—"

"I'm sorry. You're right about the sniping. That's not fair. I promise you. When I get back, we'll find someone. We'll see someone. Okay?"

"Thank you," she said in a voice barely audible.

We chatted a little more about the kids and how things were going in school. I was missing parents' weekend at Pomona, which I hated to do, but didn't see a way around.

"Make sure Claire believes me when I say I'll make it up to her," I said.

We said goodbye, but she stopped me before I clicked off.

"Jen," she said. "Watch out for this Laura."

I caught an Uber to Laura's house because I assumed we would be drinking and, sure enough, we started off with tequila cocktails. They lived in a mature neighborhood near a lake in a very nice, large, but not ostentatious, house. I hadn't been quite so obsessed with my preparation for this meeting with her, but I was conscious of wanting to impress her husband with my looks. I'm not sure why. I half wondered whether she would have told him anything about me, our past. So I guess I wanted to make sure I didn't disappoint her, in case she had built me up to him. I wore tight black jeans with strappy heels and a low-cut, sleeveless blouse. I had borrowed jewelry from my mother, who asked me why I was primping so much. She lent me a necklace and some dangly earrings. I pulled my hair back and clipped it with a large barrette.

"Who are you gettin' all gussied up for?" she had asked, her hands on her hips.

"No one, Mom. I'm having dinner with an old friend. I just want to look nice and you have such beautiful jewelry."

"Well, you might as well wear it. I don't go out anymore. I've lost my mind, you know."

"Thanks, Mom. And you haven't lost your mind, just a little of your memory."

Laura's husband, Steve, was very curious about what he referred to as my "San Francisco lifestyle." He wanted to see pictures of Mary and hear about how we met.

"Steve, stop giving her the third degree," Laura said, handing me another cocktail as we sat outside near the pool.

"It's okay," I said, showing Steve pictures on my phone.

"Wow," he said. "Is she a model?"

I laughed and said, "She's a surgeon. Orthopedics."

"Oh, god, I bet she has old guys lined up around the block for knee replacements, hip replacements."

"She's very popular," I said, clicking off my phone.

"But tell me how you met?"

"Well," I said, glancing at Laura, "I had just moved to the Bay Area—"

"From here, right? You and Laura were in the same firm?"

"We were. It was a big move for me. A big change."

Laura shifted uncomfortably in her seat. I avoided eye contact with her.

"I moved out there to take a job with a Silicon Valley startup," I said, skipping over my intermittent period of unemployment. "We worked crazy hours and had almost no time to socialize or meet people. Then one Saturday, I was complaining about that and my boss said, fine, let's all knock off work and go to this party he had been invited to in the city. My boss was gay and his friend, a gay guy with a lot of money, had a huge apartment in The Castro. So we all went."

"Were you out at that point?" Steve asked.

"Steve!" Laura glared at him.

"Sorry, I don't mean—"

"No, it's fine. I don't mind. And no, I wasn't out, but I wasn't not out, either. I knew I was gay, but I knew so few people in San Francisco that it just didn't really come up. So, anyway, I walk into this party and I see this woman across the room who is just stunning. Gorgeous. And I decide I have to meet her. I asked my boss if he knew her. He looks at me and says, 'Are you a lesbian?'

Without even thinking twice, I say 'Yes, is she?' He says yes and he tells me a little bit about her. He motions her over and makes the introduction."

"So it was love at first sight?" Laura asked, sipping her cocktail.

"Not exactly. It was definitely lust at first sight, at least on my part. But she was with someone at the time and she had a one-year-old son with this other woman. It turned out they were breaking up, but I didn't know that at the time. She called me about four months later and, well, we moved in together a few months after that."

"That was fast," Laura said.

"Well, you know the old joke…what does a lesbian bring on a first date?"

They both looked at me blankly.

"A U-Haul!"

Steve laughed and Laura shook her head.

"Did she bring her son?" he asked.

"Oh, yes. We raised him. Eli. And we have a daughter, too."

"Sounds like a lovely family," Laura said. "And you didn't even think you wanted kids."

I gave her a sharp look.

"The kids are great. But, hey, enough about me. What a beautiful place you have here."

We had dinner by the pool and I met her two children as they passed through. They were high school age. A boy and a girl. We drank red wine through the meal and I started to feel tipsy. Steve went to bed and I knew I should go, but Laura wasn't ready for the night to end.

"Stay a little longer," she said. "I want to hear more, and not just statistics. How have you been, really? Are you happy?"

I had a flashback to Paris and her asking me that question the day after we first slept together. I searched her face for any connection to that moment. I wasn't sure.

"That's a big question. Can I ask you the same thing?"

"Ah…well, I guess that's only fair."

She paused.

"I can't complain," she said. "I have everything you're supposed to want, right? How could I not be happy? That would be petulant."

"Well, I think we both know that ticking off a bunch of goals or racking up an inventory of nice things isn't the same as being happy."

Laura stared out over the pool, its lights reflecting the movement of the water into shadows on her face. We sat in silence for a moment until she turned to me, suddenly animated.

"Do you remember the time we skinny-dipped in the pool at your apartment?"

I laughed. "Yes! Your boyfriend, what was his name? Mike? Got so annoyed at us."

"Let's get in the hot tub," she said.

"Oh, no. That's a little too intimate, don't you think? In light of where we left off twenty years ago?"

"Ouch," she said. "You have every right to feel that way. But don't leave. Let's catch up a little more."

I felt uneasy, almost like I was betraying my younger self by being there.

"What are you thinking?" she asked.

"That I can't believe I'm here. In Dallas. Poolside at Laura Peters's house," I said flatly. "Not what I would have predicted."

"Well, as sorry as I am for what happened to your sister, I'm so glad you're here."

"I don't know why."

"The truth is, even though my life is full of people, I'm lonely. Seeing you, it makes me remember a time when that wasn't the case."

I could feel her unhappiness pressing in on me. It made me sad.

"What about Steve?"

"He's more like a business partner than a companion. There's not much of an emotional connection between us anymore."

"What will you do?"

"What can I do? It's too complicated to unwind all of this." She waved her hand over the surroundings.

"That's no way to live," I said.

She took a deep breath, put her head back and closed her eyes, a single tear slipping down the side of her face.

"I'm sorry," I said. "I shouldn't have said that."

"No," she said. "You're right."

She smoothed her hair away from her face, looking at me again.

"Wow, I didn't see that coming," she said, wiping away the tear. "Sorry."

"You'll figure it out. You're good at that. The next five-year plan?"

She laughed and, dipping her hand into the pool, splashed water at me.

"Stop making fun of me." She smiled.

"I'm just glad I can still make you laugh."

She locked her eyes on mine and I felt my heart accelerating, thumping into my ears, while sweat beads broke out on my forehead, a near panic attack setting in.

"Let me get you some water," she said. "You look a little flushed."

As she retreated into the kitchen, I forced several deep breaths, counting the in and out until she came back with a glass. I downed it gratefully, a little too quickly, choking as I got to the last gulp.

"Are you okay? Would you like to go into the air-conditioning? It is a little muggy."

"No, I'm fine. Maybe it's early menopause," I laughed.

"Oh, give me a break. No one who looks as luscious as you could be in menopause."

I caught my breath and felt my eyes widen as the word luscious reverberated in the space between us.

"I'm sorry," she said. "I didn't mean anything—"

"Of course not. Are you kidding?" I said, my hands gripped in my lap to stop the trembling.

We sat silent for a moment or two and I contemplated the wisdom of staying longer. She broke the reverie.

"Steve wants me to take a lover," she said. "A woman."

I raised my eyebrows, saying nothing.

"He thinks it would improve our sex life."

"And what do you think?"

"We've had threesomes," she said, stealing a shy glance at me, "with strangers from time to time. Stimulating. But a lover? I don't know. Would that make me bi—or lesbian?" she said.

I didn't respond. Didn't want to feed into her drama, especially about threesomes, given our history. I looked away, watching the steam rise off the water and thinking I wanted to get the hell out of there.

"I'm sorry to dump that on you," she said.

"Look, what you're describing—it's a little amateurish in my world. I don't mean that in a mean way, but—anyway, I'm not a therapist," I said. "My best advice to you is, figure it out. Figure out who you are and what you want. Don't live your life as someone you're not. It's such a waste."

"And the kids?"

"They'll be fine. Better off. If you're not happy, they know it. Trust me."

She sighed, and I looked at her, sure she wouldn't ever be ballsy enough to pull the trigger. I glanced at the clock on the fence behind her, shocked by how late it was.

"Oh, wow. It's after midnight. I have to go," I said, reaching for my phone.

"Let me call our driver," she said. "Uber takes forever to get to this neighborhood."

I allowed my eyes to linger on her face as she made the call. She caught my gaze and the memory of our passion flooded over me.

CHAPTER TEN

Laura and I took the overnight train from Paris to Berlin. We splurged for a nice sleeper cabin and snuggled together long enough to have sex before separating into our bunks. We strolled the streets of Berlin, holding hands, stopping in cafés, touring museums, ignoring our friends who wanted to join us. We had eyes only for each other.

One afternoon we took a picnic to the park near the Brandenburg Gate. I lay with my head in her lap while she twisted flowers into my hair. She leaned down to kiss me, slipping her hand under my shirt. Just the memory of our naked sweaty bodies pressed together in ecstasy was enough to bring me to orgasm. I buried my cry of release in her mouth, wrapping my arms around her neck and pulling her on top of me.

"Not in broad daylight," she whispered in my ear.

We laughed and lay on our blanket arm in arm. That night, we finally gave in to our friends who wanted us to meet them at an after-hours club in the Kulturbrauerei. We got there after midnight. I spotted Tom, my friend from New York, at the bar engaged in deep conversation with a beautiful young Asian man. I surprised him from behind with a big hug and he whisked me off my feet, sitting me on the bar.

"I want to introduce you to my new friend, Ian," he said.

"Nice to meet you," I said, winking at Tom.

"I've been hearing all about you and your law school exploits," Ian said in an unmistakable American accent.

"Yes, well, Tom and I were always willing to help each other get into trouble. Are you traveling as well?"

"Yes," Ian said. "I took the New York Bar—I went to Columbia."

"Awesome! Hey, meet my friend, Laura," I said as she joined us.

By now, the bartender was annoyed with me sitting in his way and I jumped down. Laura offered to buy everyone a round and then whispered in my ear.

"Is Tom gay?"

"Oh, yeah. You didn't know?"

"I didn't notice before."

"Girls," Tom said. "Ian has a girlfriend who's going to join us. Be nice to her, okay?"

"Why not?" I said, giving Tom a look.

"She's a lesbian," he whispered.

I paused for a minute, not sure why, thinking.

"You don't mind, do you?" Tom said.

"No! Why would I mind?"

"I don't know, you just look…weirded out or something."

"I've known lesbians, for god's sake," I said, frowning.

"Yeah, well, takes one to know one."

"What are you talking about?" I glared at Tom.

"Never mind."

"What was that all about," Laura asked, handing me my drink.

"Oh, nothing. Ian's girlfriend is joining us."

"I thought he was gay, too," she said, confused.

"He is. She's not that kind of girlfriend. She's…"

"What?"

"Nice, I'm sure."

Just then Elliott walked in with someone I didn't know. It had to be her. She was dressed in loose-fitting jeans held up by a chain belt, the jeans worn and ripped at one knee and under one pocket. And high top, black Converse Chucks. Her tight T-shirt showed off sinewy arms and shoulders and abs. Her short hair was straight and almost black, her skin an olive hue. In contrast to her tough girl outfit, her hands, her eyes, and nose and mouth were all delicate, almost like a doll's.

"Here she is!" Ian squealed and ran toward her, giving her a big kiss.

"Thanks for meeting her, El," Tom said.

"No problem," Elliott said. "Did you get into the exhibit?"

"We did. We owe you one, buddy."

Ian introduced us to Christine.

"We grew up together," he said. "Outside Tokyo."

"Tokyo?" I said.

"We both have Japanese moms," he said, holding hands with her. "Our dads are American. They sent us to an American school with diplomats so we would learn English with an American accent."

She laughed. "Nice to meet all of you."

"That's so interesting," I said to Christine. "Where are you living now?"

"I finished grad school at Berkeley last year," she said. "Computer science. Now I live in the city. San Francisco."

"Finally, a non-lawyer! Thank god. We're on the verge of boring each other to death," I said.

She smiled at me, looking me over. I felt my face flush crimson and was glad it was so dark in there. I glanced at Laura, who looked back with a furrowed brow and gritted teeth.

"Can I get you a drink?' Laura asked her.

"Sure," she said. "A beer is fine. Anything German on tap."

Her beer in hand, Christine planted herself next to me.

"Tom tells me you're interested in technology law."

I had taken a couple of intellectual property courses, but I had never thought too much about it. Tom, what are you up to?

"Well," I said, "uh, clearly it's one of the hottest practice areas right now. Especially where you are, in the Bay Area."

"Have you thought about coming to San Francisco? I know you're from Dallas, but is there really that much action there?"

I stole a look at Tom over her shoulder. He gave me a silly grin. I glared back. I played along.

"You know, I have been thinking about that a lot lately. My family is in Dallas, but that's not a really good reason to be there careerwise."

"You should come visit. I'd love to show you around."

She pulled a card out of her back pocket.

"Let me know," she said.

"What's up, ladies?" Laura said, joining us.

"Jen's coming to check out San Francisco," Christine said.

"Really?" Laura looked at me.

I smiled at both of them.

"We should be dancing!" I said.

I pulled both of them out on the dance floor and found them competing for the space next to me. When the music slowed to a ballad, Christine asked if Laura minded if she took the slow dance.

"Be my guest," Laura said, bowing out and retreating to the sideline.

I watched her while Christine draped her arms over me and Tom stood with that same stupid grin on his face. I looked away for a second or two and when I looked back, she was gone. I separated from Christine and ran toward Tom.

"Where is she?"

"Who?"

"Laura! For god's sake, Tom."

"I don't know. Maybe the restroom?"

I ran to the ladies' room, but she wasn't there. Shit. Where would she go? I searched the bar from end to end and outside on the terrace. No Laura.

"Fuck!" I said out loud.

"What's wrong?" Tom said, finding me looking off the terrace down the street to the main road.

"Laura's gone."

"She probably just bounced. It's late."

"I don't think so."

"Is there something you want to tell me?"

I looked at him and then at the ground.

"You're more than friends, I take it?"

I took a deep breath.

"I'm not really ready to go there. As I think you know, by the way. But…"

"You don't have to explain. If anyone understands, it's me. Why don't you go. I'm sure she's at your hotel. Call me tomorrow."

I gave him a hug and hailed a taxi. But when I got to the room, her things were gone. It was as though she'd never been there. I panicked. I had no way to get in touch with her. I couldn't imagine where she would go. I ran to the front desk. The night clerk thought he remembered her getting a taxi, but he couldn't remember where she was going. Exhausted, I collapsed into bed in tears.

The next morning, the only thing I could think to do was pack up and head for Amsterdam. That was our last stop and that was where our flight home originated. I thought she would have to end up there at least by flight time. Before I left, I checked with the front desk for a message. I couldn't believe she would disappear on me like that. I wondered if I should report her missing. I dug through my backpack looking for a phone number for any of her friends. Some of them had rented cell phones. I found one for her friend Chet.

"When was the last time you heard from her?" I asked him when I got him on the line.

"She called me last night," he said. "She said something about a change of plans. She's going home early, she said."

"Shit," I said.

"Did something happen?"

"If you hear from her again, ask her to please get a message to me through the hotel we booked in Amsterdam. Please?"

"Are you okay? Is she okay?" he asked.

"I hope so," I said and hung up.

CHAPTER ELEVEN

The driver would not arrive for another twenty minutes, so Laura poured us another drink. I felt her energy focused on me so intently that eventually I got up and began exploring the lighted gardens along the perimeter of her yard, asking questions about varieties of plants and flowers, anything to distract her. She had an encyclopedic knowledge of landscaping and escorted me through it with alacrity.

"Hey," she said as we came to the last flower bed, "there's a 10K next weekend. Are you still running?"

"Yeah," I said, cautiously. "I am."

"We could do it together."

"I'm sure you're way out of my league. I wouldn't want to slow you down."

"Don't be silly. It would be fun. Will you do it?"

By now she had taken my hands like a child begging her mom, her eyes twinkling with just a slight suggestion of mischief.

"Please?"

"If you promise me something," I said.

"Anything."

"That you will not judge me by the speed of my 10K."

She laughed, nodding and smirking at me.

"Fair enough. I'm not out to make you look bad."

"It's a date, then," I said.

The car arrived and, sitting in the back, I looked at my phone and realized that I had missed several text and voice messages from Alex. I listened to one of the messages. Alex was furious with me, but I couldn't tell what had happened. I called her, even though it was almost one in the morning.

"Where are you?" she almost shouted.

"On the way back. I told you I was having dinner at Laura's."

"Well, while you were out gallivanting with your old girlfriend, Mom took your rental car for a joy ride."

"What?"

"That's right. We're at the emergency room now. She's fine, but they're keeping her here overnight for observation."

"Shit! How did this happen?"

"You can't leave your keys where she can find them. She gets confused. She thought the car was hers and she decided she needed to go to the grocery store. Thank god she only hit a light pole and didn't kill anyone."

"Oh my god. I'm so sorry. Which hospital? I'll come there now."

I relieved Alex, telling her I would stay the rest of the night and check Mom out in the morning.

"So, how was Laura?" Alex asked, gathering up her things.

I took a deep breath.

"It was a little strange."

"Don't tell me she came on to you?"

I laughed a little, nodding.

"You are kidding me. She has some nerve."

"Yeah, she's complicated."

"I think you're being generous."

"Okay, she can be an ass."

"She's a narcissistic egomaniac."

"Alex…"

"No, Jen. Don't let her lure you in again. She's dangerous. Emotionally."

"Okay, okay."

"You're vulnerable right now because of Mary. But don't let that mess with your head."

"I got it, sis. Take a breather."

I thought about what Alex said. I knew I shouldn't think twice about Laura. Shouldn't let her back in. Not with everything that had happened between us. And not with my marriage to Mary at an inflection point. But I couldn't deny that she had a power over me that had not diminished in all these years, despite how it ended. I knew there was a line I couldn't cross without risking the family I had worked so hard to build, the life I loved so much. But Mary had put the first crack in that facade and what she had done weakened my defenses. I had started playing scenarios out in my head, then stopping myself before they went too far. It was like rehearsing, or trying it out. Imagining what it would be like without committing to follow through. That wasn't cheating, was it?

I drove Mom home from the hospital the next morning.

"What in tarnation," she said when I explained how she'd ended up in the emergency room. "What is wrong with me?"

"It's my fault, Mom. You got confused and I had left those keys right where you used to always keep yours. I'm just glad you weren't hurt."

"Lord, have mercy. Has it come to this? I have to have a guard on me all the time to keep me from doing something crazy?"

"No, no. We, I, just have to be more careful."

"How was your date?"

"My date?"

"You're all dressed up with my jewelry."

"Oh, it was nice. Not a date. Just a dinner with friends."

"You look like you took a roll in the hay—the walk of shame, dear girl."

"Mom! What do you know about that?"

I didn't bother to point out that I had spent the night in a chair in her hospital room.

"Oh, I know a few things."

She patted me on the knee. This was a side of my mother I had not seen until she developed dementia. A bawdy side that was new to me.

"Well, in this case, it was only late-night drinking."

"You're not cheating on Mary, are you?"

She frowned at me, quite serious.

"No! Nothing like that."

"Well, you better not. She's a good catch. She's lovely and a doctor, too!"

"You know, I've made a pretty good living myself, Mom. Not to take anything away from Mary."

"I know, sweetie, but having a doctor in the family is something I'm very proud of."

I shook my head in disbelief. The things that came out of her mouth these days.

"You need to help your sister, by the way."

"That's why I'm here, Mom."

"I know, but I don't think you know everything you need to know."

"Fill me in."

"You know Dave's friend Robert."

"His best man in the wedding," I said.

"Well, I think he and your sister…"

"What—Robert and Alex?"

"I think you might want to look into that."

I couldn't believe it. She must be confused. On the other hand, she could see right through me.

"Is this something new?" I asked.

"Oh, honey, you know my mind is not what it used to be. I think it's been a while, but, I lose track of time."

"Wow, this is surprising to me."

"Yes, well, you miss a lot when you're not around here very much."

"Ouch, Mom."

"You've been pretty scarce the last few years."

"I had kids at home! And you could have come to California. You never came. Almost never."

"Well, I guess I can't deny that. What's important is you're here now. And you should snoop around your sister's world a little. I worry about her."

CHAPTER TWELVE

On the train to Amsterdam, I alternated between feeling furious with Laura and worrying that our friendship was over. On one hand, I thought what she did was a monstrous manipulation. On the other hand, I thought maybe she had actually been hurt by the attention I gave Christine. In any event, it was the height of immaturity for her to run away, abandoning me and our plans without a word. So, on the whole, I was furious.

It was a day early for our hotel reservation, but they had a room, so I checked in. I asked if there were any messages for me, but the answer was no. I settled my things in the room and went out for a walk along the canals. I rented a bike and rode to the Oosterpark where I took pictures of most of the sculptures, asking other tourists to photograph me. The sun was bright, shining down on my unprotected head. I was pissed I hadn't remembered my cap. I got overheated at one point and stopped at a little outdoor café to rest. I had a beer and watched people enjoying themselves, thinking I should figure out who else was in Amsterdam so I could hook up with them. Realizing I didn't want to explore Amsterdam at night by myself and getting worked up over Laura's unbelievably selfish bullshit.

When I got back to the hotel, the front desk clerk stopped me on the way in.

"Someone is here to see you," she said.

I went around the corner to the lobby bar and there she was. I didn't smile. She looked away as soon as we made eye contact.

"Come sit," she said. "Please."

I walked to the counter and sat down on the barstool next to her.

"I'm sorry," she said.

I stared at my hands clasped in front of me. The bartender asked what I wanted and I ordered a beer.

"I'm really sorry," she said. "I hope you can forgive me."

I didn't answer right away because my instinct was to lash out, punish her, make her feel like a jerk. She deserved it, but I didn't want to risk losing track of her again. I thought she might run if I went too hard.

"What the hell happened? Why did you run like that?" I asked finally.

She sighed heavily and took a sip of her drink.

"I freaked out," she said. "I was so insanely jealous when I saw you with someone else, it hit me. I thought I was just, you know, having a little fun, messing around with you. Nothing serious. Nothing real."

I nodded.

"I realize it's a lot more than that and I don't know what to do with that. It scares me."

I stayed quiet, thinking.

"Do you understand?" she asked.

"I understand," I said. "This is not what I expected either. I was trying to do what you said in Paris. You know, go with the flow. No promises."

"And that's what you were doing. That other girl, that was… fine. I don't have any claim on you."

"We were just dancing."

"I know. I couldn't believe it—how I felt. How crazy I felt when I realized you could be with someone else. I had no idea I could feel that way."

"It's a good thing you showed up here. I was planning on never speaking to you again."

"I don't blame you," she said. "I'm really sorry."

"And now?"

"I don't know. Maybe...slow down a little? Get back to being friends?"

"Are you going home early then?"

She gripped her glass and sniffed a little.

"I don't want to, if it's okay with you. Can we finish the trip like we planned?"

"I guess so, but I don't know if I can go back to being just friends. That's not how I feel."

She was quiet, both of us staring ahead.

"Can we agree that...we won't be...physical? For the rest of the trip?"

"That's what you want?"

"I don't want to lose you, but I don't see myself...that way."

"That way. You mean gay."

"Bi. Whatever."

"Okay, if that's what you want. Let's have a good time. Pretend none of that happened."

"I'm not saying that," she said, grabbing my hand. "I'm not saying I want to forget it happened or pretend it didn't happen."

I held her hand, my heart beating into my chest so hard I started to feel faint.

"I'll do what you want," I said, "but I won't deny how I feel."

"Don't give up on me," she said, whispering into my ear as she gave me a hug.

What does that mean? I raised my glass to hers. Wasn't she the one who came on to me in the first place? It's not like I stalked her and tried to turn her gay. *She just doesn't want to face up to who she is. But I'm over all that—I know who I am.* Her eyes lingered on mine for far too long, as if she already regretted the promise to keep her hands to herself.

* * *

Laura and I were determined to enjoy every last minute of the waning days of our vacation. We rode bikes all over town, toured the canals by boat, visited the Anne Frank House and every museum, tried out several coffee houses. On our last evening, we decided to start by getting high at one of them near the Red Light District.

As we strolled through the streets, past prostitutes displaying themselves in full-length windows, advertising their attractions, Laura took my hand.

"I thought we weren't doing that," I said, annoyed at first.

"Screw it," she said. "I'm done with being a martyr. Is that okay with you?"

My resolve melted just like that, and I put my arm around her, pulling her close.

"No more whipsawing me back and forth. Agreed?"

She nodded. I led her out of the crowd and stopped under an awning. I kissed her as she pulled me forward, grasping the back of my neck and pressing so hard I got dizzy. I kissed her eyes, her cheek, her ear, her neck. I wanted to devour her. When someone yelled we should get a room, we laughed and walked quickly back to our hotel. We hadn't eaten dinner, but we didn't care. It was our last night in Europe and both of us were ravenous for each other. We couldn't stop touching and kissing and sucking and fucking. But at last, our hunger for food finally conquering our hunger for sex, we ordered room service. We sat half-naked in bed as we ate, trying not to think about our impending return to real life. We hardly slept. We talked and talked.

"What are you going to do with Mike?"

"He's picking me up at the airport," she said, frowning.

"Hmmm."

"I'll break up with him. Soon."

I sat silent, just holding her hands in mine. "What's wrong?" she asked.

"I don't know. It feels weird, thinking of you with him."

"I understand, but the truth is, we weren't even having that much sex."

I nodded, but couldn't help visualizing it.

"He probably cheated on me while I was gone anyway," she said.

"You think?"

"We've been half-assed for months. I'm sure he's been on the lookout for someone else. For a while."

"You're not sad?"

"No. The last year, we dated more for convenience than anything. With school, I didn't want to be bothered with dating someone new. And he was comfortable. It's no big deal."

"What about me?" I said, running my hand through her hair.

"You," she said, pushing me on my back, "you're a big problem."

"Is that so?"

"Seriously, Jen, I don't know what to do about this. I think I'm in love with you. But I can't be in love with you. It doesn't work in my world."

"It's not exactly my world, either."

"I know. I don't mean it that way."

"So does that mean we won't see each other? Like this, anyway?"

"Could we keep it secret?"

She kissed me, her hand pressing my throbbing groin.

"No," I said, pushing her hand away. "I don't like that idea. Live in the closet?"

"You don't have to think of it as a closet. It's just no one else's business."

"It seems like living a lie."

"I don't know how people would react to us if we came out as lesbians. It could ruin our lives. Our careers. Texas is not Paris or Berlin or Amsterdam."

I nodded, realizing how right she was. I hadn't really thought through the implications of what I wanted with her. Suddenly, it seemed hopeless.

"We could move," I said, half-smiling.

"Let's take it one day at a time. I want to be with you. I want to make it work."

We fell asleep around dawn and woke up just in time to get to the airport.

CHAPTER THIRTEEN

Shocked by Mom's accusation, I drove over to Alex's, knowing she was there after carpool.

"I'm not judging," I said, "but is it true?"

"Let's go to the study," she said. "I don't want the boys to overhear anything."

We sat at the table where she had piled up her paperwork.

"Something was going on," she said. "But it's not what you're thinking. I honestly have no idea how Mom caught on. She's like a savant these days."

"I've noticed."

She sighed, shaking her head.

"Robert came to me about a year ago and told me he was pretty sure Dave was having an affair."

"What?"

"Yeah. She's in London. She's a bookseller at a rare bookstore that Dave had dealings with."

"Why didn't you tell me about her?"

"I didn't want to believe it myself. Robert and I started snooping around on Dave, trying to confirm it or not. But we never really got to the bottom of it."

"Nothing's ever simple, is it? I guess you haven't heard anything from this person since Dave…died?"

"Robert called the bookstore, to see if he could speak to her, just on the pretense that it was a business notification. But she's out of town or something. He left a message."

"Wait, wait, wait…Now I remember. The creditor that filed the involuntary bankruptcy petition. It was Peter Harrington, a rare bookshop in London."

"Really?" Alex said. "It's in Kensington. Are you sure?"

"Yes! We need to let Laura know about this development."

"Why? What would Dave's affair, if he was having one, have to do with anything?"

"I don't know. Maybe nothing. But it's an odd coincidence, don't you think?"

"I swear to god. That man. He's going to fucking haunt me."

I gave Alex a tight hug.

"I'll see if Laura can meet with us in the morning. Try not to worry about anything for now."

I drove Alex downtown the next day.

"Isn't this weird for you? Dealing with her? I can't believe you can compartmentalize like that."

"I guess in my mind there's no point in being bitter about what happened so long ago. Things turned out great for me. It's the past. It really doesn't matter now."

Laura met us in the conference room with her paralegal and an investigator.

"Alex," Laura said, "I need to ask you some questions. They may sound intrusive, but we have to have all the facts in order to represent you—Dave's estate—as well as we can."

"I understand," Alex said, looking away.

Watching Laura command the room put me into a swoon, to the point that I had a hard time following what she was saying. I reached for a glass of water, sweat beading on my forehead and stars circling like a halo. *Stop it! Focus!* She was so much better than I had ever been. It was her calling. It was no surprise she had come so far and done so well. She paced behind a lectern that held her notes, like a professor in a classroom.

"Were you involved in the day-to-day operation of your husband's business?"

I expected Alex to say no immediately, but she hesitated.

"Not really," she said.

"What does that mean? Tell me exactly."

"Well, I would sometimes help with the books."

"The business is described as a collectibles business. Can you tell me more about what types of collectibles the business dealt in?"

"It was rare books, antiquities, and some art, that kind of thing."

"Did he take frequent trips abroad?"

She nodded. "He went to London, Paris, Berlin, Madrid, about four times a year. He was usually gone for three weeks at a time."

"Do you have any reason to believe he was dealing in anything illegal?"

"Like what?" She frowned.

"Forgeries or fakes?"

"No! Why would you think that?"

"We have to ask. The cash flow coming through his bank accounts was quite substantial. Much larger than you would expect from a trade in routine collectibles."

"I can't believe he would be involved in anything like that."

"Okay," Laura said, making notes. "When you did the books, helped with the books, what was your impression of the health of the business?"

"Money was always tight. Even though a lot of money was coming in, almost as much was going out. He was usually robbing Peter to pay Paul. Just ahead of the debt collectors. The last two years especially. We barely had enough to keep afloat."

"So he was anticipating bankruptcy?"

"He told me he was thinking about it. That he was making some moves, as he put it, just in case. But he also told me that he had a Hail Mary pass to throw, but wouldn't give me details."

"Okay. We can see that he was trying to protect some assets, without success."

"Is there any hope?" Alex asked.

"I'll do my best. We'll make the case to the trustee that you and the children need to be provided for ahead of the creditors."

"Thank you, Laura. I can't tell you how much I appreciate your help."

"I'm sorry you have to deal with it. I know how stressful it is, believe me."

"There's something else," I said to Laura, glancing at Alex.

"Go ahead," Alex said.

"There's some possibility that Dave was having an affair with a woman who worked at the London bookstore that filed the bankruptcy petition."

"At Peter Harrington?"

"Yes. Alex never got proof of it, so we don't know for sure. But their best friend, Robert, Dave's best friend, brought it up to Alex a year ago."

"That's interesting," Laura said, furrowing her brow.

"Is it important?" Alex asked.

"Yes, I think it could explain a lot," she said.

"What do you mean?" I asked.

"It has to do with the liability that triggered the involuntary bankruptcy move."

"Sounds complicated," Alex said.

"Not really. In order to file that petition, you have to have an established liability. Theirs was a claim against Dave's company for eight million dollars based on delivery of fraudulent goods. He apparently sold them a fake Shakespeare First Folio. They filed suit in Dallas several months ago and he failed to respond. So they have a judgment."

"Eight million dollars?" Alex stood up and began to pace the room.

"But what does that have to do with this alleged girlfriend?" I asked.

"They claimed that a female employee of Peter Harrington did the deal with Dave's company. It could be her."

"Unbelievable," I said.

"What a fucking bastard," Alex said.

"Do you think he was routinely trading in fakes and forgeries?" I asked.

"We're pursuing that theory, but there is more to it than that. There were so many international wire transfers, rapid-fire, over a long period of time. And yet no real money in the bank for the business itself."

"I admit that Dave has always been sketchy, but that stuff! That's a whole other level."

"Listen, you two, there's one more thing I can think of that might have something to do with all of this," Alex said.

"Go ahead," Laura said.

"God. I really thought this would all go away when he died," she said, pressing her fingers hard into her temples.

"Tell me," I said, sitting next to her and drawing her hair back away from her face.

She twisted her hands together in her lap. "I don't know details because he wouldn't tell me and I didn't really want to know, but it was like he was covering bets or something. He asked me for help about a month before he died, with a bank transaction. We were waiting for a large sum, over a million dollars, to come in from a bank in Geneva, Switzerland."

"Ha," I said. "A Swiss bank account. Interesting."

"Once it came in, he had me go to the bank and take out a million dollars in a certified check made out to him. I gave it to him and that's the last I saw of it."

"Wow."

"That's it. I don't know anything else."

I put my hand on her shoulder.

"It's okay. None of this is your fault."

"Jen's right," Laura said. "You're the victim here."

I hugged Alex and told her that Laura and I would figure this out. She needed to focus on her children and creating some kind of normalcy for them.

"Oh, I've fucked them up good," she said. "They'll pay the price, no doubt, for the sins of their father and mother."

"Alex, please. Don't go all biblical now. You've got to keep it together."

She looked at me as if seeing an unfamiliar face.

CHAPTER FOURTEEN

We came out of Customs to find Mike and Chris waiting for us on the other side of baggage claim. I felt sick, seeing him, seeing them, looking at Laura, seeing doubt in her eyes. I wanted to scream.

"Hey, you," Chris said to me, grabbing my bags and putting his arm around me. "I thought you'd never get home."

He tried to kiss me and I averted my mouth, hugging him instead. I saw Laura over his shoulder, kissing Mike, acting normal. My chest felt hollow, like my heart was scooped out. I breathed deeply, trying hard not to cry, but a tear slipped out. Chris assumed it was a tear of joy at seeing him. I wiped it away and started walking.

"I didn't know you were in town," I said.

"You don't sound too excited about it."

"I just wasn't...you know, I'm tired. I didn't plan on doing anything tonight."

"Mike and I bought stuff to make dinner for y'all. At Laura's. We thought you would like it."

He pouted a little and I considered whether it would be a good idea for the four of us to be in such close quarters. I didn't know if I could handle it.

"The guys are cooking for us," Laura said, slipping her arm into mine and squeezing. "Isn't that nice of them?"

"Sure," I said, "if you say so."

"They won't suspect a thing," she said into my ear. "Don't worry."

We rode home in Mike's king cab pickup truck, the guys in front since the back was a little cramped for Chris's 6'2" frame. Laura reached for my hand and held it across the seat. I looked at her like she was nuts, but she smiled and winked. I shook my head and looked the other way, staring out the window at the barren highway from the airport into the city. I felt a weird sense of disconnect—almost physical, like vertigo. My home now felt like enemy territory, unwelcoming and threatening in some way I couldn't quite identify yet.

"It's good to be home, I bet," Mike said. "Nothing like the good ole US of A, right?"

He looked over his shoulder for agreement.

"Right," we said at the same time, not without irony.

"I'm gonna need a shower," I said. "Drop me off at my place and I'll come over as soon as I can?"

"No," Laura said, a little too aggressively, "you can shower at my place."

"But—" I started to protest.

"No, come on, we don't want to stay up late anyway, so let's get dinner going. If you go home, you might fall asleep."

"Okay, okay."

Laura's apartment was on the ground floor and she had a terrace out back with a charcoal grill. The guys went out to work on starting up the fire while Laura and I went in to clean up and change. She came into the shower with me.

"I really can't believe you," I said as she stood behind me, soaping up my back and moving to my chest and stomach and on down.

She kissed my neck and I felt my clit bursting open like a sunflower on photo-elapsed time. I gasped and she put her hand softly over my mouth, quieting me.

"Oh my god," I said, turning and kissing her hard. "You are going to be the death of me."

"At least you'll die happy," she said, laughing.

"Let me wash your hair," I said, trading places.

She leaned back against me as I poured shampoo onto her head and massaged it in slowly.

"Mmmm," she said. "That feels good."

"Hey, what's going on in there!"

We heard a banging on the bedroom door and Chris's voice.

"Cocktails are ready! Come on."

"Jesus," I said. "He's annoying."

She rinsed her hair and I got out of the shower, watching her, wondering when I would see her like that again, if ever, already aching for the past, for another country. She caught my eye and I could tell she was thinking the same thing.

"One more kiss," she said as we toweled off and she pinned me against the tiled wall, her tongue caressing my lips and exploring the inside of my mouth.

"I love you," she said.

"How do you know?"

"I just know."

"What does it mean?"

She held me, looked at me, quiet.

"I don't know," she said finally, "but I've never felt this way before."

"Hey!" Chris again. "Are you ever coming out of there?"

"He's drunk," I said. "Chris, go away. We're coming!"

We sat outside under the stars, the wind cooling down the September night, sipping martinis and watching the guys turn steaks on the grill. I should have had some of the bread and cheese they had thoughtfully prepared, but I had no appetite. I felt the drink going to my head, combining with the jet lag. I fought off the urge to go lie down.

"Watch out!"

I jerked awake at Chris's voice, my drink spilling into my lap. I had nodded off.

"Oh, god, I am so tired. Sorry."

We sat down to dinner and I pepped up a little as I forced myself to eat. I avoided looking at Laura. I was sure I would give myself away if I did. *This is what it will be like*, I thought. Hiding. Pretending. Sneaking kisses, touches. Not for me. I guess a lot of people would find it exciting. The sex is better if it's against the rules. I didn't want that. I wanted a life with Laura. Out in the open.

"How's it going to be, working together?" Mike said.

"What do you mean?" I said, a little too defensively as the thought crossed my mind that he somehow had figured out our secret.

"You know, competition. I've heard those firms weed people out. Cutthroat. All that stuff."

"It's not as bad as all that," Laura said. "But yeah, I'll be gunning for you."

She smiled and pushed at me and we looked at each other for the first time in over an hour.

"Watch your back," I said and looked away before I melted in desire.

"But seriously," I responded to Mike. "I don't think Laura and I will compete. We're in different practice groups, so, you know."

"We probably won't even see each other much. We're on different floors."

At that point, my eyelids felt like they weighed at least twenty pounds each.

"I'm beat," I said. "I have to go home before I tip over."

"Yeah, let's get going," Chris said.

"Are you staying with your sister?" I asked him hopefully.

"Of course not. I'm staying with you."

I couldn't figure out a way not to have him come home with me without starting a fight, so I let him gather up my stuff and take it to his car. Laura walked out with us and Mike followed her.

"See you Monday," she said to me, hugging me, her tongue darting into my ear.

In the car, Chris tried to get me talking, verbally poking at me about how long I'd been away and how annoyed he was about it.

"I can't live like this," he said.

"What are you talking about?"

"You can't just go around doing whatever you want all the time without discussing things with me."

"I'm too tired to have this conversation right now."

"Well, I've had it. I won't put up with it anymore."

"Fine," I said.

"What do you mean, fine?" he shouted.

"I mean it's over."

"C'mon, Jen. You don't mean that," he said, his shout turning to a plea.

"I was going to have this conversation anyway, so it might as well be now."

We pulled up to my apartment complex and I jumped out of the car, demanding he open the trunk so I could get my things. He argued with me and tried to take back his bullying, but I insisted he give up and get going. As I watched him drive off, I realized I felt nothing. His departure from my life was a nonevent.

CHAPTER FIFTEEN

I met Laura at the Starbucks near the starting line of the 10K that Saturday morning.

"Ready?"

"I am and, hey, I wanted to ask you something," I said. "See, I'm training for a triathlon."

"What! Why didn't you tell me?"

"I don't know. It didn't seem relevant. But, anyway, I want you to push me today. I'd like to hit thirty-six."

"That's fast."

"But you're faster."

"What's your PB?" she asked.

"37.48."

"Okay. I'll pace you."

"Awesome. Thanks," I said.

"Can you have lunch after?"

"I think so. I'll check in with Mom when we're done."

True to her word, she paced me faster than I was comfortable. I struggled at the 8K mark, starting to let up a little.

"Come on!" she yelled. "You can do it!"

I blocked out the pain and focused on the group in front of us. It was the perfect day for a race. Seventy degrees. No humidity. We finished at 36.30, short of my goal, but a new PB for me. I gave her a high five as we grabbed water and a banana.

"Thanks for kicking my ass," I said. "That was great."

"Glad to help. I can work on the swimming and biking with you, too. Those are really cute, by the way," she said, admiring my shorts and lingering on my legs.

I ignored the flirtation.

"Thanks. What do you want to do for lunch?"

"Could I interest you in going over to Fort Worth?"

We got into Laura's convertible Tesla and took off.

"Nice car," I said. "You don't mess around."

"You know how it is here. You drive a lot, so it's fun to have something like this. But I admit, it's an indulgence."

"Hey, any more intel on the woman in London?"

"Let's not talk business today. Do you mind? It can wait until Monday."

"Of course."

"How is your mom, by the way?"

"She has mild dementia, but she remembers you."

"Really?"

"She warned me about you," I said, smiling.

"She remembers everything?"

"Seems like it."

She got quiet and stared straight ahead, suddenly miles away, and I thought she must be going over it all in her head, remembering the words, the tears, the pain. I was quiet, too, transported back twenty years just like that. She pulled into the barbecue place she wanted to show me. We got our lunch at the counter and sat down at a picnic-style table across from each other. She made small talk at first. She told me about her kids, how the boy was a natural athlete who played three sports. How the girl was a brainiac and wanted to be an engineer. How she and her husband had been in couples therapy for years, but never made any progress. But then her tone became more serious.

"I want to talk to you about…what happened, Jen. I want to apologize in a meaningful way."

"It's okay. Really. I don't want to relive it."

"Will you indulge me, though? Will you listen to me?"

Her eyes bore into mine, like lasers, intense, almost desperate.

"Is it that important to you?"

"It's all I can think about. Ever since you walked into my office after all these years. I feel like I can't move forward without this conversation."

I sipped my iced tea and thought about it seriously, maybe for the first time. I wasn't sure what she wanted from me. Forgiveness? Absolution? I didn't know if I could give her that. I worried that what she had to say to me was not something I wanted to hear. That we might be at odds again.

"I can understand how you must be feeling," she said. "Like this is my issue, not yours. You shouldn't have to placate me or say something to make me feel better. I get that. And that's not what I'm looking for."

"What are you looking for?"

She fumbled with her food, not looking me in the eye.

"I want to explain myself. To you. To the person who knows things about me that no one else knows. I don't need a reaction from you. All I need is for you to hear me."

I thought about it, not sure I could trust her yet, could ever trust her, when it came to this.

"I'll be honest with you," I said. "I didn't expect this and I don't know how I feel about it."

"It doesn't have to be now. You can think about it. But please, think about it."

"I'll listen," I said after several seconds, wanting to get past this conversation. Bury the whole thing. "I'll do my best to hear and understand. But I can't absolve you of anything. Don't look to me for anything like that."

"No. I can't. I won't."

"And I think you should realize that it may not help. It may lead to more questions. More confusion. And I'm no therapist."

She nodded. I glanced around at tables packed with families and raised my eyebrows in a query.

"There's a gazebo over there. In that park."

We walked across the street and sat on the bench inside the gazebo, facing each other at an angle. She drew one leg up on the bench and hugged her knee while she uncharacteristically struggled for the words she needed. She pulled loose the tie that held her hair back, shaking the perfectly highlighted locks over her face and then pushing them back. She looked small and vulnerable, so different from her presence in her office, in her suit, her armor. I felt powerful in contrast. Sure of who I was, at least. I had a flash of insight into how different my life had been as compared to hers. She lived with a strict set of rules that defined her choices, her options. It flooded back to me, how important it had been to her, twenty years before, to cultivate an image, carefully, meticulously even. She looked at me, doubt in her eyes, as I waited for her to speak.

"That day," she said. "The day everything blew up. All I could think was, my career was over. My life ruined."

I shifted in my seat, looking away from her, saying nothing.

"In my mind, no one would want to have anything to do with me if they thought that's what I was. I would be ostracized, lose my job, lose everything I had worked my whole life to achieve."

"You made that clear at the time," I said, starting to feel annoyed by the whole conversation.

"I was weak. I was a coward. What I did was wrong. I regret it. If I could go back and change it, I swear I would."

"What do you mean, exactly? What would you change?"

She looked away and I saw that her lip was trembling.

"I was in love with you. Crazy, scary in love with you. Like nothing else I've ever experienced. And I've never really gotten over you."

I felt a sharp pain reverberate through me, from my gut to my chest, as though I were a cleaned fish. Melancholy came over me. I closed my eyes and tried to come up with a response.

"I don't know what to say," was all I could manage as I opened my eyes to reengage with her.

"What a waste, huh?" she said, reaching for my hand.

I pulled away. "I don't know. I think that depends on what you would change, which you haven't said yet."

She nodded, still holding on to her upraised knee, acknowledging my point. She took a breath as though ready to launch in, then exhaled without saying a word. She stared at the ground and I thought she must have decided against sharing whatever revised version of events she had in mind.

"If I could do it over," she said, still staring down, "I would own it. I wouldn't deny it."

She raised her gaze to look me in the eye.

"I would take the consequences."

She had leaned forward as she spoke these words and I knew she meant them. I couldn't help imagining that alternative universe, considering how different things might be right now had she taken that approach.

"But the most important thing I would change," she continued, "is that I would have pursued you—us—for as far as we could go."

Without warning and without my permission, tears flooded my eyes and spilled over, hot, searing my face with surprising ferocity, the memory of my humiliation years before crashing down on me.

"I'm so sorry for what I did," she said. "Deeply, profoundly, sorry."

I couldn't manage to form a sentence and, looking away from her, did my best to quell the immense sense of loss that threatened to overwhelm me. I hadn't realized how much heartache I had buried for so long and now it had burst from its grave deep in my subconscious, scorching my insides, as though I had swallowed fire.

She touched me on the knee lightly, saying my name. She tried to put her arm around me, but I moved away.

"This is too much," I said. "I thought I was ready to hear you, but I, I wasn't prepared, I'm..." I trailed off, my throat narrowing, my thoughts muddled.

"It's okay. I understand. In some ways, I've been working on this apology for twenty years. You need time."

We sat quietly a while longer and then I said I had to get back to my mother. We rode in silence back to where we had left my car. We embraced without speaking, neither of us able to articulate our feelings any further. As I drove away, I saw Laura in my rearview mirror, watching me, just standing there with her hand on the car door, as if she didn't want to move until I had faded into the distance.

CHAPTER SIXTEEN

September turned into October as we waited for our bar results. Laura and I would meet at six thirty most mornings to take a run and, more often than not, our goodbye kiss would end with one of us pushing the other one onto a couch or a bed and stripping off her clothes. On the weekends, we would shop together and cook for friends either at her place or mine, touching each other when we could, stealing kisses, our clandestine affair playing out right under their noses. I was slowly losing my mind.

"I don't know if I can keep this up," I said one day as we ran through a park near my apartment.

She stopped at a bench and we sat down. "What do you want from me?" she said.

"You know what I want," I said, slumping forward, angry that she wouldn't just talk about it.

"We could get an apartment together," she said, touching my back.

"Oh, that's a great idea. Then I get to hear you having sex with your boyfriend. Brilliant."

"I'm breaking up with him."

"So you've said."

"That's not fair."

"You break up with Mike. Then we'll get an apartment together."

"You won't be happy until it's all out in the open," she said.

"I love you, Laura. I'm not embarrassed by that. I know this is not easy. It's obviously not 'normal.' A lot of people will be upset. But I know this is who I am and I know this is who you are. We have each other. We'll get through it."

She shook her head no.

"I'm not ready," she said. "It's all happening too fast."

I got up from the bench and started running again. As she caught up to me, I took off as fast as I could. I could only stay ahead of her for a few yards, she was so fast.

"Jen!" she shouted and I slowed down to a trot. "Please. Don't give up on me."

"Break up with him. That's the least you can do."

We threw a big bash to celebrate passing the bar. We took over the party room at my apartment building, out next to the pool. We invited some of the lawyers from our firm who were a little bit ahead of us. We hired a bartender and got a margarita machine and a keg. The alcohol was flowing.

Laura had broken up with Mike the day we got our bar results back. As she predicted, he was not the least bit resistant, and we were pretty sure he had another girlfriend already. When I had broken up with Chris, it hadn't been so easy. He called me incessantly, cried and told me I'd be sorry. I had to ask him several times to pick up his stuff from my apartment and, in the end, I packed it and sent it to him in Houston. At least I didn't have to run into him around town. He had no reason to be in Dallas without me.

The party doubled as a celebration of our newly "single" status and I allowed myself to fantasize about living with Laura under the guise of being roommates. We were already shopping for a new place.

As the party went past midnight, we were all so drunk we had no concept of how loud we were as we spilled out onto the pool deck. Several people fell, jumped, or were pushed in and, by one a.m., the cops had shut us down. A few people lived close enough to walk home. Some others slept in their cars and the rest got cabs home. Laura stayed with me.

What we didn't realize was that one of the older associates, a woman named Michelle, had passed out behind the couch in my living room. As she stumbled around in the middle of the night looking for the bathroom, she turned on the light in my bedroom and saw Laura and I lying there in a naked embrace.

"Oh my god!" she shrieked.

Laura and I jumped up, confused and disoriented, and she kept screaming.

"What the—shit. Oh, Jesus. Fuck!"

I grabbed a robe and tried to calm her down.

"The bathroom's out here," I said, ignoring the elephant in the room and getting her out of it.

I turned to Laura, who sat in what appeared to be a catatonic state, staring straight ahead, pulling the sheets up over her bare body.

"Laura?"

She looked at me, blinked several times and then got up, got dressed, and left. She hadn't said anything to me, despite my entreaties. When Michelle came out of the bathroom, I told her she could sleep on the couch if she wanted to, but she said she would call a cab. I asked her if she wanted coffee, and she said no.

"Is that…was that…you know, a one-off thing?"

"That?" I said, pointing to my bedroom.

She nodded.

"Yes," I lied, knowing I had no right to out Laura. "We were drunk. Shit happens."

"I get it," Michelle said. "I was a LUG—you know, lesbian until graduation."

"Really? Wouldn't have guessed that."

"But you aren't in school anymore. So watch yourself. Unless, of course, you want to invite a guy in. Then it's fine."

She gave me a smirk and I laughed. After she left, I couldn't get back to sleep. I was afraid of what this might have done to Laura's state of mind. It had shaken me pretty badly, like a slap in the face of my domestic fantasy. In the dark of night, Michelle's words echoing in my head, I had a bad feeling about all of it. I finally fell asleep toward daybreak.

I called Laura the minute I woke up. No answer. I called her cell phone. Still no answer. I decided to drive over to her apartment.

"Why are you here?" she said, standing at the threshold so I couldn't come in.

"Why wouldn't I be here?"

"Do you realize how fucked I am?"

"You? Why just you? And I don't think either one of us is fucked."

"Come inside. I don't want the neighbors to hear."

"Laura," I said, stepping into her apartment. "I told Michelle it was just a one-time drunk thing. The bigger issue is, how do we make this work."

Laura sighed and sat down at her kitchen counter.

"We have to cool it, Jen. For a while. We've gotten too lax. People are going to figure out what's going on."

"Yeah. I guess this means we aren't getting an apartment together."

She stared at her hands and said, "Let's give it some time. Let this incident blow over. I want to make sure there aren't any rumors about us."

"Okay, but I think we should act normal. If we suddenly aren't spending time together, that will make people wonder. We can't go from being BFFs to not speaking."

"No, you're right. You're right."

"We've already told people we're getting a place."

"No sex," she said, raising the palm of her hand to me.

"No sex," I said.

But as I said it, I moved to where she sat and stood behind her. I rubbed her shoulders, played with her hair, pulled her head back gently, and, her lips parted, I kissed her. She stood, turned toward me, and ripped my shirt open, pushing me onto the couch.

We lay there after and I whispered in her ear, "No more sex."

"I'm addicted to you," she whispered back.

We fell asleep and, when we woke up, Laura shoved at me playfully.

"Get out of here, will you? I'm hoping that when we live together I'll get sick of you and get over this whole thing."

"Good luck with that," I said, grabbing my purse and laughing as I left.

CHAPTER SEVENTEEN

Back at Mom's, I couldn't get Laura off my mind. What should I do? Should I mount a campaign to get her to leave her husband? Convince her to run away with me and start a new life? Maybe we could live in Europe. Or Central America.

Stop! Are you insane?

I went to Mom's liquor cabinet and made myself a martini. I had to forget this ridiculous fantasy. What about Mary? I felt the sharpest stab of guilt as I visualized her sitting at our kitchen counter, paying our bills, making plans with our friends, waiting for me to come home. I downed the martini and made another one. I joined Mom in her TV room.

"What's the latest?" I asked.

"These reality shows are just about the worst thing that has ever happened to television. And they're bad for the country. Who needs to see a bunch of rednecks and white trash airing all their dirty laundry in front of America. Makes me sick."

"Why are you watching?"

"I accidentally taped this show instead of what I wanted. So I thought why not? How bad could it be? Well, let me tell you, it's awful."

"Delete it."

"I was just about to. What's going on with Alex?"

"We're trying to get organized with the bankruptcy judge so we can figure out what she's going to have to live on."

"You know he had a safety deposit box," she said, looking at me out of the corner of her eye.

"No," I said, "I didn't. Where?"

"It's at a bank in Fort Worth. I think it's Southwest Bank. On Camp Bowie."

"How do you know?"

"One benefit of people thinking you don't know what's going on is that you learn all kinds of things you wouldn't otherwise. He was over here one day. Talking on his cell phone to somebody. He said he had the money in a safety deposit box. I don't know what money. But anyway, later he told me he had to go to the bank in Fort Worth. And, just being conversational, I asked what bank. I grew up there, you remember."

"You are something else, Mom."

We watched the awful reality show anyway, since Mom forgot she had intended to erase it. Soon, she was shaking me awake.

"Jenny," she said. "You fell asleep. Why don't you get to bed?"

The martinis had knocked me out.

"Good night, Mom."

Getting into bed, I picked up my cell phone to silence it when Mary's number showed up.

I answered. She wanted to know all about Laura. Every minute we had spent together. Every word we had said.

"What does she want from you?" she said.

"I don't think she wants anything from me, really. I represent the road not taken. She's decided she made a big mistake years ago and she has a lot of regret."

I could feel Mary tensing on the other end of the line.

"Is she a lesbian?"

"Who knows? She's unhappy, but she doesn't seem willing to do anything about it. She's still wrapped up in being Laura Peters and Laura Peters doesn't leave her husband, announce that she's a lesbian, and then drag her children through a nasty scandal."

I was getting angry just talking about it.

"Let's leave her to solve her own problems," I said. "You and I have enough of our own. I need to get to bed."

She tried to keep me on the line, but I said good night and hung up. Why was I so irritated with her? She had every right to ask those questions. After all, I was spending too much time with someone I had that kind of history with. It hit me. The sharp pang of guilt again. The hollowing out inside. The feeling of standing on the edge, of looking down from a dizzying height. I closed my eyes and let sleep take over.

On Monday morning, Laura called with new information on Dave's case. It was as if we had never had that bombshell of a conversation on the weekend.

"The woman Dave was having an affair with—her name is Emma—is the daughter of the bookstore's owner," she told me. "She disappeared a few months before Dave died. No one has heard from her."

"What do you think that means?" I asked.

"That she was in on the scam. And they had made plans to get away together, but either he got cold feet or something else interfered with that path."

"I never thought that guy had it in him to be involved in so much intrigue," I said.

"Those are the ones you have to watch out for."

"I wonder what she's like," I said.

"We're tracing her. We need to find her. She'll have a lot of answers."

"Like where's that money…"

"Exactly. It's probably still in Switzerland. If we can return that money to the store, this whole thing could go away."

"Do you really think so?"

"He didn't have other big obligations. Just his lease and some small vendors. It's hard to understand why he went down this road."

"Yeah. He was very disappointed in how his life turned out. He always wanted to make it big. I guess he thought he'd found a way," I said, remembering Dave huddled in his basement office, scheming on one idea after another over the years.

"It's a shame."

"And selfish. Look at all the debris following in his wake."

"Speaking of, you said you had something else," Laura said.

"Right. Mom told me about a safety deposit box that Dave apparently had in Fort Worth. Maybe there's a clue there? I'll find out whether Alex has any idea where he might keep the key."

"Please. We have to track down every lead."

I sighed heavily, the implications of all this beginning to eat into my reserves.

"Is something else wrong?" Laura asked.

"No, I, what do you mean?"

"Are you still upset about what I said Saturday?"

"Why do you say I was upset?"

"Well, you cried pretty hard. I guess I just wonder if I went too far."

"It dredged up a lot of stuff for me," I said. "And things are complicated at home."

Immediately, I was sorry I said that.

"Complicated? With Mary? What's going on?"

She sounded too eager, no doubt hoping to learn that mine was no perfect marriage either.

"Nothing. It's not important," I said.

"I've made you unhappy," she said. "By bringing up the past."

"Stop," I said. "Don't do that."

"Do what?"

"Try to manipulate me like that."

"I wouldn't do that. That's not what I'm doing."

"Okay. Look, I don't want to talk about the past. I can't handle it. I don't think you have any idea how I felt then. How I feel now."

She was silent and I knew I should hang up without saying anything more, but, for some reason I couldn't fathom, I stayed on the line.

"Jen," she said. "Please."

"Please what?"

"Please don't hate me."

"I don't hate you, Laura. I need to go."

"Wait," she said. "Let's reset for a minute. Okay? Just forget all that for now."

"As if," I said.

"Okay, fine. Just, please. I have an idea. For your triathlon training."

"Thanks, but—"

"No, really. Listen," she said. "I have an extra road bike. It will fit you. We could take a big ride this weekend. Go a little east and do some hills."

I thought about it, wary of her motives. But I really did need to train. And I knew she would kick my ass.

"Okay," I said. "Training. And training only."

"Cross my heart," she said.

Alex and I went to dinner alone that night. I asked her about the safety deposit box. She had a vague memory of Dave mentioning something about it the week before he died.

"Let me rack my brain," she said. "It'll come back to me. I know he told me where he put the key."

My sister was a strong woman, but the revelations about Dave, with the latest including a pretty strong suggestion that he was committing some serious crimes, had started to take their toll. She had a beaten-down look about her, her shoulders slumped, her hair not cut or colored for too long, her eyes bleary.

"I know this is unbelievably hard," I said, "but hang in there. We are going to come out on the other side of this just fine. I promise you."

"Thank you. I know you're doing more than you're even telling me."

"Whatever it takes," I said.

"Speaking of which, you seem to be spending more than just business time with Laura Peters. Do you think that's wise?"

"It's a good question. I can tell you Mary is not happy about it."

"I can imagine. She doesn't have anything to worry about though. Right?"

I hesitated.

"Jen?"

"Laura pushes my buttons, okay? She told me on Saturday that if she could do it all over again, she would have stayed with me."

"Seriously?" Alex said, scoffing. She leaned across the table, raising her eyebrows in a concerned arch. "That's easy enough for her to say now, but bullshit walks."

"Don't think I don't realize that," I said.

"I'm starting to worry about you."

"Why?"

"You were so off the cliff for her way back then. And it never got resolved. Yes, you moved on. But you didn't wear out the attraction. It was the biggest tease I've ever seen."

I felt a shiver of apprehension flow through my veins, hot and disorienting. Why was I going to do a bike ride with her on the weekend? Spend hours staring at her perfect ass in Lycra bike shorts?

"I'm right," she continued.

"I'm not saying you're right. But yes, there's a lot of...stuff there. It was more like an amputation than a breakup."

"Do you think you'll do it?"

"Meaning?"

"Have an affair with her."

I didn't answer. I didn't want to think about it. Didn't want my lizard brain to entertain the possibility any further. I finished my wine and said I had to go. Mom would be waiting up for me.

"Don't be mad," she said as we said good night.

"Of course not."

CHAPTER EIGHTEEN

I stepped onto the elevator, headed for the firm's library, and ran smack into Laura. A few other people also occupied the elevator, so I watched my words and body language carefully. Our break from apartment hunting had not lasted long. I told her how my end of the apartment search was going and someone chimed in about a place they knew that was coming available. We actually liked the location, so Laura took down the information and said she would call. I got off at the library floor and she kept going.

She had squeezed my hand surreptitiously and the smell of her perfume lingered on my fingers, distracting me from the research I was supposed to be doing. I had a brief due the next morning and I could see it coming—I would be up all night. Brian, the partner on the case, paged me and I picked up the house phone to speak to him. He was nervous and wanted to know the status of my papers. I calmed him down and told myself to focus.

I worked for four hours straight, then suddenly realized I was starving. It was eight p.m. and I hadn't eaten since noon. I called in an order to the sushi place across the street and headed over to pick it up. My cell phone rang as I left the building.

"What are you doing?" Laura asked.

"Grabbing some dinner and pulling an all-nighter. You?"

"I went to see that apartment," she said.

"And?"

"It's perfect. It's in Lower Greenville. A small building. Two bedrooms and one bathroom. It has a beautiful view of the pool from the balcony. There's parking and it's in our budget. We can move in at the beginning of the month."

"You're sure?"

"Yes, it's available."

"No, I mean you're sure this is what you want to do?"

"Honestly, I think it might be the only way I can keep my sanity. Seeing you every day, but not being with you every night, is driving me nuts."

"I'm excited," I said, visions of domestic bliss filling my imagination.

"Me, too."

"I have to get back to work, but let me know what you need from me."

"I'll bring the application by your office tomorrow."

The meal had made me very sleepy, so I brewed a pot of coffee in the firm eating hall and filled up my thermos. I looked at the clock. It was nine thirty. I had to move faster. I took my books to my office and started typing on the desktop. Before long, I was humming, and the text of the brief was almost finished. I started in on the footnotes and citations. By two a.m. I was done, but needed to proofread it. I set my alarm for a three-hour nap so I would have time to read it over and check everything before eight thirty a.m. when Brian would be in to review it.

"Jen," Laura said, shaking me awake as I lay in my sleeping bag on the floor of my office. "Hey, are you ready?"

"What! What time is it?"

"Seven thirty."

"Shit! I missed my alarm."

"I was worried about you, so I decided to come in early."

"Thank god. But can you help me proof? He'll be here at eight thirty."

We split the brief in half and sped through it, making corrections so fast my wrist started to ache at the keyboard.

"What's this?" Brian asked, standing at the door to my office looking at us like we were cat burglars.

"Hey, there. Laura's helping me proof the brief."

"You're not hitting my file too hard, are you?"

I couldn't tell if he was serious or not.

"I'm not billing," Laura said. "I just thought I'd help out a friend."

"Very generous of you," he said with what I thought was a little too much sarcasm.

"We're still new," I said. "Not jaded and prepared to cut each other's throats yet."

"I see," he said. "Wonder how long that will last."

"Here it comes," I said, pushing send on my email as he walked away.

"Jesus," Laura said. "He's a jerk."

"Oh my god. What a fire drill. I have to go home and shower. I feel like I slept on an airplane. Do you think anyone will miss me if I don't get back until after lunch?"

"Don't worry about it. If anyone asks, I'll tell them you went to the courthouse to pull some old filings."

"You're the best," I said, hugging her as my secretary walked by and gave me a strange look. "See you later."

I walked by the secretarial station.

"I was here all night," I said to Marla, who I shared with another associate. "I'm going home to change clothes and then to the courthouse. I have to pull some old files."

Marla gave me a look like she didn't necessarily believe me, but I didn't have the energy to enhance the credibility of it.

"I'll be back after lunch," I said and turned away before she could say anything.

Marla was a lifer at the firm. She had outlasted generations of associates, which contributed to her credible sense of superiority over someone like me. I didn't ask her for much and she didn't offer. I turned my billables in to her and she took my messages and opened my mail. I tried to stay out of her way otherwise. The other person she worked for was a third-year male associate. She brought him coffee every morning and picked up his lunch when he ate in his office. I saw her bring his dry cleaning in one time and shook my head in disbelief. She noticed and said she was only doing it because he was leaving on a business trip after work.

"That's nice of you," I had said, "but still, it seems demeaning for someone with your skills and seniority to be doing his personal errands."

She had blinked at me without responding.

When I got back that afternoon, I filled out the leasing application Laura had left for me and wrote the security deposit check. I sent it to her in the interoffice mail. I felt a flutter of nerves as I sealed the envelope, not quite believing that I was about to move in with my girlfriend.

"Love note?"

"What?" I said, looking up to see Brian standing in the hall as I placed the envelope in the tray.

"The look on your face. Made me think you're passing love notes."

I laughed a little too boisterously as I turned back toward my office door.

"No, not exactly. What's up?"

"I came by to tell you what a great job you did on the brief. It's about the best quality work I've seen from an associate in a long time."

"Thanks. Let's hope the judge agrees."

"I thought we could have a drink after work. Discuss your career."

Although it was laughably obvious that he was coming on to me, I pushed that thought away. What was wrong with these guys? He had a good-looking wife and three kids. But, then again, plenty of women wouldn't be bothered by that. As much as I didn't want to have a drink with him, I figured I shouldn't refuse.

"Sure," I said, "sounds good. Should we do happy hour? Invite the other associates?"

"Not this time. I want to focus on you. I'll see you at six thirty in the lobby."

He winked at me as he turned away and I felt an unpleasant sensation in my gut, like acid burbling around looking for something to digest. The afternoon passed quickly as I worked to catch up on the files I had ignored in order to get that brief done. I looked at my watch at 6:20 and jumped up to hit the women's room before meeting him. I brushed my hair and teeth and freshened my makeup. *Why am I primping for him?*

He was a young partner, a rising star in the litigation section. He had the power to promote me and raise my profile in the firm. If he decided to put me on a lot of his cases, it would be very good for me. I knew several people were gunning for that position, and I had to admit, I wanted it. Because I liked to win. In fact, the competition might be the only thing keeping me at this job.

As I stood next to him in the lobby before we headed out, a group of my peers, including Laura, came out of the elevator and passed us. I waved and tried to act casual, but I noticed one guy in particular looked very annoyed, no doubt making a big assumption about what I might be willing to do to advance. Laura rolled her eyes at me knowingly.

He took me to a private club at the top of a bank tower—the type that hadn't allowed women in a decade earlier. The view was nice, but the air, ripe with cigar ash and coated in aggressive aftershave, pressed in on me in an unpleasant welcome. We sat next to a floor-to- ceiling window looking out over downtown. I watched as the sun dropped down behind the Dallas skyline, casting a reddish hue over the vista. I ordered a glass of white wine. He ordered bourbon.

"You do good work," he said as we touched our glasses in a toast.

"Thanks."

"Keep it up. You'll see. It's not that hard to do great."

"What do you mean?"

"That most people are mediocre. Even at this level. If you try, if you show up, if you do your work, people will tell you you're great."

"That's it?"

"Most people let life get in their way. You can't depend on them. They get distracted. If you keep up the work ethic I saw on this brief, you're golden."

We ate slightly rubbery shrimp from the happy-hour buffet and chatted a little more about the firm and the path to partner. Then he said he had to get home to put his kids in bed. I felt a flash of guilt for thinking he might have had ideas about hooking up with me. We walked back to the parking garage in our building and he escorted me to my car.

"That's a nice outfit, by the way. You're in great shape." The slight taunt playing on his lips confirmed my original assumption about his motives.

"Thanks," I said with a flat intonation as I jumped into the car and sped away.

CHAPTER NINETEEN

When I arrived at Laura's house that weekend, she was loading her Pinarello onto the rack of her Range Rover. I whistled my approval.

"Nice bike!"

A Cannondale leaned up against the garage door. Dressed in bike gear that showcased her magnificently fit body, Laura looked like an advertisement for a Backroads trip.

"Come over here," she said. "Let me get this one fitted for you."

I complied. She measured me, then worked quickly with wrenches and screws to make the bike a perfect fit. I took it for a test ride.

"I appreciate it," I said, getting off and lifting it up to the rack. I turned to find her eyes lingering hungrily on my body as though she could devour me in one bite. I looked away quickly and took my place on the passenger's side of her vehicle.

"Perfect day, huh?" she said as we rolled out of town toward the nearest stretch of road where we could gain some elevation.

I nodded in agreement, feeling the tension in the space between us. I became conscious of the shallowness of my breath, the slight uptick in my heart rate. I sensed her desire for me, like a third passenger. I began to worry that this had been a bad idea. Maybe the worst idea I'd had lately.

"It's not easy to get good bike training in around here. I usually pack up and head down to Hill Country," she said, sipping from her water bottle and casting a sideways glance my way.

"I'm actually in pretty good shape. Lots of hills in the Bay Area. So I just need some maintenance. This will be fine."

"Yeah, I swear you look better than you did in your twenties. And you were damn fine then."

I stared out the passenger window, ignoring the comment.

"Hey, don't tell me I've pissed you off again."

I turned back to face her, determined she would not get the upper hand.

"You're not trying to seduce me, are you?"

"Always," she said, smiling.

"Shit," I said.

Soon, we pulled off the road at a rest area and trail head.

"We can do a forty-mile loop from here," she said.

And off we went. I busted ass to stay in front, demanding peak performance from my pumping quads, and soon felt my lungs burning through my chest like a raging fire. As we passed the fifth mile, she came by me on the left, easily, and I realized she had allowed me to lead in the beginning. I watched her spin with such fluidity, her head tucked in classic form, her feet making those perfect circles that ensured maximum torque. I blamed the borrowed bike for my inability to keep up, but I knew that was a lie.

"Jesus!" I shouted as we ended the loop just under two hours later. "I don't normally clock an average of more than twenty miles per hour."

"You didn't seem to have much trouble."

"I guess competing with you brings out the best in me."

"I think we've earned a nice fat lunch and a cocktail. What do you say?"

I knew I should say no and stop putting myself in the path of temptation. But the truth was, I enjoyed spending time with her and, at this point, I felt entitled to it. What was the problem with having some fun with an old friend? An old lover, you mean, debating myself.

"Sure," I said. "I don't have other plans."

Back at her place, we put the bikes away, showered, changed, and took the Tesla, top down, to Oak Cliff where she wanted to introduce me to a trendy bistro known for specialty drinks that required twenty minutes to make and cost at least $25.

"I could get used to this," she said as we sped along, eyeing me next to her, my hair blown back by the gentle breeze.

"Don't," I said. "You realize I'm married?"

"Yes."

"And so are you," I said.

"Yes."

"And you're not a lesbian, as far as I know."

"Yes. No, I mean. Maybe. I don't know."

At that I was silent. Not sure where to go.

"I just feel different around you," she said. "It's you. There's something about you in particular."

"You can't tell me you've never been attracted to another woman."

She hesitated. "Okay, you're right about that."

"I am going to be very direct with you, Laura," I said. "I am not interested in having an affair with you. Again."

She drove in silence the rest of the way and we proceeded then to have a perfectly normal friendly conversation over lunch. As though none of that flirtatious, seductive conversation had happened. Back at my mother's house, I mused over it, unsettled, confused. Something about this place, or was it just being in Laura's orbit, had me off my game. She seemed able to slip easily back and forth from seducer to adviser, drawing a firm line between them. I couldn't do that. If I didn't sort out my feelings for her, I could easily take an impulsive step in the wrong direction.

Laura called me that Monday, agitated.

"We're getting nowhere on this Emma woman," she said. "I think I'll just go to London and talk to the old man, her father, in person. My investigator is at a dead end. Will you authorize the expense?"

"Of course," I said. "It makes perfect sense."

"I think it could be helpful if you went with me."

Something like motion sickness passed through me, memories of our trip to Europe flooding my adrenal system.

"Jen?"

"Sorry, I just, but, why do you need me?"

"The old man might be more sympathetic to our case if he meets a family member who was hurt by what his daughter did."

I thought about it, wondering whether that was a good enough reason—what, to justify it to Mary? To myself?

"Let me think about it," I said.

"Okay, but I don't think we should wait more than a couple of weeks."

I had to get back to California. Had to get away from Laura. I needed to see Mary, talk things out, figure out where we were. And there was business. My partners had been patient, but I knew I was pushing it. So, while we waited for the London rendezvous to come together, I flew back to San Francisco.

"I don't understand why you have to go with her," Mary said when I told her about the situation.

"I think it could make a difference in the outcome and I want to make the most of the investment."

"I don't like it."

"I understand. But I've made up my mind."

"Jen," she said. "Will you be honest with me about something?"

"I think I'm always honest with you," I said.

She pulled me down onto the couch.

"Are you attracted to Laura? Is there still something there?"

That I didn't immediately respond with a "no" surprised me. For some reason, my analytical mind took over and tried to pick apart the questions with literal precision. I felt Mary's worry growing with every second I stayed silent.

"I don't know," I said finally. "I love you, Mary. I won't ever not love you. But what you did, it changed things. I don't know, it's like it reset everything."

She closed her eyes and let out a heavy sigh.

"In some ways," she said, "I feel like I want you to do it. To cheat on me so you can feel like we're even."

"I don't think it works that way."

"You've practically admitted you feel the temptation. So you're halfway there."

"That pisses me off. I'm honest with you and then you turn it on me."

I jerked my hand away and got up from the couch.

"I didn't mean it that way," she said, following me.

"Until this thing with Alex is sorted out, I'm going to see Laura a lot. That's just the way it is. But I have no plans to sleep with her."

"But you can't promise me?"

"This is a ridiculous conversation, Mary. Stop it."

"What about us?"

I felt like screaming, but steadied myself and said, "I need more time. I can't flip a switch. Be patient. It's the least you can do."

She pulled me to her and the ferociousness of her love for me broke my defenses so easily that I submitted to her without resistance. I caught my breath as the heat of desire radiated through me. She held me and kissed me with tender intensity as she led me into our bedroom and began to undress me. The certainty of her surgeon's hands made quick work of cloth and thread and skin on skin soon connected with exhilarating euphoria. Suddenly, my will lost, my face buried in her neck, I breathed in her scent. I kissed her with the energy of a pent-up teenager, and when I touched her thigh and pressed my hand further, she came with a primal force that left her gasping. Then, with a characteristic deftness that had always charmed me, she pushed inside me and we were one, if only for a moment. We lay there, naked, steam floating off our bodies, for a long time, falling asleep in each other's arms.

CHAPTER TWENTY

On November 1, 1996, Laura Peters and I moved into our apartment in Lower Greenville, a part of Dallas known more for its bars and restaurants than its residential nooks. We had easy access to as much entertainment as we'd ever have time for, given the work schedules we both kept.

It was a quick trip to get to work on a bicycle or by bus, but Laura loved cars. She bought a 1986 Mercedes Benz 560SL convertible, white with red leather interior, and did she ever treasure that automobile. She would drive it in every parade or vintage auto show that came anywhere near us, even though it wasn't actually vintage yet. She even joined the North Texas section of the Mercedes Benz Club of North America and went to their events whenever she could make the time.

"I swear I think you love that car more than you love me," I said one day as she prepared it for an auto club event in our neighborhood.

"Well, it's always there for me and it never talks back," she said, snapping her chamois at my leg.

I grabbed at the towel and wrenched it away, running through the parking garage toward the exit. She sprinted after me and caught me before I could get out onto the street. She pushed me against the wall and started tickling me, which she knew would cause a surrender in short order.

"I give, I give," I said, collapsing to the ground and offering up the chamois.

She grabbed it and helped me stand.

"Why don't you ride with me?"

"You've never asked before," I said. "Do you mean it?"

"Of course," she said, putting her arm around my shoulder as we walked back toward the car. "You can ride shotgun and look beautiful."

We turned a lot of heads that day as we motored along Greenville Avenue toward Goodwin, the top down, our long hair loose and trailing behind us like streamers. We both wore tight leather jackets and scarves and dark aviator sunglasses and I imagined that we were WWII dogfighters headed to battle. Word got around about two hot chicks in a Benz and before long we were pulled into a group of hard partying Benzers in a bar at the end of the route.

The men were mostly in their forties and fifties and fairly harmless. They bought us drinks and lobbied us to go out dancing. A couple of the wives showed up and welcomed us, too, happy to meet women who cared about cars like they did. I kept it to myself that I didn't have any special affection for the Benz, and off we went.

"I don't think we should let them know we're lawyers," Laura said as we headed down the sidewalk to another bar.

"Yeah," I agreed. "Probably a buzzkill. What should we be?"

She gave it few seconds' thought.

"We're both in sales," she said. "You're in high-end jewelry and I'm selling time-shares."

"Perfect," I said. "I just hope I don't get too drunk to remember that."

One of the couples, Jerry and Lorraine, took a keen interest in us.

"So you girls are roommates?" Jerry asked.

"That's right," Laura said. "We met when I tried to sell her a time-share and she outsmarted me, ha!"

"How'd you do that?" Lorraine asked me.

"I just wanted the weekend in Mexico," I said. "So I canceled the time share within the three-day rescission period."

Laura looked at me as if to say, don't sound so educated. I got the message.

"See, my brother's a lawyer and I knew all about my rights," I said, nodding sagely.

"Good for you, girl," Lorraine said, slapping me a high five.

"After that, I figured she'd be a great wing man and here we are!" Laura said as she knocked her beer glass up against Jerry's.

Jerry looked us both over like he was sizing up cattle at the stockyard.

"One of you would be just right for our son, Leroy," he said, looking right at me.

Laura spewed beer as she guffawed so hard you would have thought I was not fit to be considered.

"What's wrong," Lorraine said. "Does she already have a boyfriend?"

Laura and I exchanged glances, not quite sure which way to weave.

"Uh, well…" she said.

"I just broke up with someone recently," I jumped in, "and I'm not ready for another relationship right now."

I put on my best solemn face.

"I understand, honey," Lorraine said, rubbing my back in a nurturing way.

"What about you, then?" Jerry said to Laura.

I grinned. "Yeah, Laura, what about you?"

"What's this Leroy like? Do you have a picture?" Laura asked.

Jerry opened his wallet to show us Leroy, dressed in a college football uniform.

"Linebacker at A&M," he said. "Gradated three years ago. Tried to go pro, but got cut at the last round."

"He looks like quite a catch," Laura said. "But, it's tough for me to date right now, with all the travel I have to do in my job. I'm hardly ever around."

"Let me have your number anyway. Talk to him. You never know," Jerry said.

Laura shifted from one foot back to the other, avoiding eye contact.

"I don't know," she said. "I don't see the point."

"Are you saying you're too good for my son?" Jerry said, turning belligerent.

"No!"

"Give him your cell phone number," I said, trying to say with my eyes that I thought we should get the heck out. I figured she would switch up a number and be done with it.

"What's your number," Lorraine said, pulling out her Motorola flip phone. "I'll call it and we'll both have each other's."

"Here," Laura said, writing a number on a napkin. "Now, we have to go. Nice meeting you folks."

She grabbed my arm and pulled me after her out the door and down the street as fast as we could run. We heard Jerry calling after us that the number didn't work.

"Bitches!" he screamed.

We made it back to the Benz and jumped in without even opening the doors. We took off as Jerry stood in the middle of the street behind us, his fists chopping the air.

"Good god," I said. "Where do people get off?"

"Men are such bullies sometimes," she said. "Like we owe them all the attention in the world."

We hadn't really eaten dinner, so we pulled into the Albertsons grocery store and did some shopping. I would cook if Laura would agree to clean up after, which she did. The buzz from our drinking soon wore off and we were ravenous.

"Here," I said, popping some grapes into her mouth as we waited to check out.

"That's stealing you know," said a self-righteous voice behind us.

"Don't worry," I said, "I'll make sure to have them round up the price to make up for it. I popped a few into my mouth as I stared her down.

"You two look a little cozy to me," the woman said.

Laura whipped around on her.

"Mind your own business, lady. We're not bothering you, so leave well enough alone."

The woman opened her purse and drew out a small, white leather New Testament. I noticed the name stitched in gold at the corner. *Dorothy Park*. She opened it and started reading.

"From First Timothy," Dorothy said. "The law is not made for the righteous, but for the lawbreakers, the sexually immoral, for those practicing homosexuality—"

"Can you believe this? I feel like I'm in a *Candid Camera* episode," Laura said, turning her back on the woman and putting her hands over her ears.

"Ignore her and let's get the hell out of here."

At home, I was unsettled by the events of the day, and, though neither one of us said it out loud, I knew Laura was, too. Encounters like that made me yearn for community. For like-minded people. For other gay people. But I knew Laura didn't feel that way, at least not yet, so there was no point in bringing it up with her. She persisted in the notion that our personal life was ours alone. But, with every day that went by, I became more convinced that I needed a change.

The next day, I took off on a weeklong business trip—depositions in San Francisco. I thought I might look up that girl I had met in the bar in Berlin—Christine was her name—just for someone to have dinner with while I was there. Plus, I wouldn't mind going to a gay bar. I hadn't been to one in a very long time, and, why not? As I sat in my seat on the plane to SFO, I was overcome by a fluttery nervousness that had nothing to do with the challenging work I was charged with. I felt sure that something wonderful was going to happen to me in San Francisco!

CHAPTER TWENTY-ONE

I woke up to see Mary gazing at me lovingly, wearing a silky T-shirt, her hair messy and sexy. She smiled and touched my cheek, gently tracing the line of my jaw and reaching for my still-naked side waist. I caught her hand and kissed it, jumping up and out of bed to grab my robe.

"I'm so glad you're home," she said, straightening the covers and placing the pillows carefully.

"It's good to be home."

"Honey, I—" Mary said.

"Let's talk tonight," I said. "I have to get to work."

"I'm on call tonight, but could we catch an early dinner?"

"Let me see how the day goes."

"I'll make you breakfast."

"I really don't have time," I said. "Could you put together some fruit and nuts in a baggy?"

"Of course," she said, coming close. "I love you."

I kissed her quickly, without emotion.

"I'm jumping in the shower," I said.

Mary and I lived in Noe Valley and my offices were in Menlo Park. Could I have figured out how to take the Caltrain? Sure. And I felt guilty about not doing that. But, being both a Texan and a Californian, car culture was in my DNA, so I traveled by convertible Nissan Roadster. With the top down, the sun warming the sixty-seven-degree air, I allowed myself to relax into the calm and comfort of familiarity. The closer I got to my office, the more I felt like myself. I grew stronger with every mile, fortified by the oxygen of success filling my lungs. When I walked in, I was back, and everyone knew it.

The day passed quickly with meetings and conference calls and plans for the future. My cell phone flickered with a text from Mary and I realized it was almost five o'clock.

On my way, I wrote back.

Our house was not far from Mary's hospital, and I knew she would stay at home as long as she could. I wanted to see her. I wanted to forgive her. I wanted to move on. But in the wake of Mary's infidelity, Laura Peters had shaken me and her energy still reverberated in my head, confusing my vision of what would come next.

She greeted me at the door.

"I'm sorry, honey," she said. "I just got the call. But I left dinner for you in the oven."

I nodded and thanked her.

"I made an appointment for us," she said. "With a therapist. Someone at work recommended her."

"Good," I said.

"It's on our calendar."

"Great," I said.

"Let's try for dinner tomorrow night," she said, hoisting her backpack. "I'm sure you'll be off to work before I'm back in the morning."

I walked her to her car and gave her a kiss. In that slice of the evening, everything suddenly felt back to normal.

I had just taken the last bite of the lemon chicken Mary had made for dinner when my cell phone buzzed. I looked at the screen. Laura Peters. My mouth went dry and my satiated stomach went taut. I thought about not answering, but obligation won out.

"Can we talk schedule?" she asked, after the usual greetings and small talk.

"What are you thinking?"

"We will need a week, I think. I hope not more."

I looked at my calendar in light of the day I'd had at work.

"If I can carve out some of the time in London for my work, I could get there in ten days or so," I said.

"That should work out fine," Laura said. "We'll have chunks of time here and there when you'll be free to do anything you need to do."

"Okay, send me a calendar invite then."

"Will do, and—"

She hesitated. I waited.

"How are things at home?"

"Everything's good here," I said dismissively.

"That's great," she said, her tone tinged with what sounded like disappointment. "We'll be in touch as we get closer."

I clicked off the line and stared at the phone as if it somehow embodied a threat, a danger, a temptation. I just had to get through this and get it behind me. It's a problem to be solved and that's what I do best.

Mary and I made our first trip to the therapist later that week. Her office was on the lower level of her row house in Bernal Heights. The decor and the smell of patchouli gave it the feeling of a 1960s hookah lounge. Big puffy purple chairs and a yellow sofa that swallowed up its inhabitants sat on a deep shag carpet. Wildly colored wallpaper in pink, chartreuse, orange, and blue covered the gap between sandy-colored wainscoting and the ceiling. Pillows lay strewn all over the room and a large ornate wooden desk dominated the bay window.

Iliana introduced herself by offering us weed, her unruly red hair drawn back with what I think was a black shoelace. We both declined.

"Sit, please," she said, gesturing toward the sofa.

"Could I get some water?" I asked.

"Of course," she said, pointing to the corner where a water cooler sat draped in the vines of an ivy plant.

I brought Mary and I both a cup of water and we sat together on the yellow cushions that sank to the middle of the couch, careening us toward each other.

"So," Iliana said, leaning against her desk and planting both hands on its edge behind her. She pushed her glasses up to the bridge of her nose. "Tell me what you want."

I blinked up at her and Mary and I looked at each other blankly. I couldn't help myself. I started laughing and turned back to Iliana.

"If I could do that, I'd be standing where you are," I said.

Iliana chuckled and clapped her hands in the air.

"Let's start with another question. Do you want to stay together?"

"Absolutely," Mary said, holding my hand even tighter than she had been.

I nodded yes.

"Then our work is clear," Iliana said, turning to a bookshelf and pulling down a well-worn volume. "Read this."

She handed us the book. It was Jon Kabat-Zinn's *Wherever You Go, There You Are.*

"I want you to read this book together. And I want you to practice meditation together. We'll start today, right now."

"Wait a minute," I said. "How is that going to help us get to the bottom of why my wife cheated on me?"

Mary brought her hand to her forehead, kneading her eyebrows and sighing loudly.

Iliana smiled and said, "What Mary did has made you suffer. Meditation will help you let go of that suffering. Once you've let go of it, you can move on."

"But I want to know why! Why did she do it?"

"Knowing why someone did something in the past may be satisfying on some level, but it is not helpful in moving forward. We can't guarantee our future actions. None of us can. The world is unreliable. When faced with a dilemma, we may make a decision different from what we would have predicted in the abstract. You want to stay together. Therefore, you must let go of what is keeping you apart."

Mary and I looked at each other and, though this was not at all what I thought therapy would be, it had an appeal that, in this moment, felt right. Just listening to Iliana's voice had calmed me, opened me to a new possibility. Mary pushed my hair back away from my face and cupped her hands at my cheeks.

"Will you try? For me? For us?"

I leaned forward, pressing my head to hers.

"I will," I said.

Iliana had us pull cushions to the center of the room and sit cross-legged, our shoes off, our backs straight and our hands folded in our laps. We closed our eyes and she led us through a meditation that focused on the breath. It lasted five or ten minutes and, when I opened my eyes, I felt so relaxed, I wanted to keep going, hold on to the feeling.

"Take just five minutes a day to do this together," Iliana said. "If you can't find five minutes, find one minute. But do it every day. And read the book. I'll see you back here next week."

"She's a little nutty," I said as I drove us home, my hand on Mary's knee, her hand on mine, "but I feel so much better."

"I'm excited," Mary said. "I've wanted to try meditation for a while now. My colleague told me it was part of Iliana's approach, but I had no idea what to expect."

"Well, while you're in a Zen space, let me go ahead and tell you what's next with my sister's case."

Mary stiffened, her breath going shallow, her hand coming off mine. She folded her arms and I glanced over to notice her jaw working, grinding her teeth.

"No doubt it involves you and Laura Peters spending time together."

I did my best to hold on to the calm I'd felt in Iliana's lounge, but the well of resentment opened up inside me.

"I have to do this," I said. "And yes, I'm going to London in a week and a half and she will be there."

Mary said nothing and we drove the rest of the way home in silence.

CHAPTER TWENTY-TWO

I was booked at the Palace Hotel downtown in San Francisco because it was close to the law firm where the depositions were scheduled. It lived up to its name. The ornate lobby garden welcomed you in, its magnificent chandeliers dancing overhead. I had not yet gotten used to the posh quarters we occupied in this job, and I stood gaping at the surroundings when Brian, the partner, tapped me on the shoulder.

"Pretty sweet, huh?"

"Dang," I said. "What's not to like?"

"I thought we could have dinner tonight," he said. "Get prepped for tomorrow."

I read his look for signs of prurient interest. Nothing obvious. Why was I so on guard with him? He hadn't actually made a pass at me or said anything inappropriate. But something about him nagged at me, a signal so subtle it could easily be denied.

"Sure," I said, resigned to my fate of being alone with him. "What time?"

"Meet here at six thirty."

My room had been upgraded and I couldn't believe the size of it. Not only was there a king-sized bed and lots of fancy antique furniture, it had a sitting room, separated from the bedroom by oversized heavy wooden doors with large disc-like bronze knobs. I was in heaven. I kicked off my shoes and danced around like a four-year-old ballerina. I flopped onto the couch in the sitting room and took a big stretch. *I could get used to this,* I thought.

I had found Christine's business card in my stack of vacation memorabilia and brought it with me. I thought I should call her now, before the workday was over. Get something set up for the next night or so. I pulled the card out of my wallet. *Christine Thompson, Software Engineer, Yahoo!* Wow, I hadn't realized that's where she worked. That company had gone public the year before. She must have made a haul of cash.

I dialed the number and she answered.

"Sure, I remember you," she said. "Miss Texas."

I laughed. "Not exactly, but thanks. Do you have time for dinner tomorrow night? Or the next? Show me around a little?"

"Hmm. It looks like I have an open slot on my calendar tomorrow night. I'll pick you up at your hotel at five thirty. We'll start with happy hour and go from there. Sound good?"

"Perfect," I said, hanging up the phone and tingling with anticipation.

I thought about calling Laura, but she would be at the office and it wouldn't be much of a conversation anyway, so I didn't bother. Was that a twinge of guilt I felt that I hadn't mentioned getting together with Christine? Laura had gone so crazy that night in Berlin. I didn't want to set her off again. At least that's what I told myself. It felt a little like cheating—not that I would cheat with Christine. I was not attracted to her in that way. But it felt as if my lie of omission made me unfaithful somehow. If I was unfaithful, it was to the idea that I had to live the way Laura insisted. In denial. In secret. Almost in shame. That idea had begun to feel like a bad hangover, debilitating and stupid.

I got through dinner with Brian by keeping our conversation focused on our case, which was about a real estate development deal in Northern California that had gone bad. Our client was the investment bank that handled the bond issue that funded the construction. I found the terms of the deal itself more interesting than the legal issues, which worried me a little as I thought about the years stretched out in front of me doing this kind of work.

The next day's depositions came off without too much drama and I rushed back to my room to get ready for my night out. I put on my Lucky Brand jeans and a black silky tank top. I wore cowboy boots and slung a black denim jacket over my shoulder. I wore some bangles on my wrists and dangly earrings. I had ironed my hair straight that morning and I liked the look. I checked myself out in the full-length mirror and was satisfied.

Christine's black car pulled up to the entrance of the Palace and the doorman stepped quickly ahead of me to open the door. She beckoned me inside and whistled approvingly as I jumped in.

"I dig the outfit," she said, high-fiving me. "Take us to the Mission," she said to the driver.

"It's good to see you," I said. "And thanks for making the time."

"Yeah, no problem. I meant it in Berlin when I said you should check us out, the Bay Area. I don't know, something about you says you fit in here."

"That's so interesting. I don't know why you think that, but, in a weird way, I think you could be right. I've been a little restless lately."

"Are you still with that straight girl?"

I could not stop the expression of shock and surprise that came over me. She laughed.

"I guess that means yes!"

"I…what I…you don't, I mean, she's…we're not, oh, fuck, I don't know."

"I get it. It's not unusual."

"You know, this stuff is all new to me. I don't even know if I'm gay."

"Oh, c'mon!"

"What I mean is, I haven't been with anyone else. I just fell for her."

Christine smirked and shook her head.

"I'm taking you to a lesbian bar. We'll see if there's anyone else you could fall for."

My heart thumped and pounded in my ears to the point that I saw stars, my veins humming with an adrenaline flush. Amazing how her words produced a storm in my brain. I shivered a little, like you do when someone tells you a scary story, as she asked the driver to stop.

"We'll get out here," she said to him. "I don't want to pull up with this much fanfare," she confided to me. "We'll walk the last block."

We walked up 19th Street and into a bar called The Lexington Club.

"Welcome to the Lex," said a tall woman at the door. She wore dark jeans and a black cut-up T-shirt. Her hair, short, dark, and spiked, was tipped in bleached white. A stud in her nose, several on her ear, and one in her lip rounded out her look.

The dark red walls covered in playbills and other notices and the plastic chandeliers gave the place a homemade feel. It was packed with women, a smoky haze filling in the space around them. Several of them sported mohawks and face spikes. I got the once-over from one or two of them, standing out like the latest produce off the turnip truck. At least I had straightened my hair, I thought. I would die if I had come in here looking fresh out of the board room.

"Who's the new girl?"

She stood next to Christine, looking at me, one hand cradling a beer, the other hooked into the waist of her jeans. She wore a tight crew-necked shirt that emphasized her pleasantly muscular shoulders and arms and her flat stomach. Her dark hair was short, shaggy, spilling over her forehead and into her face. She pushed it back and I noticed her eyes, blue like sapphires.

"Jennifer," I said, extending my hand.

"She's my friend from Dallas," Christine added.

"Oh, Miss Texas!"

I gave Christine an admonishing frown. She held up her hands in surrender.

"I'm Frankie," she said, shaking my hand. "Welcome to SF."

Before long, the whole bar knew me as Miss Texas, and they were competing for turns to tell me why I should move to San Francisco. They bought me beers and gave me advice on new hairstyles and assured me the only place I should consider living was the Mission. When I excused myself to go to the ladies' room, they corrected me. No ladies here.

In the bathroom, the walls covered in Sharpie love notes and sinister threats, I stumbled over a couple having sex just inside the door. I apologized, but they didn't notice me, and I tried not to see too much, but I did catch a glimpse of the one girl's very realistic dildo thrusting impressively from its leather holster.

Frankie asked me to dance and we cut some pretty good moves while Missy Elliot pumped out of the DJ booth. I couldn't remember ever having felt so free, so comfortable, so...at home. The female energy, the safety, the lack of testosterone, threats, and predation, it dawned on me. *This is who I am. These are my people. My community.*

We stayed for a poetry reading delivered from the pool table improvised into a stage. The poet was an older woman with wispy gray hair and a wrinkled jowly face, heavy, but not fat. She wore a serape styled skirt and Birkenstocks. The poem was terrible.

"Let's get out of here," whispered Christine.

"Hey," said Frankie as she tapped me on the shoulder. "Call me."

She handed me a slip of paper with her number. I tucked it in my pocket and nodded goodbye. Christine and I grabbed a quick dinner at a Mexican place down the street. I thanked her for the evening and, outside, flagged a passing cab.

"You belong out here," she said as I slid into the car, her hand holding the door open to look me in the eye.

I smiled and said, "Maybe. I'll think about it."

"And that straight girl—she's going to break your heart."

"Good night," I said, my happiness fading like passing smoke.

When I got up to my room, I saw the message light flashing on the telephone. There were three messages from Laura. The first was pleasant, the second angry, the third worried. It was far too late to call her at that point. And I wasn't sure how much I would tell her about my evening anyway. At least not by telephone. Would she disapprove of me going to a lesbian bar? Dancing with other women? Being comfortable with dykes and butches and mohawks and spikes? I drifted off to sleep to the memories of new sensations.

CHAPTER TWENTY-THREE

"C'mon in here," Mary said, pulling me into our den, a room we didn't use much since the kids had gone to college. "I set it up for meditation," she said, pointing to the cushions on the floor and a stack of books by various gurus and Buddhas.

"I like it."

"I think it will help keep us on track. Do you have a minute now?"

We sat on the cushions and Mary took the Kabat-Zinn book from the stack. She read a passage and we did a breathing exercise that lasted five minutes. We sat for a few minutes more until the sound of the front door banging open brought us both to our feet.

"Mom! Mommy!"

Claire's voice, a dark mix of anger and distress, jolted us to attention and we rushed down the stairs to embrace her as she collapsed in tears and thrashing rage.

"What's happened?"

I begged for an answer, but she was beyond consoling.

"Should you give her something to calm her down?" I asked Mary.

She shook her head.

"Give her a little time."

We led her like a toddler to the living room couch where we deposited her and offered her water and tissues. More out of exhaustion than capitulation, she eventually quieted. Her face a mash of swollen eyes, reddish nose, and tangled hair, she stared at us plaintively. We waited for her to speak.

"He cheated on me," she said.

Her boyfriend of three years was left over from high school. They attended different colleges several hours apart. It had seemed to us destined to fade away. But, of course, this was not the time to point that out.

"Tell us what happened, sweetie," Mary said, holding her hand.

She sighed, blew her nose, and spoke with a growl.

"I came up to surprise him. Last night."

Mary and I exchanged glances.

"When I got to his dorm, his roommate told me he was at the Student Union. There was a concert or something, so I went to look for him."

She closed her eyes and tears flowed again. My heart ached for her.

"I found him. He was in the back of the crowd. He had his hands all over this trashy blonde, kissing her and rubbing up against her. It was disgusting."

I noted Mary staring at her hands, clasped tightly in her lap.

"What did you do, honey?" I asked.

"I came up from behind him. I grabbed his arm and pulled him off her. He turned around and raised a fist, not knowing who it was."

She paused to wipe her tears.

"When he saw me, he went limp. His hands just hung like meat hooks. He stared at me. He didn't say anything."

Mary and I waited for her to go on, united in our compassion for our brilliant, beautiful daughter.

"I screamed at him. I said awful things. I don't even remember everything I said, but I made a huge scene. I beat on his chest with my fists. He just stood there. Security came over and dragged me out. They told me not to come back in or they would have me arrested."

"Oh my god, honey," I said. "I am so sorry."

"Where have you been? Where did you spend the night?" Mary asked.

"I know some girls there. They let me crash. We got drunk and high and stayed up all night. Then I took a Lyft here."

I pulled her to me and held her tight while she sobbed into my shoulder. Eventually she quieted into sleep and I laid her on the couch, covering her with a nearby throw. I looked at my watch.

"I really have to get to the office," I said softly.

"I'll be here," Mary said.

As we turned to leave the room, Claire stirred.

"If either one of you ever cheated, I would kill you."

"Just rest now," I said.

I gave Mary a quizzical look as I gathered my things and headed for the door. By the time I got home from work that night, Claire was back to her cheerful wry and sly self.

"Ah, the resilience of youth," I said, toasting Mary with my customary white wine.

"He's an asshole," Claire said. "They are all assholes. Boys. I'm over them."

"Mm hmm," Mary said. "We'll see how long that lasts."

"Women are just inherently better humans. Look at you two. I couldn't imagine you treating each other like that. Just bald-faced treachery."

"Sweetie, it's not really fair to indict a whole gender. And plenty of women cheat. Lesbians included," Mary said.

I watched her as she said those words, feeling sympathy for her on this topic for the first time.

"Okay, fine," Claire said. "If you say so. But I'm taking a break for a while."

"Nothing wrong with that," I said.

"Hey, what's with the meditation in the den?"

"We're giving it a try," Mary said. "It's great for stress relief. And it's nice to do it together. Like having a buddy, you know, to hold you accountable."

Claire looked from one to the other of us, skeptical.

"I don't know. Is there something going on here, Mommy?"

"No," Mary said. "Nothing is going on. We're just trying something new."

"Mom?" she looked at me, her eyes narrowed.

"There's nothing to worry about."

"You need to get back to school," Mary said. "Do you want me to drive you?"

"No, that's too much. I'll take the bus in the morning."

The three of us drank wine and watched Netflix, falling asleep on the couch together.

Mary and I both went the next morning to drop Claire at the Megabus for Southern California. As we waved goodbye, I couldn't help saying, "That was ironic."

Mary caught my hand and spoke softly. "I'm ashamed of something."

"What, there's more?"

"No, I don't mean that. Can we stand here a minute? There's something I want to say to you."

I stood, my arms folded, listening.

"I can't believe this, but I had never put myself in your shoes, you know, to feel how hurt you were, by…what I did. Seeing Claire suffer like that, even for just a day, made me realize, this was so much more devastating than I thought. I've been very selfish. I didn't see it before."

"I guess that's progress," I said, smug.

"I mean it," she said. "I have a lot of work to do on myself. A lot more than I thought."

"If you say so."

"I do. Look, I don't expect you to praise me for saying it. I just want you to know that I get it. In a way I didn't before."

We drove home in silence. Then she spoke as I pulled the car into our garage. "When do you take off for London?"

"Sunday night."

"Let's get in one more session with Iliana before you go."

"Fine," I said. "I'll see you after work tonight?"

"I'm on call, so probably not."

She kissed me and got out of the car.

"Friday afternoon is good for me, for the session," I said as she lingered, watching as I let the car roll back out onto the street.

I headed to the office, still enjoying the freedom of being on my own for the forty minutes it took to get there. I thought about Mary's words as I drove and wondered if I should just forgive her and forget it ever happened. But if she was beginning to see things from my point of view, so I was glimpsing things from hers. My impression of myself as an innocent bystander in my wife's tryst had begun to dim a bit. I knew I shared some blame. So forgiving and forgetting seemed like letting myself off the hook as much as anything.

* * *

Iliana welcomed us in and pointed us to the cushions. We did a five-minute breathing exercise to "get warmed up."

"Now, tell me how you feel compared to how you felt when you came in."

"I feel calmer, for sure. But honestly, I get a little frustrated at how that evaporates the minute real life comes up," I said.

"Give me an example."

"Just last week. When we left here. We were both in a great place. Then I mentioned a trip to London, where I'll be spending a lot of time with someone I had a relationship with a long time ago. Mary went instantly to, you know, jealousy or being threatened, upset."

"Perfect," Iliana said. "Mary, tell me how you felt when this happened."

"I just, I can't help it. This woman she's talking about, they had a very intense relationship and it scares me that Jen is spending so much time with her. Especially since I, well, I did what I did."

"We all do this. You are creating suffering for yourself over something that hasn't actually happened and may never happen. Instead of going down that rabbit hole, the goal is to become aware of what's happening, stop, breathe, let it pass. We come back to the breath again and again. And that's how we build the muscle of meditation. We can use it at any time. In coming back over and over again, we become resilient, and we can bounce back from those moments where we get lost in all the crazy scenarios that we're making up."

"That sounds good, but really hard, and what about the things that have already happened? When someone has hurt you so much that you aren't sure you can come back from it?" I asked.

"We have to find a way to see it differently. Because as long as you hold on to that suffering, you will never be free."

"And I would do that how?"

"The way I find most effective is through something we call lovingkindness meditation."

She pulled a book down from her shelf.

"Here's another bit of homework. I want you to read this book as well." The book she showed us was Sharon Salzberg's *Lovingkindness*.

"Let's try this type of meditation now," she said.

She had us close our eyes and breathe deeply. Then she had us silently repeat some phrases to offer lovingkindness to ourselves.

"May I be safe, be happy, be healthy, live with ease," she said.

This felt truly ridiculous. I had packing to do. I had to make sure I had everything I needed to get my work done in London. I couldn't stop thinking about where I had last left my passport.

Then Iliana told us to think about a difficult person and offer them lovingkindness. "May you be safe, be happy, be healthy, live with ease."

Okay, this is even dumber. Why am I going to wish someone well if they've been giving me hell?

Then, suddenly, I gasped because it was Laura Peters who had come into my thoughts. I opened my eyes to banish her. My face flushed and I knew that it was crimson.

"Is everything okay?" Iliana said to me, with concern.

"Fine. Just a little indigestion."

She gave me what felt like a skeptical once-over. Mary put her hand to my head.

"You're really flushed," she said. "I hope you're not coming down with something just before your trip."

"I'm fine," I said, brushing her hand away. "I had something spicy at lunch. That's all."

"Ladies, I want you to try this technique for the next week, even though you'll be apart. Then come see me when Jen is back from London."

As Mary and I drove home, I said to her, "Are you sure this is what we need? Instead of regular therapy? Shouldn't we be attacking our problems head-on?"

"We could do both," she said.

"I don't have that much time! And neither do you. I say we try this a few more times, but I don't know."

Mary blew out her cheeks as though exasperated, "I think the idea is that you start meditating and you keep meditating. It's not like a course of chemo or something."

"Okay, fine. But it's a little like hocus-pocus to me."

She sighed and stared off into the hills.

CHAPTER TWENTY-FOUR

It was my last day in San Francisco and as I packed up to head for the airport, the telephone rang. Christine's voice greeted me.

"I have an idea for you," she said. "Some of us are putting together a trip to Washington for the inauguration next month. There's this thing called the Triangle Ball, a lesbian gala. Can you believe it?"

"Really?"

"Yeah. Frankie's coming. And some other chicks. You and your girlfriend should come."

Laura, all dressed up and in a room full of dykes, half in tuxedos…the thought of it seemed ludicrous.

"I don't know. That might be a bridge too far."

"Think about it. You never know if you'll get another chance to do something like this."

"Okay. Send me the details. I'll do my best to convince Laura."

I turned it over and over in my head as the plane cruised back to Dallas. The further I got from San Francisco, the less likely it seemed that I could ever convince Laura to take that leap. But if she wouldn't come, that didn't mean I couldn't. The thought of doing something like that without Laura's approval gave me an odd, unsettled feeling. I wanted to go and I wanted her to come with me and, by the time the plane landed, I had come up with a strategy.

"Are you out of your mind?" she said when I mentioned the Triangle Ball.

"No, as a matter of fact. This is one of the best ideas I've ever had. It will be so much fun and you'll see how real lesbians live."

"I'm not interested in lesbians." She smirked. "And anyway, this is probably a plot by that Christine to recruit you into full-on queer life and lure you to San Francisco."

"Just listen to me for a minute," I said. "You've decided you're interested in bankruptcy practice, right?"

"Yes. And what does that have to do with anything?"

"It so happens there's a three-day conference on bankruptcy the week before the inauguration. You could go, get your continuing education, charge the trip to the firm, and stay for the long weekend."

"What if we run into someone we know?"

"No one from here is going to a Democratic Presidential Inauguration."

I had her there. She looked at me sweetly, a sly smile crossing her lips.

"You're going with or without me, aren't you?"

I gave her a little shrug, my mind made up.

"So tell me," she said. "What does one wear to a lesbian inaugural ball?"

I tackled her onto the couch, smothering her with kisses until she pushed me playfully off onto the floor, telling me I was too cute for my own good.

We shopped at Neiman Marcus for fancy cocktail dresses and new heels and costume jewelry. Through Christine, we connected with some women who had a basement apartment in their house in Dupont Circle where we could stay the weekend for a reasonable price. As the time approached, even Laura vibrated with excitement, giggling at the prospect of hundreds of women dressed to the nines and dancing with each other, no man to be found.

Laura had gone ahead for the conference and I flew in Friday morning. Stepping out of the airport and into the taxi line, the biting cold of Washington in January took me by surprise. I had only been there in spring or summer, always on school trips. High school, college, and law school. After walking around all day, my chapped cheeks gave me an oddly sunburned look, so I bought a scarf from a street vendor to protect my face from the icy wind.

"Christine and her crew are at the Rathskeller," I said to Laura as we contemplated our options for that night. "She says it's right around the corner from here."

"Is it a gay place?"

"No, not that I know of. I think it's a beer place. They have a hundred different beers or something like that."

"I don't know. I don't want to commit to spend the whole night with them."

"It'll be fun. Come on. We can play it by ear from there."

The Rathskeller, a cave-like bar on the lower level of a nineteenth-century brick building, was a short walk from our apartment on O Street between 21st and 22nd. I could hear Christine's voice as we came through the doorway and caught her eye. She motioned us over to the corner where she sat with Frankie and two other women. They scooted their chairs over and someone added two more.

"Good to see you again," Christine said to Laura, extending her hand.

Laura responded and introduced herself to everyone else.

"How've you been?" Frankie asked me, her eyes floating over me with a little too much familiarity.

Laura looked at me. I hadn't exactly filled her in on all the details of my visit to San Francisco, including the fact that my get-together with Christine had featured a foray to a lesbian bar.

"Good!" I said. "Really excited about this weekend."

After our first beer, Laura tapped me and said, "Restroom," motioning for me to come with her. I followed her, grateful she hadn't bolted into the night and back to Dallas.

"What was that about?" she asked, her hand pressing the wall next to my head, her face close to mine. "That dyke."

"Nothing. I met her in San Francisco."

"So did you hook up with her?"

"Of course not. She's not even my type."

"Oh, so if she was your type—"

"No, that's not what I'm saying," I said, pressing her away by the shoulder.

"Why did she look like she had some claim on you?"

"There's nothing there. I met her at a bar. There was some dancing. That's it."

Laura dropped her arm, crossed both across her chest.

"Why didn't you tell me about it?"

I turned away from her, running my hands through my hair, heat building in my chest.

"I thought you might get pissed."

"So now you're lying to me, going behind my back?"

"That's not fair, Laura," I said, turning back to face her. "You know how I feel about being so closeted at home. I just wanted to get out. Meet other people like me. Not feel like a freak or a fake."

She took my shoulders, her face softening.

"Why couldn't you just tell me? Am I really that much of an ogre?"

I smiled, pulling her to me, kissing her.

"I just didn't want a replay of Berlin. I'm sorry."

"That woman better keep her hands off you," Laura said, grabbing my ass and pushing me against the wall. "Or she'll draw back a nub."

I laughed and pushed back at her.

"So you're the butch now?"

The door opened and two other women entered the bathroom. Laura dropped her hands instinctively and stepped to the wash basin, not making eye contact with anyone. She took a lipstick out of her pocket and applied it expertly.

"Ready?" she said, turning back to me.

Back at the table, Laura sat next to Frankie and I saw her speak to her quietly, their heads lowered toward each other. Frankie nodded and threw her head back in a loud guffaw, slapping Laura on the back. I exchanged a look with Christine, who crossed her eyes and laughed.

Meanwhile, the rest of the crew was making plans for the evening. They wanted to grab pizza slices at Trio, over on 17th Street, hit a couple of gay bars nearby, and end up at a lesbian bar called the Hung Jury. To my surprise, Laura said, "Why not," and we headed off into the ice-cold night.

I held on to Laura's winter-coat-clad arm as we walked across Dupont Circle, the empty, waterless fountain presiding over an eerily quiet, frozen landscape. We slipped and slid on the sheets of ice that covered the sidewalks, in turns rescuing each other from a fall. I didn't think I'd ever felt happier, embracing the woman I loved in the open air, unafraid of who might see. And best of all, she seemed just as happy.

Trio's pizza, a trailer-like space, beat up from years of little upkeep and even less washing down, was at least warm, the pizza oven firing in the background. Greasy, red-checked vinyl tablecloths covered a few tables toward the back. A couple of slices and more beer fortified us for the next stop, a gay bar right across the street. By now, we had melded into a posse, feeling our drinks and raising our voices, trying to outdo one another in bravado and volume.

The bar trumpets lay at the foot of a concrete stairway that spilled down from street level to a below ground space. A bouncer checking IDs and screening for trouble happily let in a pack of raucous women ready to party. We moved inside and pushed our way to the bar, the drink of choice turning to vodka. Vodka soda. Vodka grapefruit. Vodka cranberry. Vodka shots.

The room was humidly warm and packed with men, mostly young men, dancing and pulsing and sweating, some with their shirts off, rubbing and humping and sucking. Laura and I were like deer in headlights, both of us virgins in a gay bar.

"Wow," I said. "It's so awesome. None of them give a shit about us."

Laura laughed and pulled me close as we danced to the pounding club beat. My alcohol-infused brain erased all memory of any other way of life. I slid my hands up Laura's back, beneath her shirt, my fingers slipping on the sweaty surface of her skin, tracing the curve of her spine under the straps of her bra, moving to her chest and cupping both breasts as she gasped into my ear and pressed against my thigh.

"Girls!" I heard Christine's voice floating over the bodies between us. I looked up to see her waving from the front of the bar, holding a tray of shooters. I passed one hand from Laura's breast to her navel, kissing her before pulling her toward Christine and the others. We all downed the pink shooters and gathered our coats. It was time for the lesbian bar.

We had to hail cabs on 17th Street because it was too far to walk in the below-freezing weather. Laura, Christine, and I sent the others on ahead in the first taxi and waited, shivering, in the streetlight at the corner of Q Street.

"Maybe I was wrong," Christine whispered to me once we sat in the back seat of the cab. "She's totally into you."

"I sure hope so, because I'm stone in love."

"What's all that whispering," Laura said, slurring and lurching over me.

"Nothing, honey," I said. "We were just saying what a classy drunk you are."

"Jen," she said, suddenly sitting upright and squeezing my knee. "I'm gonna puke."

"Sir, stop the car!"

The taxi driver pulled over quickly and I reached across Laura to push open the door. She leaned out and vomited every ounce of her stomach contents. I pulled her back in and wiped her face with my scarf.

"I need to take her home," I said.

"Yeah," Christine said. "Next time."

Back at our basement quarters, I undressed Laura, wiped her down with a warm washcloth, and tucked her into bed. I sat for a while just taking her in, reveling in everything else that had happened that night. Then a stab of—what? Fear, regret, longing? Something gripped me and I realized that I was already, while still enjoying it, nostalgic for the freedom of this different way of life.

CHAPTER TWENTY-FIVE

"I have a bad feeling about you going over there," Alex's voice echoed into the AirPods hanging from my lobes like earrings.

"What do you mean?" I said, tossing underwear into my suitcase.

"Just that you're going to be there with her. It worries me. Please tell me you're going to watch it. Don't get yourself wrapped up with her again."

"Alex. Trust me. Nothing is going to happen. I'm in a much different place than I was back then. Mary and I actually had our first therapy session, if you can call it that."

"That's good! But that doesn't make me any less anxious."

"Everything on your end is calm, right? The kids? Mom?"

"I mean, I wouldn't say it's calm, necessarily. The kids are still struggling. Ben quit football. Harry won't do his homework. The coaches and teachers are understanding, but it stresses me out, obviously."

"Are they going to counseling?"

"They're going. I just can't tell if it's doing any good. And then there's Mom."

"What do you mean?"

"She got scammed a few days ago. On the Internet."

"No!"

"It was a typical case of phishing, and frankly anybody can fall for that. But when she realized it—when I realized it—and told her, she broke down. She cried and berated herself. Then a day later, she had no memory of it at all. Which on one hand is good, but on the other hand it could happen again."

"Maybe you should—we should—childproof her computer."

"I think we have to."

"I'm sorry you're having to deal with that."

"It's the least I can do. I'll never be able to repay you for what you're doing for me. And the kids."

"Don't be silly."

"How are you feeling about this trip? And Laura?"

"To tell you the truth, I've been deliberately not thinking about it. It's weird. It has me stirred up, you know? A lot of feelings I thought were buried for good."

"It feels very dangerous. Emotionally."

"Yeah," I agreed.

"You're still sure you have to do this?"

"I am. I will keep one thing separate from the other. I promise."

"You don't owe me a promise."

"I guess I'm making myself a promise," I said.

"Make sure you take care of yourself. That's the main thing."

I finished my packing, double-checking everything. Phone, wallet, passport. I hauled my suitcase downstairs. I heard Mary's car pull into the garage. She'd arranged to get off early so she could take me to the airport.

"Hi," she said, coming into the entry. "Let me get your bag."

She took it, hoisted it into the car, closed the trunk, hesitating for a moment before coming to my side as I opened the passenger door. I put my purse down on the seat. She pulled me to her, pressing her body to mine, our matching height providing a perfect union of parts. Her kiss was deep and sensuous, lingering and careful.

"Please come back to me," she said.

My gaze fixed on hers, I nodded. We said very little on the drive to the airport and our kiss goodbye reflected our uneasy truce.

Laura's assistant had booked us at the Sheraton Park Lane near Hyde Park. My British Airways flight had been uneventful, my business-class seat providing me with a decent night's sleep. Laura was scheduled to arrive at about the same time, and we had agreed to meet up for lunch. Memories of my first visit to London with Laura played in my head, in particular, images of the tiny room with one bed and my sleeping naked, her not caring. The innocence of that moment made me smile.

As I waited for the elevator to take me to my upgraded suite, I caught sight of Laura at the check-in desk. Her hair, tousled from the overnight flight, fell forward, partially covering her glasses, worn, as I knew, only when contacts were uncomfortable. I saw the clerk motion in my direction and Laura turned to wave to me, smiling.

"Wait," she said when she saw the elevator door open.

She walked quickly toward me, her suitcase and a litigation bag in tow. She threw her arms around me like a long-lost friend, which, I thought to myself, was not what she was, and asked about my flight.

"It was nice. Uneventful. The best kind."

"Let's meet in the lobby at one—does that work for you?" She smiled at me, her eyes peeking over the glasses, so fetching.

I nodded agreement and we stepped off on the same floor. I sighed, overcome by a bout of nerves at the thought of being in such intimate quarters with her for days. She didn't seem to notice as she nonchalantly opened the door to her room, directly across from mine.

* * *

Laura brought a thick manila folder to the lunch table. She pulled out a very expensive-looking brochure on the rare bookstore—Peter Harrington. I flipped through it, impressed by the heavy paper and the detailed illustrations of book covers and ancient looking folios. I could almost smell the mustiness of such a collection just from looking at these representations.

"Very high class," I said.

"Yes, they were a good mark."

"When's our first meeting?"

"We will be sitting down with the solicitor who represents the bookstore. My office contacted him. He knows I represent Dave's estate. We have a meeting with him tomorrow."

"What do you expect from the meeting?"

"We want to learn everything we can from him. About the transaction Dave did with the store. About the woman, Emma."

"But is he likely to tell us much? After all, it's his client Dave stole from."

"We need to convince him that we are determined to, and have a shot at, getting that money back for his client. The bankruptcy isn't going to help him with that."

"Should I be a potted plant or is there something in particular you want me to do or say?"

She laughed. "Follow my lead."

We got a second wind after lunch and decided to take a walk in Hyde Park. Laura hugged her coat tight around her in the crisp, cool air. When she spoke to me, she looked straight ahead in a way that struck me as nervous, anxious, almost shy.

"Being here, does it bring back memories of that trip we took?" she asked.

I smiled. "Of course. I thought about it on the plane over."

"Seems like a million years ago."

"Our innocence was so sweet," I said. "Everything was brand new."

"There's nothing else like that, you know? That feeling of discovering something so unexpected, that swallows you up, whole. I remember feeling like we were the only two people in the world."

She stole a look at me and continued, "It's like it's still here, in a way, not between us now, of course, but that it exists, somewhere in the ether. A unique experience. Can you feel it?"

"Singular," I said. "A coming of age. It happens once."

"I'm glad I had that with you," Laura said, reaching for my hand.

I grasped it quickly and let go, but a tingling lingered on my fingertips. We walked on, past lovers on a bench who snuggled under a blanket in the sun, past a food cart, and a park café. The sun began to set and the air cooled to cold as we made our way back to the hotel. She had stirred my emotions again and I felt my breath coming in shallow sips, fought with it, trying to calm it with deep inhales. Her silent presence by my side occupied more space in my head with every step. When we reached the hotel at last, I felt exhausted by the effort of containing my surging desires.

On the elevator ride, we stood on opposite sides of the cab, my gaze locking with hers in a temporary surrender to the passion that had refused to subside. We parted on the hallway, headed to our respective rooms, each murmuring about work to catch up on. But when the door closed behind me, I didn't hear it latch. As I looked back, her hand pushed it open. I called her name as I fell into her arms.

After furiously making out like teenagers behind the bleachers, we dropped our coats to the floor and flung shoes to the side. Slowing down, Laura took both my hands in hers, lifted them to her lips, kissed each finger in the space between knuckles, making a study of every dimple. Then she placed my hands to the back of her neck, freeing hers to begin my undressing. First, the buttons of my blouse came open, one by one, the silky garment slipping to the floor.

Next, the zipper of my trousers, the latch of my bra, and all the while, my tongue explored her mouth, my kisses traced her features, her neck, the ridge of her shoulder.

She moved us to the bed, propped me against the pillows and stood to shed her own clothes, me watching her like a striptease, her inspecting my nude body, open and waiting, pulsing with anticipation. I marveled at the definition in her anatomy, every muscle teased to the end of its feminine rope, her belly carved into sixes, her breasts high and upturned. I fought to hold on to my orgasm as she pushed my legs apart and touched her mouth to me and I arched to meet her, without intention, exploding into her like an aching virgin, so fast, so hard, so loud.

With waves of pleasure still reverberating through me, I pulled her up to face me, smiled and pressed my forehead to hers, breathing in the smell of sex and reaching my hand between her wet-with-sweat thighs, to find the invitation to come in. She exhaled into my ear, the heat and moisture of her breath urging me on as I pushed deeper into her, then, my excitement renewed, we came together in a waterfall of sensation.

CHAPTER TWENTY-SIX

The Triangle Ball, a presidential inaugural ball for lesbians, had been held once before, in 1993 for Bill Clinton's first inauguration. Melissa Etheridge "came out" during the festivities. Ours took place in the atrium of a glass-walled office building in downtown Washington. Three, or was it four, levels stretched up, teeming with women in cocktail dresses, ball gowns, and tuxes. A DJ spun dance music and champagne flowed. So many women jammed the space, their bodies heating up the night like a wildfire, that I imagined we could easily melt the snow that piled outside.

Laura and I stood on the third level, holding hands, looking down over the stunning crowd below.

"I feel like I'm on a movie set," Laura said. "This is crazy."

"Who knew there were this many lesbians in the world? Let alone in one place."

"Hey, look at Christine down there. Isn't that Melissa Etheridge she's talking to?"

"Oh my god," I said. "Let's get down there!"

We clunked down the steps in our heels as quickly as we could, doing our best to keep Christine in sight. I caught her eye and gestured to her to introduce us.

"C'mon!" she mouthed.

Breathless, we arrived at her side and right in front of us was Melissa, much shorter than I had expected. Christine made the introduction.

"I'm your biggest fan," Laura gushed as I looked at her with disbelief. I'd never even heard her listen to Melissa. "Can we get a picture?"

"Why not?" Melissa said, her arm slipping effortlessly around Laura's waist.

I jumped to Melissa's other side and someone snapped the picture. I noticed it was a young guy who looked like a professional photographer and asked him if I could get his card, order a copy of the photo.

"Sure," he said, handing me a card. "Just go online."

I looked at the card, which said *The Washington Post*. My tongue tingled with an odd dryness as I involuntarily hissed, "Shit." Was our photograph going to appear in *The Washington Post*? At a lesbian party? I stuffed the card in my purse as beads of sweat formed on my upper lip.

"What's wrong with you," Laura said, noticing my agitation. "Have you had too much to drink?"

"No," I snapped. "Nothing. I'm just a little overwhelmed by all of this."

"Hey," said Christine, approaching from behind us, her arms draped over both our shoulders, "come over here. There's someone else I want to introduce you to."

She pulled us to a crowd of women circled up in what appeared to be a conspiratorial conversation.

"I don't mean to interrupt," Christine said, pushing into the circle.

"You don't mean to, but that's exactly what you're doing," said an attractive dark-haired woman, smiling, curls tumbling from the crown of her head to her shoulders, glasses halfway down her nose.

"Yeah, well, that's me," Christine replied. "As you know."

"Yes, indeed. I do. Who are these lovely ladies?"

"Friends from Texas," Christine said. "I want you to meet them. They might be interested in Legacy."

"Oh, fantastic," she replied, rocking back on her heels.

"Jen, Laura, meet Andrea."

"What part of Texas?"

"Dallas," Laura said. "We're lawyers."

"Right, well, everybody's a lawyer these days. Welcome to DC."

"Thanks!" I said. "It's freezing!"

"It's hot in here, though," Andrea joked, making eyes at a passing pair of young women shod in high heels and wearing strapless gowns.

After appreciating the young beauties, Christine turned her attention back to us.

"Tell them about Legacy," she said. "Don't you have some women in Dallas?"

"We have women in Dallas. Yes, we do. Quite a few."

"What is Legacy?" Laura asked.

"It's a nonprofit we put together a few years ago. We raise money for scholarships. For lesbians. We do some great events. You should come to the next one we do in Dallas."

"I'd love to!" I said.

Laura shot me an odd look, which snapped me back into her reality. Of course, she would never get involved with a lesbian group in Dallas.

"Fantastic," Andrea said. "Let me get your email address. I'll put you on the list."

I wrote my information out on a slip of paper and Andrea stuffed it into her pocket.

"I hope you're not really going to follow up on that," Laura said as we moved on, standing at the bar for another drink.

I shrugged. "Probably not."

She shook her head at me. "You can't take the chance. What don't you understand?"

I looked away; at the floor, anywhere but at her. I fumed. I thought about walking away, finding a group to attach to, but I didn't have the guts. I didn't want to leave Laura. I wanted to stay with Laura. I wanted to be with her in every sense of the word.

"Let's not fight," she said, taking my hand. "We're here now. Enjoy it while it lasts!"

I melted and, drinks in hand, we landed on the dance floor near the DJ booth. Laura pulled me close, her arm tight at my waist, her mouth on my neck, sucking a hickey, then kissing me, then whispering in my ear.

"That stairwell over there," she said, her breath short. "I'm so hot for you, I can't wait."

The door closed and I wondered faintly whether it had locked behind us, but there was no time to contemplate. She pulled her slinky skintight dress up past her thighs and pressed against me. I backed against the wall to brace myself as she pressed harder. When my hand slipped down into the lace of her panties, the sound of her climax reverberated through the stairwell, amplified to a comedic crescendo that made us laugh to the point of tears.

She dropped to her knees, but I pushed her away.

"No," I said. "Not here. I can't do it."

"Why not?"

"I just…I keep thinking someone is going to walk up on us."

"So what?"

"You're insatiable," I said, kissing her, pulling her to her feet.

"Shit," she said, trying the door and finding it locked.

We took the stairs down to the ground level and came out into the icy air of the alley behind the building. Without our coats, and with light flaky droplets of snow falling from the sky, we were shivering instantly, running to the corner and back around to the entrance. The bouncer, a tall, broad bull dyke, laughed explosively when we told her we had gotten locked into the stairwell.

"Oh, to be young again," she said. "And in love."

Back inside, we warmed up by dancing and drinking and when the music stopped at two a.m., we were still keyed up.

"There's an after-hours party at the Hung Jury," someone said.

"Let's go. You can't leave town without checking that box," Christine said.

We got into one of the cabs that had lined up outside and took the short ride to the lesbian bar. Laura was pleasantly drunk, but I had a quickening pulse at the thought of our time here winding down. We had a flight the next afternoon and I couldn't stave off the dread of returning to my closet.

The bar was packed with women, most of whom had not been at the ball and so were dressed casually in jeans and leather. As Laura's head bobbed at the bar, a feminine woman in a skirt and tight sweater approached me. Her light-brown hair was layered and reached a couple of inches below her ears. She wore dangly earrings and a gold choker.

"Can I buy you a drink?" she asked.

I shifted, feeling anxious and awkward.

"That's my girlfriend," I said, nodding toward Laura.

"I'll buy her a drink, too," the woman said. "You look like you're from out of town. I'm just being friendly."

"Sure," I said, smiling. "Why not. I'm Jen, by the way."

"Sharon," she said, extending her hand.

Laura perked up and I put my arm around her.

"This is Sharon," I said. "She's buying us a drink."

"Nice," Laura said, her eyes half-mast. "That's nice."

Sharon and I sipped vodka sodas while Laura nursed a whiskey.

"I own a printing company," Sharon said when I asked. "We're a government contractor. I do most of my business with the Commerce Department."

"Wow," I said. "How did you get into that?"

"I went to school here—GW. I did a project for a business school class. A business plan for exactly what I'm doing now. My professor helped me raise the money to get it started."

"Awesome."

"You said you're a lawyer?"

"Yeah."

"You don't seem too enthusiastic."

"You know, I think I would be better in business, honestly."

"Don't wait. It's risky and if you get too comfortable in a law firm, you'll never do it."

I clinked her glass with mine.

"Good advice."

When I turned back to Laura, her head was on the bar and she was out, snoring softly.

"I think it's time to go home," I said, laughing and giving Sharon a farewell wave.

CHAPTER TWENTY-SEVEN

I roused to find Laura asleep in my hotel bed and experienced a gripping in my gut like nothing I'd felt before. Oh my god, I thought, how could I have done this? Adrenaline poured through my veins at a pace so intense I had to close my eyes to calm my pounding temples. I felt helpless, unable to move, unsure what to do next. She stirred.

"Hey," she said, reaching for me.

"I…Laura, I don't…"

"It's okay," she said. "I know this is not exactly, you know, well…"

"Fuck," I said.

She sat up, pulled sheets to her chin. I realized, with a shock of sudden embarrassment, that I had no clothes on. I grabbed a robe from the chair and threw it quickly over my treacherous body, the body that had surrendered all to the touch of this Aphrodite. I did not dare look at her.

"Jen," she said, prodding for a response.

"Yes," I whispered.

"That was amazing."

"Don't remind me," I groaned. "Shit."

She laughed and tugged at the belt of my robe.

"It's only sex."

I met her eyes and knew she meant it.

"Right," I said.

"Fucking amazing, mind-blowing, rarely ever experienced sex, but still, only sex."

"Like an epic tennis match, for example?" I said, growing angry.

She cocked her head back against the headboard, narrowing her eyes and smirking.

"That's not what I meant."

"Well, what did you mean? Because when I think about what happened here, it's loaded with implications. I don't casually sleep with someone just because I get the urge. For me to give in to that temptation means I betrayed someone. And I haven't betrayed her before. It's a big fucking deal to me."

She kneaded her brow, took some time.

"I'm sorry," she said. "I didn't mean to be flippant. I know you don't...that you're serious about your commitment to... your wife."

"I'm getting in the shower," I said, standing and moving toward the bathroom. "You should go."

"Jen," she said. "Please. I don't want to leave it this way."

"Look, I don't blame you for this," I said. "I wanted it every bit as much, maybe more, than you did, which scares me. I have to figure that out."

I closed the bathroom door behind me, turned on the shower, dropped the robe, stepped under the water. Memories of Laura twenty years before flooded over me, so vivid I could feel her hands on my body as I so often had back then, the shower fuck being one of our favorites. Before I knew it, my own hands did the work and I orgasmed through tears of regret.

I stayed in my room that evening with a room service hamburger, afraid of seeing her, of even speaking with her. At just before ten, the telephone in my room rang and, as I reached for it, my hand shook. I answered with an unsteady hello, my throat suddenly seared dry as though I were breathing in hot sauna air.

"Hey," she said, softly.

"Hey," I responded with a choke.

"Your cell phone is off."

"I know," I said.

"You didn't want to talk to me?"

I breathed deeply, exhaling into the phone.

"I'm...I'm scared," I said, my voice barely a whisper.

"Jenny," she said. "Will you let me come in?"

I blinked back tears. "I don't think that's a good idea."

"I promise. I just want to talk. I think we should talk."

Something about her urgency annoyed me and I found myself speaking a little too loud. "What is there to talk about? This is ridiculous, impossible, fucked up."

"I know. I know, but I don't want to leave it like that. Please."

"Laura, this is too much for me. I'm very fucked up right now."

She paused and I could tell she was trying to slow things down. She spoke softly. Lovingly.

"I'm not trying to push you. I just want to find some...some calm. To recenter."

The tactic worked. My pulse slowed down and I realized I wanted the same thing. When I spoke, I spoke with confidence.

"Promise that you will not touch me. That if I touch you, you will slap me away."

She laughed, breaking the tension. "Okay. I agree to your terms."

We sat in straight-backed chairs at the table in my room, me wearing sweats and a long-sleeved T-shirt. She in jeans and a white button-down. A pitcher of water sat on the table between us.

"Let's just talk about what you're feeling," she said, pouring us each a glass of water.

"I can't hold these two ideas in my head at the same time," I said. "I know a lot of people can, but I'm not one of them. I can't be married to Mary and have an affair with you."

"Is that what's happening?"

"I know you look at this as an event, but that's not how it works for me."

"What do you mean?"

"I mean that…having…sleeping with you…raises a very basic question for me. Doing that, giving in like that, means there's something much bigger going on. I'm not wired that way. The duality. The compartment for this, the one for that. It's all a whole piece for me."

"I see what you mean," she said.

"And you don't feel that way?"

After a few seconds of reflection, she said, "No, I don't. But I don't think it's a parallel to your situation. This doesn't feel like cheating to me."

"If you slept with a man, would it feel like cheating?"

"No," she said quickly. "Steve and I give each other that freedom."

"So Steve would be perfectly fine if you had an ongoing relationship with me?"

"Is this about me and him or is this about you and Mary?"

I rubbed my eyes and tugged at my hair. "I want to scream."

"Go ahead!"

"I'm so burned out on this. I can't think. It's like bees buzzing in here," I said, holding my head.

"You could…officially separate. Give yourself some space."

I looked at her, searching for signs of irony, and found none. I nodded.

"Space," I said, "would be good."

"Are you going to abandon our official mission?"

"I think maybe I should."

"I understand," she said. "I'll be fine here and of course I'll let you know the result. But, I just want to make sure this isn't the end of…of some kind of…friendship. Or whatever you want to call it. I realize that's asking a lot. I get it. But, having you in my life again, I don't know, it's like I'm awake for the first time in a long time."

As I looked at her, my thoughts overshadowed her words, almost muffling them entirely. Yet I heard their meaning, knew my attraction to her was primal and possibly dangerous, steeped as it was in so much impossibility.

"I won't make any promises," I said. "I can't do that right now. Maybe ever. But I understand what you're saying."

She met me in the lobby the next day to see me off.

"Travel safe," she said and hugged me very close. "I love you," she whispered hotly.

Then she was gone.

I stared into the space she had just occupied, dumbfounded.

CHAPTER TWENTY-EIGHT

As the plane touched down in Dallas with a jolt, I had a similar sensation in my psyche, back in the prison of my hometown after a weekend of gay freedom in Washington. Even Laura seemed melancholy and neither one of us had much to say as we located her car in the parking garage and loaded in our luggage.

My thoughts turned to the heaviness of my routine—getting up at six a.m. the following morning, dressing in a suit for work, trudging into that office tower with a thousand other people, grinding away in the windowless library, sitting in Brian's office on an interminable conference call. The words of the woman in the bar, Sharon was her name, echoed in my head. *Don't wait too long. Get out while you can.*

"What's on your mind?" Laura asked. "You seem like you're worried about something."

"Not worried, really," I said. "Just, I don't know, work isn't what I thought it would be, I guess. I don't know if it's right for me."

"You haven't really given it a chance," she said. "And we're on the bottom rung. It's going to be torture for a while, no matter what."

"Yes, but you have specific goals. You have a reason for going through it. I don't."

"Since the day we met, you've admitted you don't know what you want. You don't have a plan. So, either get a plan, or stop complaining about it."

"Fine. But don't ask me what's on my mind if you don't want to know."

She took a deep breath. "Fair enough. Look, I think we're both a little on edge coming home after such a great weekend."

I looked at her, a little surprised she acknowledged that.

"Did you ever imagine there were that many 'normal' girls," I said, "girls like us, who were gay? With girlfriends?"

"Not in a million years," she said, shaking her head.

"It's possible," I said. "To live that way. Now we know for sure."

She shook her head sharply. "No. Not for me."

"Why do you say that?"

"Look, Jen. I'm tired of having this conversation. I can't be that girl. If that's what you need, we should—"

"What? Break up? That implies we're together."

She took the next exit off the highway, pulled the car into a gas station, put it in park, and got out.

"What are you doing?"

She threw the keys into my lap.

"I can't do this right now. I need some space. Take the car and I'll call a cab."

I got out of the car and stood as close to her as I dared.

"Don't be ridiculous," I whispered loudly. "Get back in the car. This is crazy. Let's just forget all about it."

She looked at me with eyes full of fear, almost panic. Her whole body was taut, as though she might blow apart if she didn't manage this just right. After what felt like an eternity, she walked slowly back to the car and sat on the passenger's side. We rode the rest of the way home in silence. Exhausted, we went straight to bed, to our separate rooms.

The next day, as I paid for my coffee at the shop in the lobby of our office building, I came across the slip of paper with Andrea's phone number and email address. I felt my heart rate pick up as I thought about asking her for the names of lesbians near me. *Am I really going to follow through on it?* It seemed so strange. Laura would not like it.

Later that afternoon, after debating with myself for too long, I sent Andrea an email, though I hesitated a second or two over the send button. I checked my email obsessively for the rest of the day. At last, when I got home and logged into the computer in my bedroom, I had a response.

Get in touch with this woman named Dee, the email said. *She does a chick happy hour. You'll meet a bunch of people.*

I stared at Dee's contact information. *I don't know.* It felt like dangerous territory. Like coming out of the shadows and into the glaring sunlight without your clothes. I thanked Andrea and said I would get in touch with Dee.

"Hey, you," Laura said from the hallway, peeking into my room. "What's up?"

I quickly clicked my screen off.

"Hey, how was your day?"

"They put me in second chair on the biggest bankruptcy case we have right now."

"Great! That's fantastic."

"Yeah, I'm excited, but...I've been thinking about yesterday—"

I stayed silent, waiting for her to continue. She stepped into the room, sitting down on my bed.

"I feel...like we're starting to go in different directions and...I'm having a hard time with it."

I closed my eyes. I felt sick. *Is she breaking up with me?*

"What are you saying?" I asked.

"Just that I see what kind of life you want and I know I can't give that to you."

I steadied myself, determined not to break down.

"You mean you won't let yourself have that life."

"It's not what I want."

"How can you be so sure?"

"Do you have time for a story?" she asked, taking my hand and turning it over in both of hers.

I squeezed her hand. "Of course."

"I've never told you this before, but, when I was a kid, I was very close to my grandmother. My father's mother. She was our babysitter up until I was twelve. Then she died, unfortunately."

"I'm so sorry," I said, noticing tears forming at the rims of her eyes.

"I was her favorite. As least, I think I was," she said, smiling. "Anyway, she saw something in me. She sat me down—this was not long before she died. She said 'I see how you act around that girlfriend of yours. How you look at her.' I couldn't believe it. I felt so ashamed. I did have a crush on this girl down the street. She was a year older. But I had no idea anyone could see that, let alone my grandmother."

She paused, and I could see in her eyes that she was reliving the memory.

"I was so horrified, I stared at the floor, frozen. 'You can't ever act on those feelings,' she said. 'And it's not because it's wrong. It's because this world won't ever let you be happy that way.' Then I snuck a look at her, still not really ready to face her. 'I know,' she said. 'I know because I am the same way.'"

"Really!" I gasped. "Oh my god."

"She had been in love with another girl in high school. Her father caught them, doing what, she didn't say, but you can imagine. He threatened to throw her out of the house, cut her off, kill her plans for college. 'I never allowed myself to feel those feelings again. It will cost you everything,' she said to me. 'You must promise me you will forget about girls. Find yourself a nice boy and live a normal life.'"

She stared at the floor as she spoke these last words.

"Laura—" I wanted to comfort her; to think of something brilliant to say.

"It haunts me. That promise I made her that day."

I sat next to her and put my arm around her, but she didn't melt into me like I expected.

"That's heavy," I said.

"I know it's internalized homophobia. I get it. And I understand you don't have that problem and I envy you."

"It's not like I want to make a big announcement or start protesting in the streets. I just don't want to live a lie," I said.

"I know that," Laura said. "I can see what's happening. I wish I could be the person you need."

"You are the person I need. The person I want," I said, a sense of dread coming over me, suffocating me.

"Jenny, this is not going to get better. I have to find a way to let you go. You have to live the life you want."

She choked out those last few words and started sobbing, burying her head in my chest and holding me, almost crushing me with her intensity. I went into shock, or something like it. I couldn't cry, couldn't move, couldn't think. It was as though my insides had been hollowed out by an invisible bore that took down the infrastructure of my body and left me collapsing into myself. Apparently, I passed out and fell onto the floor, which is where I came to with Laura, terrified, hovering over me.

My eyes refused to focus at first as I heard her speaking, but couldn't process the words. I managed to sit up on the floor, my back against the bed. Laura ran from the room and returned quickly with a glass of water, kneeling and holding it to my lips.

"You scared me," she said. "Are you okay?"

I nodded and gulped the water. She smoothed my hair and looked at me intently, her beautiful eyes full of affection.

"I feel so alone," I said finally.

She sat next to me on the floor, holding my hand.

"I wish I'd been born brave, and fearless, and fierce, like you," she said. "Then I'd never let you go."

I turned to her and she kissed me, and it didn't feel like she had any intentions of letting me go. My stomach growled as my appetite suddenly returned in full force.

CHAPTER TWENTY-NINE

Mary saw right through me and I knew it.

"You slept with her," she said as we stood in our kitchen.

I said nothing, staring past the sink, out the window. *What have I done?* The moorings had come off. I drifted. No rudder. No wind for my sail.

"Jennifer!"

I turned. "I'm sorry."

"Did you do it to hurt me?"

"No!"

"Then you did it because? You wanted her? You're in love with her?"

"I...I don't know. It just happened. I didn't plan it. I don't know."

Mary collapsed into a chair like a tossed-off blanket, bent in half, gripping her sides, howling like a trapped animal.

"Whatever this is," she whispered hoarsely, "the hold she has over you, it's killing me. I don't know what to do. I can't go on like this."

"Mary," I said, kneeling beside her, taking her in my arms, holding her close as she continued to sob into me. "Please. Stop. I never meant for this to happen."

"What do you see in her?"

"It's not like that, I—"

"What does she have that I don't have?"

"Nothing!"

"I don't understand what's happening, Jen," she said, searching my face, her tears subsiding.

"It was...a moment of weakness," I said.

"No. It's more than that. It's so much more than that. And that's what I don't understand. Where is this going?"

I stared into her eyes, wishing I could have hidden my treachery. Lied about it. To protect her. Wishing I could lie at that moment.

"I don't know."

"You're scaring me," she said, standing, looking at me like I was an intruder. "I'm starting to think you could actually be dismantling our life. I can't believe it!"

"Mary, please, slow down," I said, her panic seeping into me. "I'm not doing anything. I slept with her. It happened. That's it."

"But that's not what you said a minute ago. You said you don't know where it's going."

"I'm jet-lagged. I'm exhausted. I'm overwhelmed."

"You can't see her again. Period."

I looked at her, feeling like a chastised teenager, and rebelling like one.

"I cannot make that promise."

She turned her back, left the room, and slammed the door as hard as she could, the reverberations stinging me like stones in the face. Was I dismantling our life? I allowed myself to consider it, imagining, if only for a moment, being without her, going my own way, separating. It felt neither right nor wrong. Only foreign.

I heard the garage door open, the sound of Mary's car screeching out onto the street.

I left for Dallas two days later. To help Alex with Mom. Fortunately, Laura was still in London. Mary had gone to work at the hospital after our encounter and she hadn't been home or contacted me since. She ignored my texts and calls. I felt empty. Broken. Alone.

I was sitting at my makeshift desk in Mom's house when Laura's number lit up my cell phone for the third time in an hour. I finally answered, thinking maybe it actually had something to do with Alex's case.

"You sound awful," she said. "What's wrong?"

"I don't know. Stress, I guess. I'm feeling it from a lot of different directions right now."

"Yeah," she said. "I haven't helped with that, I know."

The sound of her voice made it impossible not to envision her in that London hotel room, in my bed.

"I'm trying not to think about it," I said.

"I understand. I just wanted to fill you in on what I've learned so far," she said. "Which is that this woman, Emma, appears to have been an active participant in the folio fraud."

"Really? She defrauded her own father?"

"It looks like it. They think she's in France now because she's a French citizen. Her mother was French and she was born in Paris while her father was on a fellowship at the Sorbonne."

"What about the money? Do they think she has it?"

"It's probably in the Swiss bank. Her mother was from a very wealthy family and had set up a trust for her at the bank when she was born. It may be difficult to get the bank to cooperate, even though privacy laws are much less favorable to secrecy now."

"What's the next step?"

"I've had success in getting their solicitor to trust me. They are doing their best to track Emma down and they've agreed that, once they find her, I can interview her. I'm hoping that will be within the week. In the meantime, I'm working from here."

"That sounds very promising."

"I'm hoping to bring you some good news."

"Thank you. I could use it."

"Before you go, there's something else."

"Okay."

She hesitated.

"I've been thinking nonstop about what happened when you were here. I can't get it out of my head."

"Well, like you said, it was spectacular sex," I said, annoyed. "And I told you, I've been trying not to think about it."

"Stop. That's not what I'm talking about."

"Then what?"

"The connection. The intimacy. The way I feel when I'm with you. It's like nothing else I've ever felt."

"I really cannot imagine where you're going with this. It's not like we could ever…I don't even know…It's crazy talk," I said, growing impatient.

"I know. I know. It's so not fair for me to even say these things," she said with a heavy sigh.

My heart thawed just a little, sensing that she really was in pain, not just indulging herself at my expense. But only a little.

"You say it's not fair for you to say these things. Fair to who? Me? You? Your husband? My wife?"

"All of us, I guess."

"Because your feelings for me could never cause you to take a stand, leave your husband, make a life with me. And what about that childhood promise to your grandmother?"

"You're really putting the screws to me, aren't you?"

"You called me. With your declarations of love, passion, whatever it is you say you've never felt before."

"You're right to be skeptical. I've certainly given you every reason to be."

"Every reason," I said.

"I know it will take a lot to win your trust."

I pondered that statement. Did she plan to win my trust? Was that even possible?

"I don't even know what to say to that."

"How long will you be in Dallas?"

"I'm not sure. Alex really needs my help. And I can work from here for a while."

"I want to see you," she whispered, and I could almost feel her breath in my ear.

"Laura—"

"Please."

"I have to go now," I said, clicking off the phone before I gave in to her in a way I would most certainly regret.

"Jen," Alex said, startling me out of my haze.

"Hey, I didn't know you were here," I said, standing to greet her.

"Why did you come back from London so quickly? What happened?"

"I think a 'how are you' would have been in order."

"That's what I'm wondering, too," said Mom, walking up behind Alex. "Something's not right. I can tell."

"What is this? An intervention?" I said with a forced laugh, looking from one to the other.

"Maybe," Alex said, her arms crossed like an angry parent. "If you're thinking about getting involved with Laura Peters."

I turned away from their gaze, an odd feeling of shame coming over me.

"I appreciate your concern," I said.

"How is Mary?" Alex asked.

"Yes," Mom chimed in, "how is my sweet girl?"

"Please," I almost shouted, feeling claustrophobic with these two closing in on me. "Things are not great, okay? Things are falling apart. Maybe for good. I don't know."

"No!" Mom gasped, sinking to a chair.

"Can you distract her?" I said to Alex through gritted teeth.

She nodded and took Mom into the den where I knew she would soon forget everything that had just been said.

"Sorry," Alex said, coming back. "We're just rooting for your marriage, you know? But I realize it's not that simple."

I slumped at my desk, looking up at her through bleary eyes.

"I keep telling myself that if Mary hadn't cheated on me, I would never have given in to Laura like that. But, the truth is, I'm not so sure."

"So you did sleep with her."

"Is that awful?"

"I'm not here to judge you. Have sex with whoever you want. But, you have a great thing going with Mary. I just don't know why you would risk it. Not for Laura Peters. Not after what she did to you—"

"I know! What's wrong with me?"

"Don't blame yourself. She's a predator. And you're vulnerable."

"I think predator is a little too strong. She's self-indulgent for sure. And she's used to getting what she wants."

"You've always given her the pass," Alex said. "I don't understand how someone so smart can be so dumb."

"It's a blind spot," I said with a wry grin.

"This wouldn't have happened if you hadn't reconnected with her because of me," Alex said. "Why don't you disconnect? Get away from her. I can take it from here."

"First, don't blame yourself for any of this. And second, I think this is a little more complicated than me just disappearing back to SF. I've pretty much blown that."

"What have you done? Don't tell me you confessed."

I looked at her forlornly.

"Oh, Jesus, Jen."

"I know!"

"What were you thinking?"

"I wasn't. She knew. By looking at me. She just knew. I couldn't lie to her."

"What are you going to do now?"

"I don't have a clue. I'm just numb."

"The whole fucking world is going to hell," Alex said, flopping onto the couch.

"I'm thinking about a separation," I said, stealing a look in Alex's direction.

She nodded fatalistically.

CHAPTER THIRTY

I was keyed up. Nervous as a cat. I was going to Dee's Chick Happy Hour at a lesbian bar called Sue Ellen's. I didn't know what to wear. Should I go ultra femme? Should I dress down? Should I go straight from work in my suit? What if I run into someone I know?

I hadn't mentioned it to Laura. Ever since the near-breakup conversation, she and I had been pretty much avoiding each other. I was doing my level best to give her the cold shoulder. To see if she was really serious about staying in the closet. Or maybe she would decide she's not gay at all. It was killing me, but I really believed that if she experienced life without me for long enough, she would come crawling back. It had been a week so far, but she was busy with her trial, so it was too soon to tell.

As for my fashion dilemma, I ended up taking a change of clothes with me to work so that I could go straight from there to happy hour. I chose dark-blue jeans, a strappy black top and cowboy boots. I wore my hair loose, letting it fall to its natural length at my shoulder. Not much makeup. Just some mascara and lipstick. As I crossed the lobby of our building, headed to the parking elevators, I ran into Laura with the rest of her team. One of the guys whistled at me.

"Where are you off to?" Laura asked, trying hard, I could tell, to sound casual.

"Just meeting some friends for happy hour," I said, smiling and waving to the group as I walked on.

"I don't know which angle I like better," said the guy who had whistled. "From the front or from the back."

Laura swatted at him. "Inappropriate!"

I turned to give her a last look and she met my gaze with something between fear and disapproval.

It was a beautiful early-spring evening and the doors to Sue Ellen's were open to the air. I walked in feeling like I stood out as an obvious newbie. These women were so comfortable with themselves, so full of confidence. I asked someone to point me in Dee's direction.

"Hey, new girl," she drawled in her heavy Texas twang. "Come on in here and meet everybody."

Sue Ellen's was a nice open space with a high ceiling, lots of neon lights, a big service bar and a large dance floor in the middle. The place was packed. A DJ played dance tunes and plenty of women were moving to the music. Dee introduced me to her crowd.

"You're new to town?" asked a woman named Marcie.

"No, I'm from here, but…"

"New to the life?"

"I guess, yeah, you could say that. I'm sort of just getting used to all of this."

"Are you out?" Marcie asked.

I hesitated.

"No. I'm not. Well, at least, not here. I have friends in San Francisco and DC who I've been, you know, out and about with. But not here. Not until now."

"Are you seeing someone?"

"Do you mind if I get a drink?" I asked, moving toward the bar.

"Sorry for the third degree," Marcie said.

"Really," said a woman named Crystal. "She's gonna think this in an inquisition."

I laughed, saying, "Oh, it's fine. I don't mind. But I don't really have an answer to that question. It's a little complicated."

"We've all been there," Crystal said. "My first girlfriend and I were completely in the closet for three years. It was hell."

I ordered a glass of white wine and rejoined the conversation.

"Do you mind if I ask what happened?" I asked Crystal. "At the end of the three years?"

"She moved away. We broke up. I came out and she's still not out, as far as I know."

"What about your work? They were okay with it?"

"I work for myself. I'm a freelance photographer. It's a pretty liberal crowd I work with. Lots of gays, actually."

"Really? I can't imagine. I'm in a big law firm. I don't think it would go over well at all."

"Hey," Crystal said, "you want to dance?"

I put my glass down on a bar table.

"Sure. Why not?"

We danced to the Spice Girls, Sheryl Crow, Whitney, Madonna. There were five or six of us all dancing together and I had a blast, enjoying the relief, if temporary, from my homophobic anxieties and worries. The group invited me to join them for dinner nearby.

Eight or nine of us all sat together at one big table, eating spaghetti and drinking red wine. I couldn't quite believe it. That I was sitting at a restaurant in my hometown with a bunch of lesbians. It was a dream come true.

I paced myself on the drinking because I had to drive home. As I paid my share of the bill, Crystal handed me her phone number.

"If you ever want to talk…" she said.

"Thanks," I said. "I appreciate it."

I got home around eleven to find Laura just coming in from an evening run, her skin glistening, rivulets of sweat cutting across the definition of her muscles, her shorts tight across her rock-hard thighs. Her hair was pulled to a high ponytail, damp ringlets kissing her neck. I resisted the urge to caress them. I closed my eyes, instructing my blood to stop surging.

"Hey," I said, stepping into the apartment behind her. "A little late for a run."

"What do you think you're doing?" she said, turning to confront me.

"What do you mean?"

"I know you got together with that woman. The one they told us about when we were in DC."

"Okay. Well, you're right about that. But so what?"

"You can't do that. It's too risky. Someone might see you. And blow the whole thing up."

"What whole thing, exactly?"

"Stop being obtuse, Jen. Your career. And mine. Our life."

I threw my jacket on a chair and moved toward the kitchen, suddenly desperate for water. She followed me.

"As you well know, this is not my idea of a real life," I said. "It was only a week ago that you were breaking up with me because you know I don't want to live in the closet. It won't work."

"I disagree with you. I've thought a lot about this. We can be together without being out in the open. People have been doing it for centuries."

"Yes, but the world is changing. Not to mention, how long do you think we can keep living together without raising suspicion? A year? Maybe two?"

I turned away from her and walked toward my room, growing increasingly agitated.

"I don't know why you have to plot out our entire future," she said. "Why can't we take one day at a time?"

I turned on her, incredulous.

"You? The woman with the five-year plan? The husband and kids? Give me a break."

"Hey," she said, reaching for my hand. "I know I've been sending mixed signals. When I saw you in the lobby tonight, oh my god, I couldn't think about anything else all night."

She paused, waiting for me to respond, to agree, to disagree, but I just stood there, watching her, saying nothing. She took the glass of water from my hand. She tingled the skin of my bare arms as her fingers slid up to the straps of my top, pushing them off.

"Stop," I said. "I'm not in the mood."

She kissed my neck, my chest, the top of my breasts. I pushed her away.

"I mean it, Laura. You can't keep playing this game with me. It hurts too much."

"I would never hurt you," she said. "You know that."

"No, I don't. I know the exact opposite. That's where this is headed."

She pressed her fingers to my lips, gently. Clutched me in her sweaty arms. Slipped my top over my head and quickly unlatched my bra, which dropped to my feet like a flag of surrender.

I wanted to stop her. I really did. I despised my lack of willpower in the face of her lustful hunger for me. She pushed me into my bedroom, onto my bed, struggled to strip off her soaking wet shirt and sports bra as she straddled me, her thighs pressing against mine. She dangled her breasts against my nipples as she kissed me, tugging at my jeans, which were too tight to pull off without my help.

I pushed the jeans and panties down off my hips and she pulled them the rest of the way, tossing them across the room, along with her shorts. She lay on top of me, one arm holding me slightly off the bed as she sucked my neck and thrust herself into me. I took her breasts in my hands, devouring each in turn, as I quickly lost track of every reason why this was a bad idea. We romped with unusual energy, as though we'd long been separated by time and miles.

Some time later, as we lay naked and exhausted on my mangled duvet, I turned on my side to face her, and she me.

"You make me crazy," I said.

"Ditto."

"You should come with me to Chick Happy Hour next week."

She jumped off the bed, grabbing her clothes off the floor.

"Good night," she said and left my room.

CHAPTER THIRTY-ONE

An hour after Alex had gone, I found myself still sitting at my desk, staring blankly at the wall, waiting for inspiration on a business email that had dogged me all day. Mary's silent treatment had begun to distract me from everything else. It was completely contrary to my many years of experience with her, for her to be so cold. When my cell phone vibrated with her number, I grabbed it and swiped immediately.

"Hey," I said. "You had me worried."

"Yeah, right."

"Honey, don't…"

"Wow," she said. "Do you realize how long it's been since you called me that?"

"Yeah," I said. "I'm sorry…"

"You should be," she said. "But that's not why I'm calling."

"Is something wrong?"

"It's not an emergency, but it's urgent. We have a roof leak. There was a major storm night before last and our bedroom got soaked."

"Fantastic. Did you report it to insurance?"

"I did. They sent somebody over this morning."

"What can I do to help?"

"We have to decide whether to stick with the asphalt shingles or go ahead and do the clay roof we've always wanted to do. The price difference is ginormous."

I weighed my response carefully, silently, remembering the time before the troubles, when plans for improving our home were one of our fondest pastimes. Now, this stark choice seemed a metaphor for our life together. Go with the asphalt and admit it's over. Pick the clay and gloss over the rift.

"Jen? Are you there?"

"I'm here. What do you think?"

"I think the timing is fucking ironic," she said. "I don't know if I'll be married to you in a year, much less living in this house."

"You said it's not an emergency. Is there something we can do while we think about it?"

"They've already done a temporary tarp thing. And it's not supposed to rain for the next week, according to the weather forecast."

"Okay, well—"

"I have the next few days off," she said, cutting me short. "I was thinking of coming to visit."

She spoke softly, causing my pulse to quicken as I envisioned her sitting on a stool at our kitchen bar, sketching on an art pad, as was her habit, probably drawing silhouettes of women. I suddenly realized how anxious I was to see her, to be with her.

"I'd like that," I said, my temperature rising, my blood surging, the return of a familiar feeling that had been absent for too long. "How soon can you get here?"

* * *

"Mary!" Mom cried out as the two of us walked through the door of her house. "I'm so happy to see you. This daughter of mine doesn't know how good she has it, being married to you."

I raised my arms in a plea of "no contest" as I shook my head in disbelief. "What, now you're an advocate for gay marriage?"

"I'm an advocate for yours, anyway," she said impishly.

"I guess the next thing I know, you'll be campaigning for a comprehensive ENDA," I said.

"What's that, honey?" Mom asked me innocently.

"Never mind," I said, laughing.

"I'm so glad to see you, Mom," Mary said. "You might be the best thing about this marriage."

Mom narrowed her eyes at me over Mary's shoulder as she gave her a hug, reducing me to my twelve-year-old self. I half expected her to send me to my room. I sulked as I watched them bend their heads over Mom's latest crocheted pillow cover.

"I guess I'll go back to work then," I said. "Since you two are so busy."

"No," Mary said. "Come with me."

She wanted to get some fresh air and exercise after being encapsulated in an airplane for several hours. We walked briskly to the local public recreational complex near Mom's house. It teemed with middle school soccer players, girls and boys, at least four different games going on simultaneously. Moms and dads hollered and admonished their offspring with frightening intensity.

"When I grew up here, it was all about football," I said.

"Thank god that's changing. Too many brain traumas."

I wanted to distract her from any deeper conversation. I wasn't ready for it. I was still trying to process so much conflicting thought. That last talk in London with Laura kept coming back. *Why was I so rigid?* Maybe it was wrong-headed to think in terms of monogamy. Wasn't that what was causing all my problems? *Why was it so important?*

"I know what you're thinking," Mary said, touching my arm and stopping me along the path next to the playground equipment.

"You do?"

"I know you. You lead with your head. You have to understand things intellectually. And you haven't been able figure this out. You're paralyzed."

I nodded in agreement. Just then, a soccer ball came flying right at my head. I butted it back to the midfielder nearest me and she fist-pumped at me in delight. Mary smirked at me as if to say, you're not getting out of this conversation.

She crossed her arms and continued, "If Laura was available, free, willing, would you prefer her?"

I didn't say no fast enough. Mary looked at me in disgust and started quickly down the path.

"No," I said, catching up to her. "Of course not."

"You had to think about it."

"That's not what I was thinking about."

"Then what?"

"I was thinking about monogamy. The fact that my insistence on monogamy is what I'm hung up on."

"And where are you going with that?"

"Isn't that what's causing my problem with what you did? Your problem with what I did?"

Her face contracted in a painful grimace. "Why can't you just view the mutual cheating as making us even?"

"I just can't," I said.

"Why not?"

"Because I don't know whether or not I would have done the same thing even if your thing had never happened."

"Well, I think you're mistaken. Clearly, this was cause and effect. I cheated, so you cheated."

"You're sure?"

"No. But I want it to be true. I want it to be the same as what I did. Stupid and indulgent and meaningless."

I thought about that. Clearly, what I had done with Laura was indulgent. But was it stupid and meaningless?

"You can't say that, can you?" she asked, looking panicked. "It wasn't meaningless."

I stood open-mouthed, saying nothing.

"Are you leaving me for her?"

"No!"

"What then?"

"You said it. I'm paralyzed. I don't know what to do."

"This feels like it's coming out of left field, Jen. It's like you're suggesting an open relationship. How long have you been thinking about this?"

I hadn't thought of that term before. "Open relationship?"

"Isn't that what you're getting at?"

"No. I don't…I wasn't proposing anything. I was just asking questions."

"You're looking for a way to keep the door open with both of us. Laura and me."

"Look, this has all taken me completely by surprise. Starting with what you did."

She looked away, her arms folding over her shoulders in a huddle.

"What you did. What Laura did. What I did. I didn't see any of it coming. I need a pause."

She turned her back to me, braced herself against the chill in the air.

I dared to put my arm around her as we walked further along the path. The sun slipping down the horizon slowly brought the soccer games to an end. We took a seat on one of the benches, quiet, waiting, as if for permission to go home.

"I think we should go with the asphalt," she said after a while.

"I guess that's right," I said with a sigh.

CHAPTER THIRTY-TWO

"It's our biggest fundraiser of the year," Dee said on the other end of the line. "And it's a blast. You have to come. And bring your girlfriend!"

She had invited me to an event for Uncommon Legacy, the lesbian scholarship foundation Andrea had told me about. It was founded back in the eighties in the Hamptons in New York. I wanted to go. I would go. The way Dee described it, it would be the highlight of my social life which, because of Laura's paranoia, was increasingly restricted. I very much doubted I could get her to come with me.

"When is it?" she asked, sitting across from me during our lunch break at a deli frequented by lots of people from our office.

"Next Saturday night," I said.

She seemed to contemplate it, which had me very confused.

"Would you come?" I asked.

She sucked on a straw and pushed black beans around on her plate.

"I feel like I need to keep an eye on you," she said.

"Really?"

I searched her face for signs of humor. Finding none, I shifted uncomfortably in my seat.

"I don't think that's necessary," I said. "You should come if you want to have a good time. And meet some nice women."

"Fine," she said. "What's the dress?"

"Aren't you worried about ruining your career? Blowing everything up? Being outed? I thought that was your whole thing these days," I said in a low voice.

She glanced around the deli, but no one seemed to be paying attention to us.

"Yes. Of course I am. But, and I've been thinking about this for a while, I also have to be fair to you."

I softened, touched by this note of empathy for me. It was a first and I liked it. But, at the same time, it worried me. What if something did go wrong? It could backfire. She would hold me responsible.

"Are you sure?" I said, "Don't blame me if something goes wrong."

At that moment, our colleague Michelle, the one who had stumbled in on us at my apartment that night, walked into the deli.

"You two again," she said. "Seems like you're inseparable."

"Hey," Laura said, gathering her dirty dishes and rising from her chair. "I was just leaving, actually. Take my seat. I have a client call."

"I wouldn't mind," Michelle said, looking to me for approval.

"Sure," I said. "I have some time if you want company."

Laura gave me an anguished look as she left the deli, as if to say "I told you so." I looked away, determined not to engage. Michelle returned to the table with a sandwich and an attitude.

"People are talking, you know," she said.

"Talking?"

"About the two of you."

"I don't know what you mean," I said, sipping water and trying to stay cool.

"I get it if you don't want to talk about it. And I don't have a problem with it, by the way. I'm just telling you that some people think there's something going on between you and Laura."

I looked her in the eye, swallowed, said nothing. She took a bite of her sandwich and chewed slowly, seeming to read my silence as an acknowledgment of the truth of her assertion. I broke the tension by laughing easily and rolling my eyes.

"I think people don't have enough to do," I said. "It's a good story, but it's not true."

At home that night, Laura turned sullen after I told her about the conversation with Michelle.

"I thought I handled it pretty well," I said, trying to get through to her, to cheer her up.

She sat balled up on the couch, rocking back and forth, staring with unfocused eyes.

"Laura," I said, sitting next to her.

"I don't know what to do," she said. "I'm feeling like a caged animal."

Her fear seeped into me like a noxious gas, closing up my throat until I realized I was literally holding my breath. I said nothing and neither did she. Eventually, she got up and went to her room. I fell asleep on the couch, waking up at two in the morning, more than ever feeling fear and dread. The kind of anxiety that looms large in the middle of the night. I noticed the light coming from under Laura's bedroom door. I opened it slowly, assuming she had fallen asleep, but there she sat, wide-eyed, against the pillows in her bed. She made a tiny ironic smile of her lips and I came in. She patted the bed next to her and I sat there.

She put her arm around me and I cuddled into her like a four-year-old. We slept that way until dawn.

On Saturday night, we dressed excitedly for the Legacy party, pushing away fears and trepidations about the chances we were taking.

"How do I look?" Laura asked.

"Smokin' hot, baby," I said, nodding approval at her tight sweater, short skirt, and cowboy boots. "You better stay close to me."

"Where else would I be?" she said, pulling me to her with her hands on my ass and kissing me sweetly.

The party, at the bar Sue Ellen's, was packed. The place throbbed with energy as women of all shapes and sizes and colors packed the dance floor. I introduced Laura to the women I had met before and, after a while, a group of us found ourselves outside passing a joint. I hadn't smoked since Amsterdam, and it didn't take much to get me high.

Laura took a long drag and quickly ascended to a very pleasant state of mind. Back inside, she slow-danced with her arms draped over me, her tongue lapping up the sweat on my neck. We stayed until the lights came on, signaling the end of the night.

"You gals know how to party," Dee said as we gathered our things to leave.

"You know how to throw one," I said. "We had a great time."

"Should I put you on the list for Chick Happy Hour?" Dee asked Laura.

"No, thanks," Laura said quickly. "Jen can let me know."

As we stepped out onto the sidewalk outside the bar, I heard a man's voice call Laura's name. We both turned in that direction and our hands, which had been clasped, suddenly pulled loose.

"Jolm," she said. "Hi. It's been a while."

Jolm, tall, dark-skinned, and slim in tight black jeans and a form fitting T-shirt, stood next to another, very similar-looking, young man.

"I wouldn't have expected to see you here," he said, nodding at Sue Ellen's. I looked on nervously as Laura seemed to process a response.

"Who's your friend?" she asked.

"This is Curt," he said. "We've been together for almost a year. What about you?"

She shook Curt's hand and I, annoyed that she hadn't introduced me already, stepped forward to do it myself. We chatted for a minute or two and I learned that Jolm had been two years ahead of Laura at law school.

"We're not—" Laura started, but then stopped.

"You're not out," Jolm said.

"No," she said. "And I would appreciate it if…"

"Don't worry," he said. "I understand. This hasn't been easy for me. As a matter of fact, it's been shitty."

"What do you mean?" I asked.

Laura mentioned the name of his firm, a rival to ours, as if that explained it.

"They've made it clear I'm not supposed to 'act gay,'" he said. "They tolerate me because I've been able to generate a lot of business. And I'm the only Black guy in the firm."

They invited us over for a drink at Jolm's apartment, which was nearby. To my surprise, Laura agreed and we joined them for a cognac, sitting on the balcony that overlooked the downtown skyline. She held my hand in front of them and suddenly it occurred to me that we had never been affectionate in front of anyone either one of us actually knew, from our real lives. But rather than feeling happy about that, I felt strangely sad, anxious, confused.

"That was nice," I said as we taxied home.

"Yeah," Laura said. "It's funny. I always thought he was gay, but he never, you know, was obvious."

"There's a community here. We could be a part of it, you know."

"I knew you were going to say that."

"Well, it's true."

"Around and around we go again," she said, folding her arms.

I drifted into my own thoughts, weary of this game we were playing. Exhausted by the effort of holding up my end of it. As if she read my thoughts, Laura whispered hotly into my ear, "Don't give up on me."

It had become her mantra.

CHAPTER THIRTY-THREE

Mary had left the next morning with plans in hand to replace our roof with asphalt shingles, a conclusion that left me feeling out of sorts even as I knew it made sense. She had taken an Uber and I had taken my daily run. Now, at one in the afternoon, I still hadn't been able to eat anything. No appetite. No hunger pangs. The gallon of coffee I had consumed began to eat into the lining of my stomach. I couldn't work. I left my mother in her usual spot in front of the television and took a walk.

I had fallen into a habit of dressing in yoga pants and sports bras every day, not bothering to wear real clothes as long as I was operating solely out of my mother's house. I was beginning to feel out of touch with my work, my partners, my life in San Francisco. Was I slipping? *Are you kidding? Jesus, give yourself a break.*

Just then, the cell phone in my pocket buzzed. It was Alex.

"I found the key," she said.

"The safety deposit box?"

"Yes. Should we go today?"

"I'll be by for you in a few."

As we drove toward downtown Fort Worth—Mom had been right about the location—Alex asked me for the latest from London.

"They are still trying to locate Emma. They know for sure now that she's somewhere in France, but they still don't know exactly where."

"And you and Laura? How's that going?"

I looked at her sharply.

"That's mean."

"I didn't intend it to be mean. I'm just wondering if, now that you're officially separated—"

"It's not official. We don't have a separation agreement."

"You know what I mean."

"Laura and I are not pursuing anything."

"Has she given up?"

"I don't want to talk about this right now. Please."

"Fine," she said.

My mood darkened as we sped along the highway past Hobby Lobby, Ruby Tuesday, Red Lobster, LA Fitness, California Pizza Kitchen, over and over and over. Downtown Fort Worth provided some relief from chain-store hell as we passed through the historic stockyards on our way to the bank. Once there, we quickly got down to business. Alex opened the safety deposit box. Inside was a thin envelope and a small key keeper. The envelope contained a letter. It was addressed to Alex from Dave.

"'Honey,'" Alex read, "'I'm sorry. It was the perfect plan. Until it wasn't. I failed you. Failed the kids. Everything has gone wrong and I can't face going to prison so, yeah, I'm taking the coward's way out. But I did manage to put away a few dollars for you and the kids. You'll have to get it back into the country, but you'll figure that out. The key goes to another safety deposit box. In London. Tell the boys I loved them. Dave.'"

Alex stared at the letter, seemingly unmoved.

"Are you okay?" I asked.

She looked at me, anger in her eyes. "What an asshole. He actually planned it."

I hugged her. "I'm sorry."

"I might have forgiven him if he'd done it in the heat of a moment," she said, crumpling the letter and tossing it into a nearby trash can.

I opened the key keeper to find a small piece of paper next to the key with the words "Barclays Bank London; 73 Russell Square."

"I guess I'm going back to London," I said.

I didn't mention it to Mary. We weren't talking and I didn't see any reason to reopen communication over another foreign encounter with Laura.

"When will you get here?" Laura said after I had explained what I knew. "I can't wait to see you."

"Yeah," I said. "Me, too. I'm taking the flight tomorrow afternoon. So I'll see you the next day."

My heart pounded in my chest as I imagined her on the other end of the line, sitting on the bed in her hotel room. It was late, so I saw her in her silk robe, naked underneath, running her hand through that cascading mane of hair.

"Should I get you a room? Or…"

"No," I said quickly. "I'll do it."

"You should plan on coming with me to France. We are narrowing down the possibilities. It's looking like Lyon."

"Ahh. Maybe."

"Why not?" she said. "If you're coming all this way."

"I'll think about it."

I flew to London the next day and checked in at the Park Lane. Laura met me for coffee in the Palm Court.

"You could have sent this over with a courier, you know," she said, one eyebrow raised, holding the small package Alex and I had retrieved from the security deposit box.

"Yes, I could have," I said, staring her down.

"But you didn't."

"No."

"You wanted to see me then?"

"I don't know where this is going," I said. "I'm flying blind."

She nodded. We were silent for a moment, both sampling the coffee.

"It feels good," she said. "Being here with you."

"Let's talk business," I said.

"Okay," she said, pushing back from our tête-à-tête to an upright posture. "I've made an appointment at the bank for this afternoon."

I took a sip of coffee before saying, "What are you doing until our appointment?"

She looked at me as if trying to read my thoughts.

"I was thinking of taking in an exhibit at the Tate. There's a Nan Goldin show called *The Ballad of Sexual Dependency*."

"Like 'The Threepenny Opera,'" I said, referring to the song of that same name.

"Yes," she said, pulling a torn magazine page from her purse. "This says that the artist describes the show as 'capturing the struggle in relationships between intimacy and autonomy...and what makes coupling so difficult.'"

She looked up at me and we held each other's gaze until finally I blinked, saying, "I'd love to see it."

We caught a cab and arrived just as the museum opened. The crowd was light and we were able to move deliberately through the exhibit, taking it all in. Some of the photographs were so moving, I had to linger for several minutes. One in particular overwhelmed me with a heavy sadness. It was called *Nan and Brian in Bed, New York City, 1983*. The artist is the subject of the photograph, along with her lover. She is clothed, at least as far as we can see, which is only from the waist up, her head against a pillow, one hand under her cheek, looking at his back. He sits on the edge of the bed, shirtless and smoking a cigarette, staring away from her.

"Do you think he's just raped her?" I said.

"That's dark," Laura said.

"What do you think then?"

"Maybe they've had an argument. Maybe she wasn't interested in sex. Or he wasn't."

"It's very provocative," I said, moving on, thinking of the artist's words about intimacy and autonomy.

We finished our tour of the exhibit just before noon.

"I'm starved," Laura said as we exited the show. "We have time for lunch at Level 9."

"I love that place."

I had the gazpacho and the cod. Laura had the tuna tartare and grilled cauliflower.

"Oh…my…god," I said. "So good."

Over a glass of wine, we continued to discuss the show.

"Would you say that sexual dependency leads to bad decision making?" I asked.

"How do you define sexual dependency?"

"The urge to have sex, the desire for someone's body, a craving, that clouds your head somehow, if you let it."

"Isn't there an emotional component?" Laura asked. "It isn't just physical."

"Yes, of course. Desire is the emotion. Sex is the physical expression."

"Dependency is a difficult word. It suggests weakness or addiction," Laura said.

"But that's what she's getting at, right? Can you be intimate with someone while holding on to your autonomy? Can you be a couple without losing your individual self?"

"I would say that the answer to those questions is yes, if you're highly evolved. Most people aren't."

"What about you?" I asked.

She hesitated before saying, "Are we talking about us?"

At that moment the server arrived with the bill. We paid it and caught a cab to the bank.

"Holy shit," I said, staring at the pile of cash I'd just dumped out of the large safety deposit box the clerk had left us with.

Laura quickly counted stacks of hundreds. "One million," she said.

"I don't know what I was expecting, but this wasn't it. I thought he might have skimmed a hundred thousand."

"It's impressive, actually," Laura said. "I don't know how he thought he would get away with it."

"And leaving it for Alex? What did he think she was going to do with it?"

"Delusional," Laura agreed, staring at the cash, deep in thought.

"What are you thinking?"

"This has to have been part of the eight million dollars that Dave and Emma conned out of her father. Where's the rest of it?"

"In Emma's Swiss bank account?"

"Exactly," Laura said. "We have to find her. Until we do, we're stuck."

"Should we go to Paris, then? Your people seem sure she's somewhere in France."

"So you *will* come."

She gave me a satisfied smile.

"Why not? I want to meet the woman who could fall that hard for my brother-in-law."

"I don't think that's why you want to come."

"Oh, really? Well, I guess you think it's because you're irresistible."

"Stop," she said, laughing. "Don't tell me I'm that big of an asshole."

"No comment," I said, raising my brows.

"Let's leave tonight," she said. "Where should we stay?"

She took my hand and I didn't pull it back. I felt exhilarated and out of control. Like I was being sucked into a vortex, drawn to her for better or worse.

CHAPTER THIRTY-FOUR

As we rolled into spring, my sister, Alex, had just arrived back home from a study abroad in Spain. I hadn't seen her for almost half a year. I had volunteered to pick her up from the airport so our parents wouldn't have to be bothered. I screamed when I saw her come through the gates after passport control.

"It's so good to see you," I said as I hugged her, taking one of her bags off her shoulder. "It feels like forever."

"You look great," she said. "Something's working well for you."

I flushed, feeling suddenly guilty about having kept my relationship with Laura a secret from her.

"I've been running a lot," I said.

"Ah."

"Hey," I said. "Let's grab something to eat before I take you home. We have a lot to catch up on."

We drove to our favorite hole-in-the-wall Mexican place near Mom and Dad's house. My palms dampened and my throat dried as I thought about the conversation I had planned to have with her. We ordered our usual, authentic pork tamales, black bean soup, and Spanish rice.

"What's bothering you?" Alex asked after a few minutes.

"What makes you think something is bothering me?"

"I can tell. You're distracted. What is it?"

I stared at my food, only half consumed, and felt no appetite. I hadn't thought it would be this hard.

"I've met someone," I said, plunging in after a silence that had reached the edge of uncomfortable.

"Really?" she said, excited. "Tell me."

"It's, uh, someone I met at work."

"Ooooo, an office romance. Sounds complicated."

I raised my hand to my brow, chuckling a little. "Complicated. Yes. That's a good word."

"What's he like? Same age? Where'd he go to school?"

I ran my tongue along my lips, took a breath, steadied my voice.

"That's the thing. This is, it's not, it's just that, well, it's not a man."

I stole a look at her, my head bowed toward my plate. She seemed confused and I turned away, wishing I could disappear. Regretting the whole thing.

"Oh," she said as if suddenly understanding my implication. "Oh!"

She reached across the table and grabbed my hand.

"You're gay," she said with glee.

"Quiet," I said, horrified she'd said it out loud.

"I always thought you might be," she said, almost as if congratulating herself.

"What? Why?"

"Little things. Here and there. Over the years."

"Like what? Give me an example," I insisted.

"The movie posters you had in your room in high school."

"What about them?"

"*Fried Green Tomatoes? Entre Nous? Thelma and Louise?* And then there was Melissa Etheridge."

"So what?"

"Most girls had posters of guys—New Kids on the Block, Boyz 2 Men, Seal."

"I don't think that proves anything."

"Why are you arguing with me? You're telling me you're in love with a woman."

"I never said I was in love."

"I can tell."

I looked at her, sighed, took a sip of iced tea.

"Fine," I said. "Maybe I am."

She asked me to tell her all about Laura and so I did.

"When will you tell Mom and Dad?"

"Ugh. Never."

"Oh, c'mon."

"Why should I? You heard what I said about Laura. I don't know where the relationship is going. So why bring them into it?"

"Because if it's not her, it will be someone else," she said, sitting back, her arms folded.

"When I'm ready," I said, feeling hungry again and eagerly finishing my plate.

*   *   *

"I'd like you to come over to my parents' place," I said to Laura a few days later. "They're giving Alex a little coming home party."

She was in the middle of folding laundry in the living room. She stopped in mid-crease and looked at me like I had suggested a root canal.

"Your parents?"

"I'd like you to meet them. And my sister."

"I don't know. Isn't that weird?"

"Why would it be weird? They've met dozens of my friends."

"Yeah, but I'm not—"

I raised an eyebrow. "You're not?"

"You know what I mean."

"What are you worried about?"

She picked up a T-shirt and folded it neatly.

"I just think, I don't know. It might be obvious."

"I don't mind," I said. "Anyway, I told Alex."

"What?" she said, dropping the towel she had picked up from the pile on the couch. "Why would you do that?"

"Because I needed to tell her. She's my sister. I needed to talk to someone."

"Great," she said.

"C'mon," I said. "It'll be fun. My dad has a great wine cellar. You won't believe it."

I picked up a T-shirt and started folding.

"Here," she said, taking it from me. "Let me show you how to do that right."

I smiled as she earnestly showed me how to do the perfect department store fold.

"Fine," she said. "Just this once."

"Yay," I said, grabbing her around the waist and kissing her. "Thank you."

"Spoiled brat," she said, hugging me tight.

My parents had a beautiful large backyard with an expansive tiled patio and a pool. My mother was a devoted gardener and the vegetation was always magnificently maintained. The late-spring weather was perfect for a party. It started with swimming in the late afternoon. Laura sat tensely in the passenger's seat and didn't say a word on the way out there and I worried that maybe it hadn't been the best idea to bring her.

"This will be fun," I said as I got out of the car. "I promise."

She sat motionless in her seat and I half considered just sending her home. I leaned into her window.

"Are you coming?" I asked gently.

She took a deep breath and put her hand tentatively on the door handle. She swung the door open slowly and got out, reaching into the back seat for her bag of extra clothes.

"Please get me a drink right away," she said as we walked side by side to the front steps.

I opened the door to find my mother arranging flowers in the entryway, decked out as usual in a darling outfit purchased just for the occasion. She threw her arms around me as though she hadn't seen me in years.

"I'm Marilyn Adair," she said to Laura, extending her hand. "Welcome."

"So nice to meet you, Mrs. Adair," Laura said as my heart melted at the sight of her in my childhood home.

"Do you need to change?" Mom asked us. "Alex is out there with a bunch of her friends."

I took Laura upstairs to change in my girlhood bedroom, which my mother had meticulously kept as I left it at age eighteen.

"Oh my god," she said, pointing at the posters on the wall. "Little baby dyke Jen!"

"Stop! That's so rude."

"Except that it's true," she laughed. "Are you sure you didn't have a girlfriend in high school?"

"I was homecoming queen, babe. Full-on hetero."

"I want to see pictures! Now!"

"No time for that. You'll have to come back another time."

Back downstairs, I grabbed a couple of towels off the bench near the patio door and Laura and I joined the group outside. I introduced Laura to Alex, giving Alex a stern look when she seemed to scrutinize her a little too closely. The party was a mix of guys and girls who Alex had gone to high school with and a few friends from college who lived in the area. I hollered hello to everyone, shouting Laura's name to whoever was paying attention and headed for the keg to pull a beer for her. I made sure she met a few people and then left her on her own to socialize with the ones I had known best.

"Your friend is hot," said Jimmy, one of Alex's high school boyfriends. "Is she single?"

"No," I said. "She's seeing someone. I think it's pretty serious."

I noticed that Alex had made her way over to Laura and had her cornered in what looked like an inquisition. I bounded over to investigate.

"What's up?" I said to Alex, smiling tightly.

"We're just getting acquainted," she said. "Did you know that Laura was the captain of the drill team in high school?"

"Really? How did I not know that?"

"Maybe you need to ask more questions," Laura said.

Just then, someone did a cannonball into the pool and sent a spray of water all over us.

"Get in! It's time for volleyball!"

It was Jimmy. He managed to get Laura on his side of the net. One too many times, he used the game as an excuse to dunk her or put his hands on her. I yelled at him to lay off and everyone looked at me like I was speaking German.

"Calm down," Alex whispered in my ear. "You don't want to act like that."

I saw my mother looking out at us from her chaise at the side of the pool. Her eyes shifted between Laura and me. A feeling of nausea came over me and I rushed out of the pool and into the house. It was a near panic attack. I locked myself in the powder room and talked myself down. A knock on the door roused me.

"Hey," said Alex.

"Jesus," I said, opening the door. "I cannot believe I overreacted like that."

"You're not exactly a poker face. But I don't think anyone really paid that much attention."

"Except Mom," I said.

"Yeah, there's that. You're not going to get much past her."

"Do you think she knows?"

"I feel like mothers always know. But she won't say anything unless you do. That way, she can go on in denial."

"Well, anyway, what do you think of Laura?"

She smiled, nodding approvingly. "She's beautiful. And really smart. Not bad for your first time out."

"I wish I knew where it was going."

"You might want to slow that part down."

"What do you mean?"

"You've already said she's super in the closet. And now that I've met her, I see that. So, I guess what I mean is, I'm not sure it's going where you want it to go."

I nodded reluctantly, sighing and heading back out to check on my closeted girlfriend. There she was, full-on flirting with a huddle of admiring college boys.

"Didn't you want to see my dad's wine collection?" I said to her, dragging her away.

"Sure, but that was unnecessarily rude."

"Look, they didn't even notice," I said, pointing to the boys, who were already horseplaying in the pool.

"That was fun," she said as we rode back home.

"Glad you enjoyed it. You were the belle of the ball."

She glanced sideways at me.

"Are you annoyed?"

"A little. But I guess I'm getting used to it."

"Used to what?"

"These games we play when we're around other people."

She didn't say anything and I left it at that. But I couldn't stop thinking about it, seething as I went over it again and again. All of her attention had been focused on creating the image she wanted to project to a group of strangers, many of whom she'd never see again. All the while, ignoring me. By the time we got home, I was in a proper bad mood and went straight to my room without a word.

CHAPTER THIRTY-FIVE

We flew to Paris that night and opted to stay at the Shangri-La, a far cry from the cramped spaces that had been our only option twenty years before. I was transported by the magnificent grand staircase rising out of the lobby like a scene from a storybook wedding.

I got settled in my room, then called Laura to invite her to go out for a walk. The air, refreshing in its sharpness, brightened my mood and I almost giggled with delight as we passed through the majestic streets leading to the Eiffel Tower.

"There's nothing like it," Laura said, pulling her pea jacket tighter, its collar caressing her neck.

"This is where I fell in love with you," I said, surprising myself.

She looked at me, smiling shyly, "Likewise."

We walked along in silence, me not wanting to spoil the moment with analysis. It was all I could do to stop from grasping her hand and running headlong into the night and into a different life. I could feel her energy, too, boiling up to the surface next to me. But somehow we got back to the hotel without ever touching.

We were to spend the next day in Paris, then head to Lyon by the TGV the day after. Laura's investigators had found Emma there and were monitoring her movements. We would have to hope she would agree to meet with us.

Laura and I said good night in the hallway and went our separate ways chastely.

When I woke the next morning, I had a message from Claire. Cryptic, just asking me to call. It was ten p.m. in California, so I called her back.

"What are you doing?" she asked roughly.

"Well," I said. "I'm working. Helping Alex, really."

"But you're in Paris."

"Yes, we're tracking someone down in France."

"We?"

"The lawyer who's helping us. I'm with her."

"The one who's your ex?"

I hesitated.

"Claire, are you concerned about something?"

"I'm concerned about you cheating on Mommy."

"First of all, I'm not cheating. But you know Mommy and I are taking a little time apart right now."

"Mom! This is so awful. You need to come home. You need to fix it."

Her sniffles had turned to a roar of tears.

"Claire, honey, please. Don't worry about this. Mommy and I will be fine. You will be fine."

"I just don't understand."

"I know. I know. I'm not sure I do either. But, sweetie, I will be home soon and we can talk about this in person. Okay?"

"Promise me."

"Promise what, honey?"

"That you will try. Try really hard."

"I promise. Now get some sleep."

I hung up, feeling suddenly jet-lagged and disoriented. The room phone rang and it was Laura, calling from downstairs.

"I booked us a bicycle tour today. It looks like so much fun."

"Great idea. I'll be down shortly."

The day was spectacularly sunny without much wind. Perfect for bike riding. We met up with our group at a nearby bike shop. Juliet, our guide, was a diminutive twenty-something who spoke beautifully accented English. In explaining our route and the day, she emphasized the importance of "the hand."

"The most important of the thing," she said, "is the hand."

She demonstrated by holding her arm out with her palm facing opposite, as if forbidding anyone to advance.

"When we goes through the intersection, you must use the hand. Nobody gonna challenge the hand. Show me."

We all followed suit with "the hand." And off we went. We started at Place de l'Alma with yet another amazing view of the Eiffel Tower, past the Flamme de la Liberté, along Avenue George V, then down the Champs-Élysées with the Arc de Triomphe behind us.

We stopped on the Avenue Winston Churchill with the Grand Palais to our right and the Petit Palais to our left. As our guide recited historical facts and figures, I noticed Laura's gaze lingering on me.

"What?" I asked.

She smiled. "Nothing really. Just memories."

I had a flashback to the absolute abandon with which we had pursued our attraction back then. It seemed so innocent now. So uncomplicated. A place we could never return to.

Our route took us past the Tuileries, the Musée d'Orsay, and the Louvre. We took a lot of pictures along the way, posing in selfies and in photos taken by our fellow tourists. In front of Notre-Dame, our guide took a group shot.

"Please no Facebook," I said to Laura as we scrolled through the selfies. "Or Instagram."

"I'm not on any social media," she said. "You?"

"Only because of Claire. When she was in high school, we had to sign up in order to communicate with the parents' group. The last thing I need is her seeing posts of me and you in Paris."

"Is there a problem?"

"She called me this morning. She's just very upset about Mary and me. She's starting to suspect there's a problem."

Laura pocketed her phone.

"Is there a problem?"

"Not one I want to talk about right now."

"I understand. My kids aren't exactly happy with me either."

"What's going on? You haven't said anything?"

"Nothing official. There's just a bit of a chill in the air in our house. Kids always know."

"I'm sorry," I said.

"Don't be. Let's not ruin this beautiful day with all that!"

We continued the tour along Pont d'Arcole and ended at the Hôtel de Ville de Paris.

"I'm starved," Laura said as we turned our bikes into the tour shop. "What if we grab sandwiches and some wine and take a picnic in the Tuileries?"

"Perfect," I said. "I saw a boulangerie next to a wine shop just around the corner."

Our picnic secured, we made our way to the gardens. I had picked up a tablecloth at the wine shop and we used it to spread out on under one of the magnificent trees. The food and wine and the warm sun conspired to bring a heaviness to my eyelids that I couldn't fight, and I laid down, apologizing that I had to nap for a while.

Laura said she didn't mind, and when I opened my eyes some twenty or thirty minutes later, she lay propped up on her side, close to me, looking at me. I worried that she would try to kiss me. Then I worried that she would not try to kiss me.

She rolled over away from me and said, "We should probably get back to the hotel. I have some work I really have to get to and a few things I need to do ahead of tomorrow."

I don't know if it was the jet lag or the wine or the sun, but I felt out of sorts as we walked through the lobby of the hotel. I could not put my finger on it. Maybe it was the call from Claire. I shook it off and figured I would feel better the next day. I begged off having dinner with Laura and stayed in my room for the evening.

I slept fitfully, worried about oversleeping for our early train the next day. I finally got out of bed at five, packing, then scrolling on my phone as a distraction. I ordered room service for breakfast, then met Laura in the lobby at six thirty. Our seven thirty train would get us to Lyon by nine a.m.

On the train, we sat in seats facing each other and talked through the plans for the day. Laura had gone through a series of conversations with the attorney for Emma's father, and had persuaded them to agree to a reconciliation with Emma, if she would return the $8 million. If we could get Emma to agree with this plan, her father would allow us to keep the $1 million that Dave meant for Alex.

"My investigators have an eye on Emma. I think our best bet is simply to approach her with a knock on the door," Laura said.

"Really? What if she just slams it in our faces?"

"I don't know. Based on what I've learned about her, I think we might have a chance."

"What's she like?"

"Very sheltered. She's in her forties and has never really lived away from her father before. She's worked for him since she left university. She's had few romantic interests, so the relationship with Dave was likely quite a big step out of the box for her. An affair with a married man. Very much out of character."

"Sounds like Dave took advantage of her. It's sad. Pathetic, really."

"She no doubt thought she'd found her knight in shining armor."

"She hasn't contacted her father in all this time?"

"No. Maybe she assumes he's disowned her. He has very high expectations, apparently, and she's not wrong to think he might cut her off. But he's feeble now and concerned that he doesn't have much time left. He wants to patch things up and pass on the responsibility for the shop. That seems to be what he cares about most."

Laura and I both had other work to do, so, for most of the rest of the ride, we each worked on our laptops and phones. I couldn't help noticing how natural I felt sitting there with her. How comfortable. She glanced up at me at one point and gave me a knowing smile, as if she had the same thought.

CHAPTER THIRTY-SIX

I was just reaching for my six thirty alarm one morning later that week when I heard Laura scream in a wail unlike anything I'd ever experienced.

"What? Oh my god!"

I rushed down the hall, glimpsed her collapsing onto the floor, her telephone dangling from its cord like a fallen sparrow. Her cries pierced the morning quiet like a siren.

"What happened? What's wrong?"

I knelt down beside her, at a loss. She couldn't stop crying long enough to speak. I picked up the abandoned telephone.

"Hello?"

"Who is this?"

"This is Laura's roommate. Jen."

"This is her brother, Matt. I just called to tell her that dad died of a heart attack during the night."

I gasped. "I'm so sorry."

"Thanks," he said. "This was a complete shock. Laura was really close with our dad. Maybe you could hang around until she calms down?"

"Of course! I'll be here. Don't worry."

I took down Matt's phone number just in case and sat next to Laura, who had by then gotten up off the floor. I put my arm around her shoulder, doing my best to comfort her. I was clueless as to what to do. I hadn't experienced a death before and I couldn't think of anything helpful to say.

"I'm so sorry," I said, I don't know how many times.

"I have to get to Kansas City right away," she said.

"I'll come with you," I said, seizing on the first idea that came to mind.

She turned toward me, staring through bleary, bloodshot eyes.

"It's nice of you, but you don't need to."

"Yes, I do. You're in no shape to make the arrangements. I can take care of everything. I'll do it right now. We'll leave on the first flight."

She barely nodded, closed her eyes, slumped onto my chest, and cried softly. I rocked her for a while, then laid her down on her unmade bed. She rolled into a fetal position and I pulled the sheet over her.

We got a flight out of DFW that afternoon. The flight was short and before we knew it, our taxi was pulling into Laura's parents' driveway. Their home was in an upscale neighborhood on the Kansas side of town. It was just before nine p.m. Laura had been quiet, almost silent, the whole way, but she seemed comforted by my presence. Matt, a thin, fit man with a receding hairline who I judged to be in his late twenties, met us at the door and helped with our luggage, looking from Laura to me and back again with what felt like a quick assessment of our relationship.

Laura went immediately to her mother while Matt showed me to the room set aside for Laura and me. I kept repeating my "I'm so sorry" line as I followed him up the carpeted stairs to a hallway lined with family portraits. I caught sight of one of Laura at sixteen, I guessed, and felt my heart thump so hard in my chest I thought Matt might hear.

"You don't have to be so sorry," he said. "At least not for me. The man and I hated each other."

"Oh," I said, shocked by his attitude.

"You'll have to share," he said, opening the door to a small room only big enough for a double bed and a dresser. "We're a little short on accommodations at this point."

"Don't be silly. Laura and I have shared more than one room on our travels."

"I bet you have, honey," he said with a wink, twirling a set of keys through his fingers.

He's—gay? Oh my god. Laura had never mentioned this!

"No, I didn't mean—"

"I know my sister," he interrupted. "There's towels in the bathroom down the hall. Come join us in the family room when you're ready."

I unpacked my things into an empty drawer in the dresser, then took my toiletries to the bathroom in the hall. I brushed my teeth and hair and put on mascara and lipstick. Before today, I hadn't expected to meet Laura's family at all, much less under these circumstances. This had all happened so quickly, I hadn't prepared for it and I suddenly felt panicked. I gave myself a hard look in the mirror and thought, *don't do anything stupid.*

Following the sound of voices in hushed tones, and the smell of brewing coffee, I found my way to the family room. I recognized Laura's mother immediately, and not only because she was the center of attention. She was a perfect older version of Laura. She looked up at me, as though feeling the weight of my stare, and I instantly diverted my gaze.

"Introduce me to your friend," I heard her say, and suddenly Laura was by my side, providing my name, rank, and serial number very matter-of-factly.

"I'm sorry we're meeting under these circumstances, Mrs. Peters. Please accept my condolences."

"Thank you for being there for Laura. I know she is very fond of you."

Laura moved back to her side and Mrs. Peters returned her attention to the small group of attendees surrounding her. *Laura is very fond of me.* I clung to that thought as I backed away, bowing as though exiting an audience with the queen. My awkwardness brought Matt to my rescue.

"Here," he said, handing me a drink. "It came out of a snifter, but I think it's Maker's."

"Thank you," I said, gripping his hand. "Could we get some air? I'm feeling a little overheated."

He took me to a porch off the side of the house. A smoker's stand sat at the far end of the decking, and he walked toward it, lighting a cigarette.

"How long have you and Laura been together?"

I laughed. "Together? You mean roommates?"

"If that's what you want to call it."

He smiled into his drink while I tried to gauge how sure he was about his assumption.

"We met on the first day of work. Right out of school. So we've known each other almost a year."

Remember, don't do anything stupid. Like confess to Laura's brother that we are, in fact, lesbians. I changed the subject.

"What's your story?" I asked him. "Do you live here in Kansas City?"

I noticed his shoulders slump as he said, "Yes. I'm here. Temporarily."

"As in here?" I gestured to the house behind us.

"Temporarily," he confirmed glumly.

I decided not to press further, happy I had thrown him off my trail, and, after he finished his cigarette, suggested we go in search of a snack. Back inside, the gathering was beginning to break up and I found Laura in the kitchen with her two younger sisters, to whom I was introduced. Rachel, twenty-three, and Carrie, twenty-one, gave evidence to the strength of the family gene pool. They were beautiful and smart, pursuing medical and law degrees, respectively.

We munched on barbecue and baked beans while the sisters discussed funeral arrangements and how to help their mom sort through her finances. When Matt wandered in, the air seemed to stiffen. I looked from Laura to Rachel to Carrie, waiting for someone to speak. I exchanged a look with Matt, who shrugged.

"You had a big fight with him," Rachel said at last.

"And?"

"You were the last person to see him alive," Laura said. "What was the fight about?"

"What do you think?" Matt hissed at the three of them. "The usual. How I can't finish anything. How I can't keep a job. How I'm a fag!"

"Matt!" Carrie said. "Dad never called you that."

"He didn't have to. You know it's what he thought."

"Well…" Rachel said with a slight smile, "you are gay."

"That's not the point," Laura said, glancing ever-so-fleetingly at me. "The point is, yours was the last conversation he had. Did he say anything else? Did he seem unwell? Did he know he was about to die?"

Matt dragged his hand across the top of his head, scratching at the crown. I noticed that all three sisters had folded their arms and assumed the air of a firing squad, or at least that's what it felt like to me.

"All I remember is that he was in a bad mood. He seemed pissed that I was back at home. He got so wound up about it, I couldn't take it. I walked out in the middle of his rant." He looked at his sisters intently, saying, "It's not my fault."

"Of course it's not your fault," said Mrs. Peters, who had come into the room while Matt was speaking. "He was on new medication for his cholesterol. It didn't agree with him. He was taken too soon, but it wasn't anyone's fault."

She put her arms around Matt and held him close. He cried as she comforted him.

"Your father loved you," she said. "He worried about you. You were his boy and he wanted the best for you."

The sisters gathered round and the family drew together, making my presence ever more superfluous. I tiptoed out and made my way back to the bedroom, wondering why I had thought it was a good idea to come here. Matt had seen right through me and now I worried that we wouldn't pull off the best friend thing with everyone else. Exhausted from the stress of the day, I took my clothes off and got under the covers, too tired to wash my face or put on pajamas. I was sound asleep when Laura's warm body, pressed against mine, woke me.

The next morning as we dressed for breakfast, I couldn't help saying, "You never told me you have a gay brother. And everyone seems to acknowledge it. Even your mom."

She sighed deeply and looked annoyed.

"Yeah, well, everyone sort of accepted it over time."

"But...I had the impression you feel that you could never—"

"It's different with me," she cut me off.

"Because?"

"Because of the promise I made. Now, let's go. We're late."

CHAPTER THIRTY-SEVEN

Upon our arrival in Lyon, we discovered the city's cab drivers were on strike. That included rideshare companies. The day was gray with a drizzle of rain hanging over us. But our hotel was only a twenty-minute walk, so we set off, dragging our cases behind us over the damp cobblestoned plaza in front of the train station and across a town square or two. The hotel was a converted monastery sitting on the edge of Vieux Lyon, not far from the river. They stored our luggage as we were too early to check in, and we went off in search of a covered outdoor café where we could have a coffee and plot our course.

"She's staying in this neighborhood," Laura said, pointing to a map she had pulled from her bag. "We can walk there."

"And then what?"

"Her place is a brownstone with a door right on the street. According to my investigators, she's there by herself. No servants. I say we knock on the door."

"Do you have a picture of her?"

"Yes. Here," she said, showing me a 4x6 photo of a nondescript, slightly plump, woman.

"Interesting. Not what I would have guessed."

"The femme fatale is often unassuming," Laura said, a slight smile on her lips as she tucked the photo back into her purse.

"I'm trying to imagine what Alex would say to her if she were here. Does she even know Alex exits?"

"There's a lot we don't know. We don't even know if she knew he was married. He could have told her anything."

"I'm sure it was an elaborate lie, whatever he told her."

"Well, today's goal is to gain her trust, which won't be easy. My plan won't work unless she trusts us completely."

"And what is your plan?"

"Just watch it unfold," Laura said, squeezing my hand.

We finished our coffee and started out in the direction of Emma's house. We walked slowly, me because I dreaded the confrontation we were about to make. Laura, I assume, because she was rehearsing her lines. The idea of meeting the flesh and blood person who was directly involved in the undoing of my brother-in-law, however pathetic he was, unnerved me.

"This is such a beautiful city, even on a day like today," Laura said, instinctively trying to lift the mood.

"It's one of my favorites," I said. "In the whole world. I came here to visit a friend a few years ago. She's a scientist with the World Health Organization."

"Is she still here?"

"No. She's back in the States. We know each other through work. I met her when she was advising one of our VC companies on a patent application."

At the next corner, Laura touched my elbow to stop me.

"It's right down there," she said, pointing to a row of brownstones.

I took a deep breath and noticed Laura do the same as we set off purposefully down the block. But as we approached within a few feet of the door, it opened and out came a frumpily dressed forty-something woman whose dark hair was streaked with gray, shopping bag in hand, almost barreling into us. I recognized her from the photo. She froze with apprehension.

"Excuse me," she said in French. "There is not normally a lot of foot traffic on this block."

"Don't worry about it," Laura said, also in French. Then, switching to English, "We actually were just about to knock on your door."

"You're American," she said, gripping her bag close to her chest.

"Yes. We'd like to talk with you."

"What about? This is very irregular."

"Could we go inside? We just want to talk. I think you can guess why."

Her eyes darted from me to Laura and back. Then, seeming resigned to the situation, she took her keys from her pocket.

"Fine," she said. "But only for a few minutes. I have shopping to do."

We followed her inside and into her drawing room. The house smelled slightly mildewy, as if it had suffered more than one occasion of water intrusion.

"I would offer you a spot of tea, but I really don't want to prolong this."

"Thank you, Emma. It's not necessary. It's not like we're here on a social visit," Laura said.

"Why are you here? Who are you? How do you know me?"

"May we sit?"

"Yes, of course. I apologize."

Laura and I sat on an overstuffed loveseat while Emma faced us from a wingback chair across a tea table.

"My name is Laura Peters. I'm an attorney from Dallas, Texas. This," Laura said, gesturing to me, "is Jennifer Adair. Her sister, Alexandra Jackson, is the widow of Dave Jackson."

Emma went pale, her hand covering her mouth and tears forming on the rims of her eyes. She stared at the floor, the news sinking in.

"He has died?"

"At his own hand," Laura said.

"Oh my god."

"I know you've suffered a loss," I said, surprised by the huskiness of my own voice as I struggled with a suddenly contracted throat. "My sister and her children have suffered a great deal, as you can imagine."

Laura and I, as if on cue, remained silent, waiting for Emma to respond. A number of seconds went by.

"I'm very sorry," she said at last. "For your sister. I actually didn't know that he had a wife and a family, though it doesn't surprise me."

My eyes met Laura's and I nodded.

"I thought as much," I said. "Dave always had a convenient definition of the truth."

Emma got up, reaching for a nearby tea towel, and buried her face in it, crying painfully for what felt like an age. Finally, Laura got up and touched her shoulder, asking if she would like some water. When she nodded, Laura went off in search of the kitchen. Emma looked over at me through swollen eyes.

"How many?" She hesitated. "How many children did he have?"

"Two boys," I said. "Ben is sixteen. Harry is thirteen."

"I never meant to hurt anyone," she said meekly. "Well, except my father, that is."

Her posture shifted, her back straight, her head held high. Her gaze hardened. Laura came back in at that moment, handing her a glass of water.

"Thank you," she said curtly. "Now, what else is there to discuss?"

Laura opened her briefcase, pulling a file from it and shuffling through a sheaf of paper. "It has been alleged that you and Dave engaged in a scheme to defraud your father of eight million dollars," Laura said.

Emma took a sharp breath, but her expression did not change, and she said nothing.

"The discovery of that fraud by your father's solicitor led to the bankruptcy of Dave's company and, ultimately, to his suicide."

Emma slumped forward into her tea towel again, sniffling and shaking her head as if denying what had happened. That this sad, disheveled woman was in any way responsible for my sister's current chaos seemed so incongruous.

"Emma," I said, leaning toward her hunched frame. "I really would like to hear your side of this story. I think it would help Alex. She's struggling to understand. To heal."

Emma assumed her more formal posture again and spoke evenly, her eyes meeting ours with a certain strength.

"I haven't admitted to anything other than having a romantic relationship with Mr. Jackson. What happened to his company. What happened to him. Has nothing to do with me."

Laura pressed her hand to mine, knowing that I was agitated by this, and responded calmly.

"Of course. We understand. And we are not asking for any kind of admission. What we're interested in, is what went on between you and Dave. How long you were together. What were your plans for the future."

"But why? I can't imagine that Mrs. Jackson wants to hear all of that. Are you building a case against me?"

"No," I said. "Not at all."

"We can give you a release if you like."

She waved that idea away.

"You know my father is pursuing charges against me in London?"

"Yes," said Laura. "We do know that. We assume that's why you're here in France, where you can't be extradited because you are a French citizen."

"You have done your homework," Emma said. "In which case, I'm sure there is much more you already know and I can guess what you're really after."

I wasn't sure where she was going with that and said nothing. Laura also sat silent, waiting.

"Dave and I were together for about two years. He had been a customer of the bookstore for a few years before that. Always charming. Never mentioning anything about his personal life. Eventually he started asking me to tea. Then to the theater. Art openings. Museum exhibitions."

She teared up at this point, but went on.

"Eventually I went back to his hotel room. We became lovers. Then we started to talk about the future. He told me he wanted to live in Europe. He said he had a lot of business debts and needed a way to pay them off."

"Well, that part is true," I said.

"I wanted to help, but my father is a controlling bugger. He's always kept me totally under his thumb, using his money. Unfortunately, I let myself become too dependent on him over the years. Once I was involved with Dave, I began to feel trapped in my father's world. I wanted out."

"Who came up with the idea to fool your father with a fake Shakespeare?"

"That was me, actually," Emma said with a smile. "Some years ago, we had a customer, a Shakespeare collector, who was desperate to find that folio. We could never locate it. It seemed the perfect bait for my father. Dave, as a long-standing trading partner, had my father's trust, so when he claimed to have procured a copy, I thought my father would be ecstatic. And so he was."

"Very clever," Laura said. "But I'm curious, how did you plan to get around the fact that the fraud would be obvious to the collector?"

Emma sighed, pulling at her scarf and becoming agitated.

"The plan was for Dave and I to leave immediately for France upon receipt of the wired funds in Switzerland. But, at the last minute, Dave went back to Texas. I did as planned and came here. I never saw Dave again. I assumed he changed his mind about us."

"I'm really sorry that my asshole of a brother-in-law took advantage of you," I said. "I hate to say it, but you're better off without him."

Tears fell into her lap as she gave up on her towel.

"I'm exhausted," she said. "I just want to get back to some semblance of my life before all of this."

"I can help you with that," Laura said, touching her shoulder reassuringly.

I had never been more attracted to her than in that moment.

CHAPTER THIRTY-EIGHT

I couldn't help myself. We had been back from Kansas City for a week, having come back the day after the funeral. I knew I should be more sensitive to Laura's bereavement, but the discovery that her brother was gay and pretty much accepted by her family had really started to get to me. I confronted her over leftover spaghetti and meatballs that we had pulled out of the fridge on arriving home from work at nine p.m.

"Your family doesn't seem so homophobic to me," I said, plunging in.

She looked at me over a fork full of pasta hovering near her lips. She dropped the fork.

"You spend a few days with my family, during a funeral, and suddenly you know everything there is to know?"

"No! I don't mean that. I'm not trying to start a fight. I just thought we could talk about it."

"There's nothing to talk about."

"But he's—"

"Jennifer. I don't want to discuss it."

She got up and left the room.

"Aren't you going to finish eating? Please, Laura. Don't do this. Come back."

I went down the hall, sticking my head into her doorway. She stood with her back to me, arms folded.

"I'm sorry," I said. "I'm really sorry."

"You are so obtuse," she said, turning to face me. "My father is dead and all you can think about is how I shouldn't be in the fucking closet."

"I know, I know! Let me take it back. Please," I begged.

"You are so selfish."

"I know. Can we just start over? Come back and finish dinner."

"I'm not hungry."

"Honey," I cajoled. "If you don't eat, you're going to wake up in the middle of the night hungry and even more unhappy with me."

I tried taking her hand and she slapped it away.

"Fine. But don't bring that up again. When I'm ready to talk about it, if ever, I'll let you know."

I sighed in relief and silently scolded myself for the incident. *Timing. Your timing is terrible.*

* * *

"We need a vacation," I said as we sat lounging in the living room that weekend. "Look at this. It looks like fun."

I had pulled an advertisement out of the *Dallas Morning News* about a camping music festival in West Virginia.

"Camping?"

"I think it would be a blast. I know how to camp."

"'All Good.' What is a jam band?"

"You know. Like the Grateful Dead."

"No. I have no idea what that's like."

"Well, you're gonna find out."

She studied the details in the ad and tossed it back me.

"Buy the VIP tickets."

I pumped my fist with a "yes" and jumped up to make the phone call.

We would need to procure camping equipment and I went about that with gusto, going overboard, especially when it was not clear that we would ever go on a camping trip after this one, in picking up every little tool and comfort I could find. I bought blow-up mattresses to go under the sleeping bags and a coffee pot that sits over a campfire (even though the VIP camp would have a hospitality suite serving coffee every morning). I bought "flooring" for the tent and battery-operated torch lights to create a pathway to our door.

"This is ridiculous," Laura said, looking at the pile of purchases in the middle of the living room. "How many trips did you have to make? We can't fit this in either of our cars."

"I know! We're renting a minivan."

"Of course we are."

"Hey, I invited Jolm and Curt to come and they're in."

"Really? I wouldn't have thought it was their scene."

"It's Curt. He's totally into jam band music and he also likes to, you know." I put a pinched finger and thumb to my mouth, mimicking a puff on a joint.

"All of us in the minivan?"

"No! They're gonna fly. I guess there's an airport pretty close by."

"And why are we not flying?"

"Because this is a road trip. I want to take the whole week."

"Ugh. Maybe this wasn't such a good idea."

"Oh, c'mon. You'll love it. I promise."

"This is a hell of a long way, Jen," Laura said, studying the map the week before our trip to All Good.

"It's a good two days. Nashville looks about halfway."

"Not exactly the vacation of my dreams."

"Would you stop complaining? Really. It's annoying. Aren't you the one who loves driving?"

She held her hands up in surrender.

"Okay, fine. I'll get my head around it. And no, I love cars, not driving."

"I've got a cooler. We can pack food and drinks and snacks. We'll be there before you know it."

We left on Saturday, planning to get to Nashville that night, stay two nights, then make stops in Lexington, Cincinnati, and maybe Charleston WVA, planning to roll into Morgantown by midday Thursday, when the early-bird festival was set to begin.

Five hours later, just outside of Little Rock, we stopped for gas. But when I turned the engine to start up again, nothing happened. Click. Click. Click.

"Now what," I said.

"Sounds like the alternator," Laura said. "That's just great."

Laura had AAA, and we were able to get the van towed to a repair shop, but it cost us three hours. In the ninety-degree humid heat of June. With nowhere to wait except a small patch of grassy dirt under a scrawny poplar tree. Laura was mostly silent, which I took as a blessing. I paid for the repair. With six hours left, we decided Nashville would have to wait. We found a decent roadside motel at the halfway point, Laura's bad mood tightening around my neck like a python.

"I want my own bed," she said as I walked to the motel's office.

I got a room with two doubles. She slammed her bag onto the luggage rack and dug out her toiletries. Saying nothing and acting like I wasn't there, she proceeded to take a shower and get ready for bed. She got in the bed, grabbing a book and turning on the reading light over her shoulder.

"It's not my fault the car broke down," I said.

"Can you not see that I'm reading?" she said without looking up.

"Why are you giving me the silent treatment? It's manipulative."

She slammed the book shut.

"Why can't you just let me have some time to myself? You're dragging me across the country to some godforsaken field somewhere in the blazing heat. I want some peace and quiet right now."

It was all I could do to stop myself from snatching the book out of her hand and throwing it across the room.

"Fine," I screamed, "I'm sleeping in the van."

With that, I left the room, slamming the door so hard I thought I might have broken the jamb. I already felt like an idiot for that move and, once I was in the van trying to get comfortable, I really regretted it. I pulled one of our sleeping bags into the front seat and somehow got settled on the floorboard. I was drifting in and out of sleep for what seemed like hours. Then I heard it. Someone was trying to break into the van. My eyes wide with fear, I noticed a glint of metal under the passenger's seat. It was a handgun.

I knew Laura had a license, but I had no idea she actually had a gun, much less had brought it along. But at that moment, I didn't think about all that. I retrieved the gun, stood up on my knees and pointed it in the direction of the lockpicker.

"Hey!"

I cocked the gun. The guy turned and ran and I started shaking so hard I thought I might shoot by accident. I managed to uncock the gun and I sat, my heart racing, for I don't know how long. I put the gun back under the seat and ran back up to the room. It was two a.m. I had left without a key, so I had to knock.

"Laura, please. Let me in."

She opened the door with an angry stare, but I fell into her arms.

"Someone tried to break in," I choked out in a husky voice, on the verge of tears.

She held me.

"Oh my god," she said. "Are you okay?"

"I found your gun," I said.

"Good."

"We should call the police."

"We'll take care of it in the morning," she said, still holding on to me. "I'm sorry. I'm sorry I was such an ass."

She insisted I sleep in the bed with her and she kept a hand on me all night.

Laura drove from Little Rock to Nashville, her hand on my knee for most of the way. I was still freaked out about my encounter the night before, and exhausted from having slept so poorly.

"Hey," she said. "Look at me."

I tried to smile.

"I want to apologize again. I'm actually really looking forward to the festival. I've been reading up on some of the bands."

"Really?"

"There's a LISTSERV on AOL for jam bands."

I shook my head and laughed.

"You are such a geek."

We stayed at a nice hotel in Nashville and, after a long soaking bath, I felt much better. We strolled around town and ended up at a barbecue spot in Lower Broadway. After dinner, we hopped from bar to bar taking in the music and the vibe.

"This was definitely worth a stop," Laura said, sipping a light beer and moving to the music.

"Hey, gals," said a thirty-something woman with a smoker's voice, coming toward us with a postcard in her hand. "Come on over later."

I looked at the card, which was an advertisement for a women's party at a bar not far from there. Clearly for lesbians.

"Do we look gay?" I said to Laura, not kidding.

"Well, maybe you do," Laura said, laughing.

"You think it's funny, huh?" I smiled.

"I'm just happy to be alive."

"I need to freeze this. I haven't seen you this relaxed in forever."

"It's good to be away from home," she said, draining the bottle.

CHAPTER THIRTY-NINE

We had left Emma with a promise to come back the next day with a plan to resolve things between her and her father.

"I hope we can pull this off," I said.

"Leave it to me," Laura said. "I have a call arranged with the solicitor at six p.m. After that, I'd like to take you on a date, if you'll allow me."

"A date?"

"Yes," she said. "A real live lesbian date."

I blinked in amazement.

"Lesbian? Where am I? Mars?"

"I'm serious. Will you go out with me?"

I laughed and nodded cautiously.

"I'll pick you up at eight. Dress for it."

I stared with a bit of apprehension as she turned and sprinted up the stairway to her room.

Dress for it, she had said. *Hmm.*

I stared at my wardrobe, wondering which way to go. Sexy and feminine? Hot and edgy? Professional and demure? After too much thought, I settled on hot and edgy. Tight black jeans, a cropped black linen shirt, knee boots, chunky jewelry.

Before getting dressed, I drew a very hot bath and settled in to relax, closing my eyes. It was midmorning back home in San Francisco and I couldn't help thinking of Mary, where she would be now, what she would be doing. I saw her in the operating room at UCSF Medical Center where she had practiced for several years. I imagined her in the locker room after the procedure, dropping her scrubs and stepping into the shower. Then, unbidden and unwelcome, I saw the young intern step in behind her.

"No," I shouted, striking the surface of my bath water and sloshing it out all over the floor. "Fuck," I said, suppressing the tears that tried to escape. It felt as real as if I'd seen it in the flesh. I knew it was possible that it was in fact real. I took a few deep breaths and a sip of the white bordeaux I'd poured. Sadness settled over me like a thick fog.

By the time I'd finished the wine, I had forced myself to snap out of my funk. Staring at my reflection in the mirror, I knew I had work to do. I blew my hair straight and applied more makeup than usual in an attempt to liven up what appeared to me as ashen pallor. The lipstick, which I normally skipped, helped the most. When Laura knocked on the door, I was suited up for the game.

"Is something wrong," she asked the second she saw me.

I think I grimaced at that.

"I mean, trust me. You look fantastic. But you seem sad."

"It's nothing. I think I'm just a little homesick."

"Missing Mary, I assume."

"Something like that."

"Well, let me see if I can take your mind off her. And no business tonight, either."

With that, she took my arm and escorted me down that amazing staircase and out onto the streets of Lyon. We strolled arm in arm until we reached an open-air restaurant situated in a park square.

"This place is supposed to be amazing," she said as we were seated at a table on the grass. "Everything is straight from the farm."

My mood improved quickly as we sat under a starry sky sipping an amazing rhone and eating the most delectable meal. Laura was quite animated, reciting all kinds of facts about the region.

"Lyon is the gastronomy capital of France, which is saying a lot since the whole country is known for its cuisine," she said. "Oh, and it's also the place where the motion-picture camera was invented."

"Aren't you a font of information," I said with a grin.

She smiled and we sat quietly for a few moments until I broke the awkward silence.

"You called this a lesbian date. How did you mean that?"

She blushed and said, "I don't know really. I guess I'm just trying to get used to thinking of myself that way."

"As a lesbian? Really? What is happening right now?"

"You have every right to react this way. I know I have a very bad track record."

I nodded my head slowly, trying to absorb what I was hearing.

"I don't know what to say, Laura."

"What would you think if I told you I've asked for a divorce?"

I did my best to hide my shock. I had been sure she would never turn her world upside down. Topple her picture-perfect family.

"Wow. One surprise after another. How are you feeling?"

"I feel at peace. It was a decision I had been putting off for too long."

"What about Steve? And the kids? How are they taking it?"

"Steve is more or less fine with it, I think. I mean, the devil's in the details, but he's been waiting for this shoe to drop for a while. As for the kids, well, we haven't told them yet. It's not great timing for Josh. He graduates this year. I don't want to take the spotlight off of him until we're done with all of the celebrating."

"Wow. I'm sorry. I mean, it's hard no matter what. Even if it's what you want."

"I don't mean to pry, but how are things with you and Mary?"

I sighed, "It's not technically official, but there's definitely been a bit of a cooling off."

"What do you mean, exactly?"

"Well, I was pretty transparent with her about what happened in London. So, you can imagine how that went over."

I stared into my wineglass, not wanting to meet her gaze just then.

"Go on," she said.

"I couldn't tell her…I couldn't promise, I had to admit I still have feelings for you."

"That's my Jenny," Laura said. "Honest to a fault. I've always loved that about you."

"Yeah, well, as you know, it's gotten me into a fair amount of trouble over the years."

She winced. "Yeah. I'm really sorry. About your split, I mean. I know you weren't looking for trouble when you reconnected with me."

"How can you be so sure?"

Our eyes locked and she seemed to search my face for an indication of my meaning. Just then, the server returned with the credit card machine and she paid the bill. I stood and walked briskly away from the table.

"Wait," she said, coming after me. "Are you saying…?"

I shook my head. "It's late. We've had a lot of wine. Let's not have this conversation now."

At breakfast the next morning, we were all business. Laura filled me in on the results of her discussion with the London lawyers the day before. Emma's father would agree to forgive and forget if she would return the money. Laura had successfully made the argument that, since Alex had legitimate claims against Emma, she should be allowed to keep the one million dollars Dave had skimmed for her as a full settlement.

Now we just had to convince Emma to agree to this arrangement, even though it would put her back into the life she had hoped to escape. But without Dave, she seemed unlikely to move forward with a life of permanent exile. We met her at a coffee shop near her home.

"I don't know," Emma said when we gave her the news. "Living under my father's thumb is its own life sentence."

"Maybe so," Laura said, "but let me tell you what you'll be dealing with if you decide to go it on your own. If you start spending any of the stolen cash, he'll find where you've hidden it. He'll freeze it. And he owns the house you live in. He could sell it. And then there's Alex, Dave's wife. We would be forced to pursue you on fraud charges, which we could do here in France. It would prevent you from ever traveling to the US. Your world would get smaller and smaller."

"Fine," Emma said angrily, "you've made your point. I suppose it's the only way out."

"I'll let your father's lawyers know."

"I'm sure in the long run it's the right thing," I said. "I wish you the best."

"Good luck," Laura said, as we rose to leave.

"Oh, Ms. Adair?"

"Yes?"

"Please give your sister my sincerest condolences. I never wanted to hurt anyone."

"Thank you," I said, nodding an acknowledgment.

"Well, Counselor," I said as we walked back to our hotel, "you certainly pulled off an amazing resolution to this fiasco. I can't say that I'm surprised."

"It was my pleasure. I'm so happy I was able to do something for you and your family."

"We have to celebrate with Alex when we get back home."

"Home?" Laura smiled.

"You know what I mean," I said, but it had shocked me, too.

"A celebration is definitely in order. I'll make the arrangements."

"No, please. You've done so much. Let me take care of it."

"Jenny," she said, turning serious, "I want to ask you something about what you said last night."

"No, please. I really don't think we should talk about it. Not yet."

"Not yet." She smiled. "I interpret that to mean that we will talk about it when the time is right."

"Okay, well interpret it how you like, my friend. By the time we've both worked through everything we have to resolve, we'll be lucky to remember what we were talking about."

When we got to the front door of our hotel, she grabbed my hand and swung my arm like we were childhood girlfriends.

"No matter what happens, I don't want to lose touch with you again. Ever."

"Pinkie swear?"

We grasped the pinkie fingers of our right hands together and laughed, kissing sweetly before going inside.

CHAPTER FORTY

Thursday morning, we left Morgantown and headed for the festival grounds. On the dirt road at the base of Marvin's Mountaintop, we found a good-sized line up of vehicles already waiting to get in. People were tumbling out of their cars and campers and vans. Music blared from sound systems and boom boxes. Weed smoke drifted over the crowd like fog over San Francisco, casting a pleasant buzz in its wake. The air on the sunny warm day was weighted with humidity.

I put the van in park and we got out to stretch our legs. A trio nearby cranked out bluegrass tunes on a banjo, fiddle, and washboard. A gathering of dancers congregated around them. A passerby handed me a beer pulled from a keg.

"Not bad, huh?" I said to Laura, lifting my beer with a nod.

"Not bad at all," she said, reaching inside the van to take a can of light beer from the cooler.

In an hour or so the line began to move as the festival grounds opened. We separated into the VIP lane, drove through the gate, got tagged with our special bracelets, and quickly gained access, picking up a goodie bag of souvenirs on the way. The VIP camping section sat at the top of the hillside overlooking the main stage. The VIP lounge, perched on the edge of the hill, was a wooden structure housing a bar that doubled as a coffee and breakfast station. A deck extending off to the side offered chairs and tables.

We pitched our tent in a spot toward the back, near the woods and furthest away from the lounge. We saved a spot for Jolm and Curt, who would arrive that evening.

"This is a masterpiece," I said, admiring our campsite, which included a covered seating area and a lighted pathway. "I knew we needed all this stuff."

Laura took my picture standing in front of my handiwork and then we took off to explore the best of the grounds. A gravel road extended from the hilltop and wound down through the main festival area, past music stages and camp sites. Food trucks and stands along with vendors of all sorts lined much of the road. I stopped to buy a wide-brimmed hat and some neckerchiefs to protect me from the sun. Laura picked up an herbal iced tea. Music washed over us from all directions, some live, some recorded.

On the well-trodden path that connected the main grounds to the furthest flung stage and ran past the public restrooms and showers, we noticed something interesting. Some of the people walking by would drop what seemed like code words into the air in a tone somewhere between a whisper and a normal voice.

"What are they saying?" I asked.

"I think they're talking about drugs. They're selling."

"Ahh," I said. "Okay. I see it now."

I noticed discreet transactions taking place off to the side of the road, cash changing hands for small bags or plastic tabs. It had the feel of an informal marketplace.

"It's like a silk road for drugs!" Laura laughed.

"Should we go shopping?"

Laura gave me a sharp look. "You?"

"I'm kidding. But I bet Curt will be into it."

We headed back to our campsite, expecting the boys to arrive soon. We picked up Jack & Cokes at the lounge and sat watching the crowd fill in on the hillside below, which acted like an amphitheater for the main stage. The first band was tuning up. I tried to hold Laura's hand, but she pushed mine away.

"It's pretty chill here, you know," I said. "These are a bunch of hippies and Deadheads."

"Maybe once the sun goes down," she said without irony.

I sipped my drink in silence.

"What's the name of this band?" Laura said.

"The String Cheese Incident," I said, getting up to stroll around and try to get past my annoyance at her.

"Where're you going?"

"I'll be back."

I walked to the opposite side of the VIP area, for the first time giving some serious thought to how long I wanted to stay in this relationship, if you could call it that. It was more like a one-way street that moved in her direction only. And she was the cop directing the traffic on top of that. The sun slipped down behind the hills to the west, the air cooling, the band jamming.

I felt Laura's arms around me, her face nuzzled into my neck, her lips gentle. "I know I make you crazy," she said.

I said nothing and she pulled me a little closer, draping a stadium blanket around both of us. She slipped one hand into my cutoffs, the other under my shirt, slid her finger over my clit and cupped my vulva, penetrating the instantly lubricated vagina. I gasped and shuddered, my glutes contracting, pushing me harder against her fingers.

"That's not fair," I said, collapsing to the ground. "And I'm still mad at you."

"The boys are here," she said, reaching a hand out to help me up.

My arms bristled in the almost-cold air. Laura offered me the blanket and I accepted, the sting of her manipulation still irritating me. I shook it off for the time being as we approached the campsite and greeted Jolm and Curt.

The four of us listened to the bands, one after another, into the night, drinking beer and getting high, laughing at anything and everything. The starry sky was filled with beach balls bouncing into and over the crowd. Flags and banners waved, a stilt walker made his way through the crowd along with a Chinese New Year-style dragon. A psychedelic video played on the background of the stage. It must have been after two in the morning when we made our way back to our tents and turned in for the night. Laura tried to snuggle with me, but I pushed her away. I felt dangerously close to a breaking point with her, even in the numbing haze of alcohol and weed.

I woke the next morning with a feeling of dread gnawing into my stomach. I couldn't remember if we'd had a fight, or I had just wanted to fight with her. I had a vague feeling I might owe her an apology.

"Good morning," I said gingerly as she rolled over and stretched awake.

"You acted like an ass," she said. "It was so embarrassing."

"What are you talking about?"

"You don't even remember," she said with disdain.

"Okay, well, I might have been overserved."

"No excuse."

"Will you just tell me what I did or said or what happened? I can't remember walking back up here at the end of the night."

"You were screaming at me. In front of everyone."

It began to come back to me piece by piece and I felt that pain in my stomach coming on hard.

"Saying I was a fake, a fraud, in the closet. Blah blah blah."

"I'm sorry," I said, dropping my head into my hands and sighing heavily.

"You should be. You made such a scene."

"You are, though."

"What?"

"In the closet."

"I can't believe you," she said, crawling over me roughly to get out of the tent.

My head throbbed like a sprinter's pulse and I suddenly had to get out into the air. The brightness of the sun hit me so hard I staggered and almost fell.

"A little rough this morning?"

It was Jolm. I nodded and dug into our cooler for a bottle of water. I drank it down in one long draw.

"I guess I got a little aggressive last night," I said.

"You could say that," he said gently.

"Was it as bad as she says?"

"You were loud and clear about how you felt and, let's be honest, you weren't wrong."

I searched his face for signs of support. He was her friend, after all.

"Has she always been this way?"

He chuckled. "I don't know about always, but she's been... struggling, I guess, ever since I've known her. I'm sorry."

"Sorry for what?"

"That she's making this so hard for you."

"I'm starting to wonder if it's...worth it."

He nodded thoughtfully and, grabbing his souvenir cup, said, "Want some coffee?"

We walked up to the lounge to get coffee and breakfast. Laura was sitting with Curt, sipping a cup. She looked up at me, a little contritely I thought, and motioned for me to sit down. She held my hand in her lap as if demonstrating a new bravery.

"I know I have a lot of shit to deal with. But I don't want to be bullied."

"Fair enough," I said. "But I can't wait forever."

She relaxed her grip on my hand and I slipped it away. I noticed Jolm looking on and suggested, as cheerily as I could muster, that we explore the shops in the "village" down the mountain.

I bordered on morose for the rest of the weekend and mostly avoided being alone with Laura. But, staring down a very long road trip back to Texas, I knew I had to at least get to neutral with her. I asked her to take a walk with me on the afternoon of our last day.

"It's a long ride home," I said. "Can we have a truce?"

"I'm not fighting with you," she said.

I walked in silence for a few steps.

"You're fighting with who I am. With who you are."

She folded her arms and kicked at the dirt on the path we had taken into the woods.

"What does this truce look like?"

"We promise not to bring up this topic while we're on the road. And we promise each other to have a deep, no bullshit conversation about it when we get home."

We walked a little further before she responded.

"I guess that's fair."

She held her hand out to shake on the deal.

"I do love you, you know."

"I do," I said. "That's what makes this so hard."

I couldn't stop looking at her, taking in her features, every strand of hair, every freckle, the tint of suntan on her shoulders, the way the strap of her blouse slipped down close to her elbow, the short skirt hugging her hips. It was as if I thought I might not get this chance again, to drink her in, to devour her with my eyes. She leaned forward to kiss me gently, to break the spell.

CHAPTER FORTY-ONE

"I can't thank you enough," Alex said to Laura as we sat in her office after signing the papers to close out the international saga surrounding Dave's demise. "This is a huge relief. The money will really help me out. And the boys."

"I'm so glad we could bring it home. Your sister was no small part of it."

I smiled and shook my head.

"Not really. But it was fun to watch."

"I want to celebrate!" Alex said, looking at me. "Is that tacky?"

"Absolutely not! I've already got it all planned out. I've booked the private room at Fearing's for this Friday night."

"I love that place," Alex said. "You've been so good to me, Jen. I can't imagine what I would have done without you. You've made all the difference."

I smiled and squeezed Alex's hand, catching Laura's gaze out of the corner of my eye. She fixed on me, as if somehow freezing this moment, with tears threatening to breach their boundary.

"I'll miss you both," she said to us.

"But you'll come to the party," Alex said. "It wouldn't be a celebration without you."

"Of course. But I suppose after that we'll go our separate ways."

I hadn't thought about it. The pinkie swear notwithstanding, I hadn't allowed myself to consider what I would do with Laura after there was no necessity holding us together. Alex sat quiet, almost holding her breath, it seemed.

"We'll see," I said finally, standing and holding my hand out to bring our business meeting to a conclusion. "I'll let you know details about Friday night."

She held my hand a touch longer than she should have, then pulled me forward for an embrace. I could feel her filling her lungs with my scent. I pulled away gently and returned her wistful smile.

"That was awkward," Alex said as we left the office building. "She's completely in love with you."

"Maybe," I said.

"What about you?"

I hesitated.

"I don't know. I'm a little numb. So much has happened so fast."

"Is it really over with Mary?"

"I don't know. It needs resolution. But I have no idea what that looks like."

"Sounds like you need to get home. The last thing I want is for my family mess to ruin your family."

"First of all, what's happening with me and Mary would be happening anyway. The Laura piece of it just gives it a strange twist. If Mary and I are over, it has nothing to do with Laura Peters."

She looked at me skeptically, and I knew I hadn't been convincing. It wasn't dishonesty, exactly, that made me stake that claim. It was more that I wanted it to be true. I wanted to separate these two women, keeping each one in her own compartment in my mind, in my heart, not giving up either one.

I knew I couldn't do it for long and I felt a twinge of cowardice in realizing that I wanted an external force to put a stop to it.

Back at Mom's house, I made dinner for her and sat in front of the television while she ate, but I had no appetite myself.

"What's wrong, honey? Girl trouble?"

I couldn't help but laugh.

"Well, Mom, you're on to something. But, if you don't mind, I don't really want to talk about it tonight."

"Sleep on it. Everything looks less serious in the light of day."

"On that note, I think I'll turn in early. You'll be okay?"

"I'll be dancing with the stars!"

I kissed her good night and went to my room, marveling at her resilience. She had managed to lighten my mood, which was helpful when I looked at my buzzing phone and saw Mary's number.

"Hey," I said.

"Hey. You're back."

"I am."

"Why didn't you call me?"

"I wasn't sure you wanted to hear from me."

"I take it things ended well?"

"About as well as they could have."

"The amazing Laura Peters."

"C'mon, Mary. That's not fair."

"I've decided I want to meet her."

I paused to process this.

"Why?" I asked, with a lilt in my voice that made clear the bewilderment this question caused.

"Because she's haunted you for more than twenty years and she has a hold on you that astonishes me and I just want to see what it's all about."

"Mary, I don't think—"

"Jen, I'm serious. I'm coming tomorrow. See you then."

I stared at the phone, mouth agape, panic setting in.

* * *

The landline phone on the table beside my bed startled me awake. I looked at the clock to see that it was three a.m. The last-century caller ID flashed Alex's name. I snatched the receiver from its cradle.

"What is it?"

"You're not going to believe this," she sighed. "Ben has been arrested on a DUI. He's downtown at the police station."

"Oh, for god's sake," I said. "I'll go down there."

"I'm so sorry. I just thought since—"

"Don't worry. I'll bring him home."

I dressed quickly and quietly, leaving the house through the side yard door, the one furthest from my mother's room. Yet, by the time I was sitting in my car, she was standing outside her front door, calling my name. I motioned for her to get into the car, drove her to Alex's and dropped her off. Any explanation would do, so I told her I had to bail out a friend.

At the police station, I flashed my Texas Bar card and filled out the paperwork to bring Ben home. He had mostly sobered up by this time and had adopted a sullen silent facade. I tried to engage him in conversation as we headed back to my sister's house. He grunted a few unintelligible responses and then, in an outburst I did not see coming, started shouting.

"You're all a bunch of liars. You. My mom. Aunt Mary. My dad. All of you. Nobody's who they say they are. It's the biggest pile of dog shit!"

I stayed quiet and he struck out again.

"You. You're lying to my cousins and they know it."

"What are you talking about?"

He sat silent, but I was no longer in the mood to accommodate him.

"What the hell are you saying, Ben?"

"They know you're split up. They know there's some other chick."

I stopped myself from asking which chick. *Jesus.* I drove the rest of the way without speaking; he was quiet as well. The sun was coming up as we walked into Alex's. She tried to hug him, but he pushed her away and headed to his room.

"He'll be fine," I said. "But he should get therapy. He has a lot to work through."

Alex nodded. "Thanks for doing that. I'm hoping that's the last favor I need to ask for a while. Ever, actually."

"He said something."

She looked at me expectantly.

"It never occurred to me that he would be in touch with Eli and Claire."

"Facebook?"

"I don't know. But he says they know about Mary and me. And I know Mary hasn't said anything."

"Whoops."

"Speaking of Mary, she's coming here. Today!"

"Is that a good idea?"

"It's her idea. She wants to meet Laura."

"Oh, my."

I was exhausted and couldn't bear the thought of dealing with Mom. Instead, I crashed in Alex's guest room and slept until noon. I woke up thinking about my children and feeling guilty and ashamed that Mary and I had not sat down with them.

What were we thinking?

Mary's cell went straight to voice mail and I assumed she was in the air on the way here. I texted Claire and Eli separately, just checking in. Both responded in the usual way. I took a shower to clear my head. It didn't help.

Mary called me after she landed.

"I'm staying at the Montrose."

"That's probably better," I said.

"Should I make an appointment to see Laura Peters?"

"No! What the fuck. Why would you say that?"

"Because I want you to understand how serious I am."

"What the hell has gotten into you?"

"I'm tired of your self-righteous bullshit. You blow me up over what I did while you do whatever the fuck you want. I'm sick of it."

"Can you just calm down?"

"Don't tell me to calm down!"

"We need to talk to Eli and Claire. Apparently they know about all of this."

"Of course they do. There aren't any secrets in the Internet age."

"Have you said anything to them?"

"Not with any transparency."

"Meaning?"

"I've dodged a few questions."

"We should sit down with them in person."

"Fine," she said. "Now what about Laura?"

"There's a dinner Friday night. To celebrate. Laura will be there. You might as well come."

"I'll be there with bells on."

"Fuck," I said, clicking off. "Alex!"

My sister appeared quickly.

"She's coming to the dinner Friday night."

"Mary? This just gets better and better."

"What am I going to do? Now I have to tell Laura that Mary will be there."

"I think Laura would enjoy the chance to depose your wife," Alex said with an evil chuckle.

"I think I'm going to be sick," I said, doubling over in an agony that was as physical as it was emotional.

"I feel for you, but, I have to wonder, how did you let this happen?"

I jumped to my feet.

"Let it happen? How was I supposed to know that Mary would transform into a heat-seeking missile. This is so not like her."

"Makes you wonder what's going on."

"Exactly," I said, turning it over in my mind.

CHAPTER FORTY-TWO

Back home, we seemed to have, by mutual agreement, decided to avoid each other. Laura worked the longest hours I'd ever seen her work. While I, more and more disenchanted with what I was doing, attended Chick Happy Hour regularly and started hanging out with Crystal and some of the other women separately.

I took up tennis and played doubles on a weekly schedule. We played on Saturday afternoons at an apartment complex one of them lived in. Mandy, Kara, and Rebecca, all lesbians, all currently single, taught me a lot of the basics of gay culture. Mandy was a "gold star," someone who had never been with someone of the opposite sex. Kara was a lipstick lesbian, always dressed in an outfit and in makeup, even on the tennis court. Rebecca was a "player," with a reputation for seducing straight women.

"Straight?" she'd say. "Yeah, straight to bed."

Kara invited me to coffee one day during the week. She worked as a CPA at a firm close to my office. Always ready for an excuse to get out, I accepted eagerly. After some small talk, she got to her point.

"How are things with you and Laura these days?"

I shrugged.

"Not great. We're basically in a cold war right now, I guess." I told her about West Virginia. And about Laura's brother.

"I'm a little worried about you, you know, because, well, I've been there."

I listened as she told me about a woman she had dated for almost five years, who was in the closet, and was so paranoid of being outed that she insisted Kara not be out to anyone, including her own family.

"I started to feel like I was losing my sense of self. Our world just got smaller and smaller until, finally, I had a breakdown. I had to take a leave of absence from work. I did intense therapy for a long time."

"That's terrible. I'm so sorry you had to go through that."

"These women who don't want to admit they're gay can be dangerous. To your mental health. I just felt like I needed to say something to you."

"I'm glad you did," I said.

"It's just that, most people like that, they don't change. I would just hate to see you waste years of your life like that, like I did."

It hit me hard, thinking about life with Laura on an infinite loop of secrecy. Expecting her to change seemed increasingly unrealistic. But life without her also seemed impossible to contemplate. I wondered if I should go to therapy, like Kara, but I couldn't get motivated. I felt mentally and emotionally lethargic, like I was walking in a lap pool, unable to move at a normal pace.

One evening as I sat on our balcony with a glass of wine, staring out into the moonlit night, Laura came home earlier than usual.

"Can I join you," she asked, coming outside, glass in hand, still wearing the suit skirt and soft silk blouse of her work uniform.

"Sure. What brings you home early?"

"We settled that big case I've been working on. God, it feels good to relax."

She unbuttoned the blouse and put her manicured feet up on the little metal coffee table that occupied the space between us. Her scent, a combination of the misty perspiration of the day and her perfume, rich and woody, reached me and ignited my endorphins. I breathed in deeply, closing my eyes.

"Congratulations. Must be such a relief."

"What's wrong?"

I sat up straight, startled.

"Nothing. Why?"

"You sound so formal. Distant."

"No, I mean...I just—"

"I've barely seen you lately," she said, leaning closer to me. "I know I've been working crazy hours, but you're never in your office when I come around for a dinner break. Is everything okay at work?"

I shrugged.

"Same old same old."

"Maybe you should try another practice group."

"Maybe. I don't know. I've been in a funk lately. Nothing feels quite right."

"Nothing?"

I stared into my glass, which was almost empty.

"I need a refill," I said. "I'll bring the bottle out."

My heart pounded in my chest as I walked to the kitchen to retrieve the wine. *Should I bring it up now? The possibility of a breakup?*

"Jen," she said, taking the bottle from my hand as I stepped back onto the balcony. "Look at me."

She lifted my chin and leaned in to kiss me as I found my arms next to her bare skin inside the open silk shirt. I simply had no defense against my attraction to her. I ended up in her bed and the rest of the world fell away, my doubts about her suspended again.

The next day I received a cryptic message from my mother, summoning me to the house for dinner with the family the following weekend. I immediately called Alex to ask what she knew about it.

"I don't have a clue," she said. "I got the same message."

"Do you think one of them is sick?"

"I really have no idea. Do you want to drive out together?"

Alex picked me up from the office where I was actually working on a rare Saturday afternoon, and we headed to our parents' home. We chatted about Alex's recent engagement to her boyfriend, Dave, and our plans for a bachelorette getaway to Austin. Our mother greeted us at the door, dressed in her usual impeccable style—skirt, blouse, scarf, low heels, jewelry. Dad said hello from behind a newspaper in the living room as we walked through on our way to the kitchen, where we always helped with dinner. The house smelled of lemon and verbena, Mom's favorite.

Mom put on an apron and tossed a salad while gesturing to a plate of meat I was to put on the gas grill out on the patio. Alex set the table. A fleeting concern crossed my mind as I wondered why Dad wasn't in charge of the grill as usual and I worried that the reason for this visit was some health problem of his.

Seated at the table a short while later, Dad insisted he was fine and he did in fact look and seem perfectly normal, except that he hadn't met my gaze once since I'd been there. I had bitten halfway into a piece of my T-bone steak when my mother dropped her bombshell.

"I had hoped against hope, Jennifer, that my suspicions were wrong, but I have it on good authority that I was right."

I looked at Alex, my fork suspended in midair, and she returned my stare with an equally blank look. I finished chewing and swallowed hard.

"Right about what?"

"The relationship you are in. With this young woman you live with. I cannot condone it. It is a sin. The Bible makes that clear."

I dropped my fork, which landed squarely on the china plate and made a reverberating clang that hung in the air like the residual of a gong. I couldn't believe my ears. I couldn't formulate a response. I had never ever thought that my mother would confront me with this. It was so not her move. I knew she had suspected me since adolescence, but for her to say something? I looked at Alex again, who just raised her shoulders as if mystified. I then noticed that my father was fiddling nervously with his glasses. Taking them off, putting them back on, massaging them between his fingers.

"Dad," I said, "what is going on?"

Without acknowledging my question, he put his glasses down, picked up his iced tea and drank until the glass was empty, then poured himself another out of the pitcher that sat on the table.

"Sweetheart," he said, staring into the space above my head. "Your mother and I love you. I...I don't know quite what to say about this...Marilyn?"

His eyes pleaded with my mother for help.

"We can't just sit back and let you ruin your life with a choice like this," she said.

"Choice?" I was recovering from my shock and realizing that they had taken away my option of a well-planned coming out. "Do you think anyone would choose to be a member of a hated and persecuted minority? Why would I do that? This is not a choice. It's not a confession. It just is. It's who I am."

"You admit it then," Mom said, bringing a tissue to her face to dab at the tears that threatened to ruin her carefully applied makeup.

"Admit? I thought you said you knew?"

"I thought you might deny it. That you might have the decency to hide it. Especially with your sister just announcing her engagement. Think how embarrassing this is for her."

Alex perked up, shaking her head. "No, no, no. This is not about me. I have no problem with Jen being gay."

"Don't use that word in my house," Mom cried, holding her hands to her ears. She ran from the table, leaving the rest of us sitting in bewilderment.

"How did all of this blow up?" I looked at Dad. "It's not like I'm even out."

He rubbed his temples and got up from the table, walking to his chair in the living room and opening up the cabinet where he kept his reading materials. He retrieved a manilla folder and brought it over to me.

"You mother's friend Angela was showing her clippings from her trip to Washington for the inauguration last January."

I felt a stabbing pain in my solar plexus as I gingerly opened the folder. Alex stood over my shoulder as I flipped through *Washington Post* photos of Bill and Hillary, Al Gore and Tipper, Madeleine Albright, and other luminaries. In a page of gala photos, there we were, Laura and me, arm in arm, with Melissa Etheridge at the Triangle Ball, which was labelled euphemistically as a "women's gala."

"Oh my god, Jen, you never told me about that!"

"Shit," I said. "Laura will kill me if she ever finds out this was in *The Washington Post*."

"Was it fun?" Dad asked, reminding me that he was still there.

I looked up at him and saw he had the hint of a smile on his face.

"So much fun," I said quietly.

"She's very attractive," he said, picking up the photo of us, affixing his glasses for a clearer view.

Alex and I looked at each other and laughed nervously. I searched the first floor for any sign of Mom, but she had apparently left the scene.

CHAPTER FORTY-THREE

"There will be seven of us," I said to the event planner as I stood in the private room of Fearing's in the early afternoon of the day of the party. "I want to do place cards because I cannot risk the scenario of people deciding for themselves where to sit."

"That's easy enough," he said. "Just give me the names and I'll handle it."

"I guess one person will sit at the head of the table and then we can put three on each side."

I could put the boys on either side of Alex, but that would leave my two love interests on either side of Mom if I sat at the head. Or I could put the boys across from each other, Alex at the head and me across from Mary and next to Laura, with Mom next to Mary. Or I could put Mom at the head, with Mary to her right hand and me to her left. Then the boys could be next to us across from each other and Laura and Alex could face each other on that end. That was it! I sketched it out and gave it to the planner.

As I drove home to Mom's, my heart rate kept spiking and I had to wipe my sweaty palms several times, an endless series of horribles parading through my mind as I imagined tonight's possibilities. *Why on earth had I allowed this to materialize? What was wrong with me?* I thought seriously about calling it off. But then I would just have to deal with Mary anyway. I tried practicing some of the mumbo-jumbo meditation I had learned, or really not learned, in San Francisco. I couldn't tell that it made any difference.

Laura's cell phone rang through on my car's audio.

"How are you feeling?"

"Like Daniel headed into the lion's den."

"Going biblical, huh?"

"Don't joke about this! I am on the verge of cancelling."

"No, don't do that. I think this could be fun."

"That's because you're looking at this as sport. You just want to win."

She laughed.

"True. I always want to win."

"Laura, seriously. Can you please help me keep this from blowing up in my face?"

"Of course. Of course. Don't worry. Just keep reminding everyone that this is about Alex and the boys. It's not about us."

"Have you thought about what you're going to say to Mary?"

"I have a list of questions prepared."

"Oh, god."

"I'm kidding. No, I haven't thought about it, actually. I'm curious, that's all. I'm dying to observe you with the woman you've been with for twenty years."

"That does not ease my anxiety."

"Go for a run. That will relax you."

"Good advice. I'll see you tonight."

I arrived a little early with Mom and got her settled at the head of the table.

"Whose birthday is it again?" she asked for the third time.

"It's not a birthday party, Mom. It's a celebration. For Alex and the boys. We got a settlement for them and that's why we're here."

"I'm sorry. I know you've said that before. My mind is just not what it used to be."

"It's fine, Mom. Oh, look, here's Alex now."

She came in with Ben and Harry, who were dressed in brand-new sport coats and ties, their hair slicked back, hands stuffed in pockets. Ben walked gingerly as though afraid of damaging his shiny spotless loafers. Alex, made over with highlights and hair color and professional makeup, lit up the room like I hadn't seen in years.

"Sis, you look amazing!"

"Funny what a little money in the bank will do for your attitude."

"You deserve it."

"Did you win the lottery?" Mom asked with a smile.

"Something like that, Mom."

I had been obsessively checking my cell phone for text messages from either Mary or Laura, half hoping that one of them would decide not to post. When I saw them walk into the room together, chatting like they were old friends, I saw stars and thought I might find myself face-planted.

Alex said with a smirk, "At least you don't have to worry about how to introduce them."

"Why do I feel like you're enjoying this," I whispered.

"I'll give you this much," Alex said. "They're both gorgeous."

I nodded, stunned by the vision of the two of them standing next to each other, both tall and athletic, at ease in their effortless beauty.

"I see you've met."

"I know you," Mom cried out excitedly. "You're Jenny's girlfriend from way back. The one who ran her off to California."

I turned to Mom, my mouth agape. Alex knelt down beside her and quieted her with a quick acknowledgment of her memory.

"You just never know what's going to come out of her mouth," I said, looking from Laura to Mary and back.

Mary snickered while Laura stood pale and speechless, something I'd never seen before. Mary approached me, giving me a platonic kiss and then stepped over to greet Mom. Laura, who certainly would not have anticipated Mom's curveball, seemed to struggle for her next move.

"Allow me," she said finally, "Mrs. Adair, to reintroduce myself."

"Oh, my," Mom said. "Have we met? I'm so sorry. My mind is not what it used to be."

Laura looked at me and I let out a sigh.

"Don't worry about it."

"There are my boys," Alex said to Laura in a not-so-subtle attempt to break up the awkwardness.

Laura shook their hands in an exaggerated display of professionalism that obviously appealed to their egos. Ben practically swooned as he introduced himself.

"You're the lawyer, right? The one who helped us?"

"That's me."

"I might want to be a lawyer."

"Okay. Maybe you can do a little interning for me. During the summer."

"That would be awesome!"

I saw Mary flinch while Alex looked at me nervously.

"You don't have to do that," Alex said.

"Mom! Stay out of it," Ben said.

"It wouldn't be a gift," Laura said. "He'd work his ass off. Might convince him it's not what he wants to do."

She gave Ben a gentle squeeze as she said this. Mary stood, arms folded, glaring at me as if expecting me to intervene. I demurred.

"Let me check on the hors d'oeuvres—I think they should be serving by now. And let's get some champagne flowing!"

"I'd like to make a toast," Alex said as we settled into our arranged seating around the table. "Here's to my sister, Jen, without whom I would be completely lost in this world."

I smiled while shaking my head.

"Here, here," said Mary.

"Where's Dave?" Mom said. "Did we forget him?"

"He's dead, Grandma," Harry said. "You can't remember anything."

"Harry," Alex said. "Stop."

"Here's to you, Mom," Mary said. "You're the rock of this family. We love you."

"I'm so confused. Why are we here?"

"How about a toast to our amazing counselor and friend, who bailed us out of a very difficult situation, with skill and grace," I said.

"Yes," Alex enthused while the boys raised their glasses of soda.

"Friend?" Mary said to me, not quite under her breath, her voice thickened by the champagne. "Seriously?"

"Not now," I said.

"No, I think now is the time," she said, standing up. "I'd like to know, Laura. Are you Jen's friend? Is that what this is all about?"

Mary stood staring at Laura at the other end of the table. Alex seemed to shrink, almost ducking, her head bowed over her plate. The boys looked at each other gleefully, glancing from me to Laura to Mary. Mom sat still, almost as if she didn't really hear what was going on.

"Mary, sit down," I said, standing and pulling at her elbow.

She jerked away from me, going on.

"You know," she said to Laura, "the only reason she's sleeping with you is to get back at me."

A collective gasp went up around the room. Laura looked at me in shock.

"I fucked up," Mary said. "I had a slip and that's what this is all about."

"I think I should go," Laura said, gathering her purse.

Mary stepped toward her. "Oh, right, just leave. Just walk away. That's what you do."

"Mary," I shouted at her.

"I'm more than willing to have this conversation with you, but not at this party. Tonight is not about us," Laura said.

"Us? Now you and I are us?"

"Please," I said to Mary, "you're drunk and you need to back off. Just sit down and cool it."

"I'm not letting this go," she said, slumping in her chair.

Laura was almost out the door of the restaurant when I caught up to her.

"Hey, there," I said. "I'm so sorry about all of that. Are you furious?"

"You never told me she cheated on you."

"I, yeah, I guess I was afraid to let you in on that secret."

"Afraid? Why?"

"Because I would never want you to think that it had anything to do with what was going on with us."

"I would never have thought that. You're not that kind of person."

"I shouldn't have let her come."

"First of all, she's still your wife. So of course she should have come. And by the way, I'm not furious. I don't blame her for fighting for you. I…I wish I had. Is it too late?"

I felt safe enough in the dim light of the parking lot (this was Texas after all) to take her into my arms, wondering if she felt safe enough to allow me. She kissed me as passionately as she ever had in private, but we instinctively pushed away from each other when headlights approached.

"I don't know what's going to happen," I said. "I don't even know what I want. Or what Mary wants. If I were you, I would probably stay away from me."

She shook her head slowly. "I don't know if I can do that."

I walked her to her car and said goodbye, not knowing when I would see her again or under what circumstance. The party was breaking up as I came back inside. I put Mary in a taxi back to her hotel, promising the driver she would not puke in his cab, and hoping that was true. I paid the bill and found Alex outside by herself.

"Where's your crew?" I asked.

"Waiting in the car. I wanted to make sure you were okay."

"I guess I can be glad it wasn't worse. At least there were no physical blows thrown."

"I've never seen Mary tipsy, much less blackout drunk. What the hell?"

"I don't know. Do you think she wants me to be the one to pull the trigger? Ask for a divorce?"

"Maybe. Whatever the case, it's not healthy. For you or for her. I'm sorry, sis."

The next morning Mary called me with a muted apology and a declaration.

"You need to either come home or get out of the house."

She hung up on me.

CHAPTER FORTY-FOUR

"Can I get a word with you in my office?" Brian said as we passed in the hall one Monday morning not long after the fiasco at Mom's. His finely pressed Armani suit backed up the air of authority that hovered around him.

"Now?"

"Now."

I followed him to his office, growing nervous as I noted the exaggerated uprightness in his posture. He motioned for me to sit in one of his visitor chairs. I took a legal pad out of the Redweld™ folder I had with me and prepared to take notes.

"You won't need that," he said with a sigh, dropping into his chair and folding his hands together under his chin. He looked at me for what felt like forever before speaking. "What's going on with you?"

I blinked a few times, feeling my face turn red. I shook my head.

"I don't know. Nothing in particular."

"Do you realize you were about to turn over privileged information in a document request in the MacArther case?"

My heart racing, I reached instinctively for my folder.

"What?"

"My paralegal caught it."

I sat breathing shallowly, wondering if he was going to fire me, wondering if I would care.

"I'm sorry. I can't believe it. Thank god she did."

"Yes, thank god. And you can thank me for giving you another chance."

"What do I need to do?"

"Go help Kate redo the response. And don't hit my file with a single hour."

"Of course. I...I don't know what to say. Except thank you. It won't happen again."

"No, it won't. You either get your shit together or you pack it up without being asked."

I left his office, shaken, and headed to the paralegal bullpen. That was a major mistake.

Malpractice. I couldn't believe I had missed something so crucial. I approached Kate sheepishly. An affable woman in her forties, she was plump and impeccably dressed, stuck working in a windowless warehouse of desks and file drawers that smelled of moldy documents. She tried to make me feel better.

"Honey, don't feel like the Lone Ranger. This happens more than you would think. A big part of my job is making sure young associates don't screw up like that. I would have brought it to you, but I couldn't get ahold of you and Brian wanted this out the door on Saturday, so I had to tell him."

"I understand."

"I hope he wasn't too hard on you. Believe me, I've saved his ass more than once."

"He put the fear of god into me. Which I needed."

I spent the morning with Kate, going over the responses three times just to make sure there were no mistakes. The stale air in the dank room gave me a headache.

"Not everyone is cut out for this kind of work, you know," Kate said as I wearily stacked up the binders and readied the boxes for the mail room. "I know the money is good, but it's not really worth it if you're miserable, is it?"

"Is it that obvious?"

"I'm sorry. This is none of my business."

"No, please. I could use an honest conversation. I feel stupid talking about it with friends. When you've invested so much time and effort, and money, into getting to this point, it seems silly to walk away."

"Maybe you could get some counseling. You know, a therapist. Insurance will pay for it, I think."

I mulled that over for a few days and decided it couldn't hurt. It was increasingly difficult to get out of bed on time and get out the door.

"What do you think you're doing?" Laura said one morning, a steaming cup of coffee in her hand, when I was still in bed at nine a.m.

"Why aren't you already at the office?" I asked, shocked by her intrusion.

"I have to drive to Austin for a deposition this afternoon. Do you sleep in like this on a regular basis?"

I turned away from her and pulled the covers over my head.

"Seriously, you can't do this."

"Don't worry about me."

"Whether I worry or not, you're in trouble at the firm. People are talking. You're on thin ice."

I sat up and threw the bedclothes to the side.

"Fine. Okay. I get it."

"Maybe you should get some help."

"What kind of help?"

"A shrink. A counselor. Something."

I took a shower, thinking about what Kate had said. Now Laura. I knew I was in trouble. I hadn't even been exercising lately. I couldn't remember the last time I took a run. I hated work. I hated living the way I was living.

"I feel paralyzed," I told the therapist the next week at my first appointment. "I know I have to make changes, but I don't know what to do in place of what I'm doing now."

She probed for details of my childhood, any traumas, on and on. An incense stick smoldered in a dish on the desk behind her.

The couch I sat on was lower than her chair and I felt small, infantile, by comparison.

"I just want to know what to do now," I said.

"You're going to have to do some work. I can't snap my fingers and cure you."

"Cure me of what?"

"Depression. You're depressed."

"I'm just confused."

"Let's go with that. What are you confused about?"

"Everything."

"Okay, what are you most confused about?"

"Laura."

"Who is Laura?"

I gave her a truncated version, enough for her to get the point.

"Has either of you had any other homosexual relationships?"

"I don't think so. I mean, I haven't. And I don't think she has, but I actually haven't ever asked her that."

"Could this be a passing infatuation?"

"It doesn't feel like that. Would that be normal?"

"Lots of women go through a phase of attraction to other women. What is it that you find attractive about Laura?"

Lots of women go through a phase?

"Is it her breasts?"

She looked at me intently, waiting for my answer.

"I don't understand this question. I mean, I'm attracted to everything about her. Her body. Her mind. Her personality. Her essence. All of it."

"Does she remind you of your mother?"

"Jesus Christ! No!"

I reached for my things, ready to bolt from her office.

"Okay, that was a little aggressive, but please sit down. Let's finish the session."

"Being a lesbian is a real thing," I said, still standing. "If it wasn't Laura, it would be some other woman."

"How do you know?"

"Because I know. I've been attracted to other women. It's who I am."

"I just think you should be careful about throwing away your future over something that could be...a passing thing."

"So you're as homophobic as anyone else out there."

"Not at all. I have lots of gay friends. That's how I know how difficult it is."

"I'm exhausted from this kind of debate. Thanks for the session, but I won't be back."

I rushed out, her voice trailing behind me.

I have to get out of this place. Out of this town. This part of the country.

I sat in my car for a long while, just staring, unfocused, numb. I kept pushing away the thought that Laura was not only not good for me, but toxic. When I let the thought in, a freeze took hold of my heart, coupled with a pain that was crippling. As dusk turned to dark, I realized I couldn't just sit there. Metaphorically or otherwise. I had to break loose and it was only a matter of time.

When I got home, quite late, Laura rushed out of our apartment and took a few quick steps to meet me.

"Is something wrong?" I asked, frightened by the look on her face.

"I couldn't figure out where you were and no one seemed to know."

She put her arms around me, hugging me and whispering in my ear.

"You scared me."

"I went to see a therapist."

"How was it?"

"Awful," I said, pushing past her and into the apartment.

"Tell me about it," she said, sitting next to me where I had flopped exhausted onto the couch.

"She was terrible. She asked me ridiculous questions and dismissed my attraction to women as a phase."

"You told her?"

"Of course I told her. That was the whole point."

"I thought you were getting help for your depression."

"Why does everybody think I'm depressed?"

She got up, saying, "Let me get you a drink."

"Thanks. And I'm not depressed. I'm confused, but I'm not depressed."

She brought me a glass of white wine and put a bowl of nuts on the coffee table.

"What can I do to help?"

I took a sip and stared into the wineglass.

"I think…maybe we should…I don't know, maybe I should move out for a while."

Laura sat motionless beside me. I was shocked the words had come out. They seemed to hang in the air, like cloud cover.

"I really don't like that idea," she said.

"Tell me why you don't like it."

She sipped from her glass and said quietly, "You know why."

"I know you might worry that we couldn't come up with a credible explanation for why I moved out."

"That's not it," she almost shouted. "I love you. You know that."

I shook my head.

"Maybe you do, but your love has me very confused. This right here is my problem. Not work. This situation. You. Me. Us."

She jumped up, pacing the floor.

"I haven't been giving you enough attention lately. I'm sorry for that. Work has just been so crazy. Let's have a date night this weekend."

I felt my resolve waning, my decision, which I had been on the cusp of declaring, fading into reconsideration.

"If I say yes, that doesn't mean I've changed my mind."

"I don't think you've actually made up your mind yet."

Her powers of persuasion, her desire to win, to come out on top, were all ganging up on me. She wanted to drag me into her room for make-up sex, but I wouldn't let her touch me. I had to create some space. Had to stop letting her make all of the decisions.

CHAPTER FORTY-FIVE

My phone rang a day or two later and I was surprised to hear Laura's voice.

"Hey," she said. "I know you're probably headed back to SF soon, but there's one more thing you should squeeze in before you go."

"Yeah, I am pretty much wrapped up here at this point. But what do you have in mind?"

"There's a triathlon in Galveston this weekend. I think you'd do well."

"An ocean swim?"

"You can do it!"

"I don't know."

"Oh, c'mon. I already signed us up and got us rooms. Separate rooms. It's really a fun one."

I thought for a moment or two and decided it would be a nice way to say goodbye to Laura, which I needed to do.

"Okay, I'm in."

"I'll pick you up Friday morning."

* * *

"Where are you off to?" Mom asked as I carried my gear out the door to Laura's car.

"Galveston. We're doing a triathlon."

"Who's doing what?"

"It's a race. Three different sports. Swimming, biking, running."

"Sounds crazy to me."

"Well, you're not wrong."

"Is that Laura out there?"

"Yes," I said, always amazed when she could pull a random memory trick. "She talked me into this."

"Well, be careful. You get a little addled when you're around her."

"You think?"

She winked at me.

"Don't forget your marriage vows."

"I thought you didn't believe in gay marriage."

"Stop arguing with me."

She gave me a kiss goodbye and waved to Laura.

"Your mom is something else," Laura said when I recounted what just happened.

"Uncanny, actually."

We smiled at each other, but the atmosphere was one of constraint, as though we both knew we needed to stop playing this cat-and-mouse game. I had to finish things with Mary, or not, and we both knew it.

* * *

The motel-style beach accommodations at Galveston were mediocre, but I didn't care. It was nice to be on the ocean. The salt air. The smell of marine life. After I dropped my gear in the room, I went for a walk alone, along the edge of the ocean beach, feeling the slosh of cool water on my bare feet.

The Galveston event was a standard one, following Olympic guidelines: a 1.5K swim, a 40K bike ride, and a 6.2K run. I was nervous, but also confident. Throughout all the ups and downs of the last few months, one thing had remained constant: my training. So I was ready.

Laura and I had a pasta dinner at a nearby Italian spot and headed to our rooms for an early night. We had to be at the swim start at seven a.m. I had just closed my eyes when my phone lit up with Mary's number.

"What the fuck do you think you're doing?"

She screamed so loud I had to hold the phone away from my ear.

"Mom told me! You're off with her again. I can't believe you!"

"Stop, wait a minute."

"I hate you!"

"Mary, stop! You're wrong. Nothing is going on here. I'm doing this event. That's it."

"I don't believe you! You haven't been the same ever since you left for Texas."

"Mary, nothing is happening right now. I was just lying down to get—"

"Listen to me, Jen. I've had it. This is it. I'm done with you making me look like a fool."

"Mary—"

She was gone. I was exhausted and couldn't think about her or us or anything else.

I woke at five thirty feeling strangely energized and determined to kick some ass in every leg of the race. Laura was in a higher-ranked group on every leg, so I only saw her from a distance at the swim start and not at all after that. I poured every ounce of my determination into each swim stroke, each pedal stroke, each heel strike.

When I reached the finish line, I knew I had done well, but I was absolutely astounded to learn that I had finished third overall in my cohort. I was screaming with exhilaration when Laura found me and hugged me tight, both of us crying. She had finished second in her group.

After celebrating for a while on the beach with the other competitors, we went back to the motel, cleaned up, and got on the road. We were both anxious to get back. I told her about Mary's call.

"I'm sorry," she said. "That sucks."

"Yeah. Mom's memory has an interesting way of sharpening around certain topics."

"You don't blame her?"

"No, of course not. But it was just unfortunate."

We rode in silence for a while and then Laura said she had something she needed to say to me.

"Steve and I have a court date to finalize our divorce," she said. "It's a short wait here in Texas, as you may remember."

I hadn't really believed she'd go through with it.

"Oh," I said, "so final. And you're sure?"

"Absolutely. I feel relieved. Happy, actually."

"Good. That's good."

"Jen, I, well, I need you to know that I am in love with you. I know that now for sure. And, I know it's not convenient. I know you're not free. But I want you to know that, if that changes, it's my deepest desire, the deepest desire I've ever had, to be in a public and committed relationship with you."

I didn't know what to say. I was stunned.

"I don't expect you to say anything right now. And I realize that you might think I'm the most self-obsessed asshole you've ever known."

She paused as if waiting for me to argue. When I said nothing, she continued, "I couldn't let you leave not knowing that I've changed. That I'm not ashamed to be who I am. Not anymore."

I couldn't seem to process my emotions. I closed my eyes and before long, I was asleep. I woke up when we arrived at my mother's house.

"Jen, please say something."

"I have to think. I have to figure some things out. Believe me, I appreciate what a big step this is for you. I'm proud of you. And, of course, I'm flattered that you think you want to be with me."

"I do want to be with you. It's one of the few things I'm sure about."

"Okay. Give me some time."

"Go to dinner with me before you go home to San Francisco. I want to say a proper goodbye."

I agreed and gathered my things from her car.

"You kicked ass today, by the way. I'm proud of you."

I smiled and walked stiffly up the driveway.

Mom looked at me sheepishly over her coffee the next morning. She still had some of her wits.

"Did you win your race?"

"I did the best I've ever done. I came in third out of a group of seventy-five."

"Good for you, honey!"

"Thanks, Mom."

"I told Mary about it."

"I know."

"Was that wrong?"

I sipped my coffee. I couldn't get mad at her.

"No. Not wrong. But she took it wrong."

"You need to go home. Try to make things right with her. She's such a lovely girl. You owe it to yourself. Whatever happens, happens. But know that you did everything you could."

"Okay, Mom."

On my last night in Dallas, Laura took me to the French Room at the Adolphus Hotel for a chef's tasting menu. The historic hotel in downtown Dallas was one of my favorites. She chose the wine pairing as well. Sitting in a private corner, far from any other patrons, we started with champagne.

"Here's to the future, whatever it may hold," she said.

By the third course we had started talking about our trip to Europe more than twenty years before, reliving the highs and lows.

"What were you thinking? About us, I mean. While we were on that trip," I said. "I always wondered."

She drew a deep breath and seemed to float into the past for a moment.

"I remember being so happy and so terrified at the same time. I think I imagined that we could somehow have a life parallel to the conventional one. It seemed plausible at the time. In the haze of what I thought of as an impossible love."

By the fifth course and the third wine pairing I was feeling quite dreamy.

"Thank you for this. It's very sweet. And a perfect way to say goodbye for a while."

"No, don't say that."

She reached her hand across the table for mine. I tried to resist, but she insisted.

"I don't want to lose you again."

"But I have to—"

"I know. You have to see it through with her. But I know you love me. I've seen it these past few months. It's you and I who are meant to be together."

I shook my head and drew my hand back.

"I don't want to mislead you. I haven't made that decision."

"You're honest. And you're loyal. I admire that. It makes me love you that much more. But once you've gone back and done what you need to do, I believe you'll be ready for us."

I sipped another glass of wine and let her words sink in.

"And when you're ready, I want you to have this."

She pulled out a ring box and opened it, displaying a beautiful sapphire and diamond engagement ring.

"Oh my god, Laura. It's beautiful, but no, this is too much."

"I want to marry you."

I shook my head, almost laughing at how ludicrous this was. "You know I can't say yes to you. Not now."

"I want you to know how serious I am. How committed I am. Don't have any doubts about it. Promise me?"

The wine was getting to my head. And Laura's full-court press had me spinning. "I hear you. And I believe you," I said finally. "But right now, I need to go home."

She put me in an Uber back to my mom's, kissing me on the forehead as she buckled me in.

CHAPTER FORTY-SIX

Our date that weekend was a bust. In typical Laura fashion, she wanted to wipe the slate clean and push ahead without actually dealing with our issues.

"I can't take this much longer," I said. "I'm not sure you get that. We're going to have to split up if you can't find a way to come out."

She glared at me, looked away angrily. Then she softened.

"I'm sorry. I just can't. I know I'm losing you, but I can't. I think I would literally die if I had to admit who I am. What I am."

Tears came fast and furious as she buried her face in her napkin. I didn't know how to help her. Her self-hatred was exhausting me and I knew I was dangerously close to not caring anymore.

"I guess you don't care," she said, looking up into my stone-faced expression.

I looked down, but I couldn't think of anything useful to say. We rode home in silence and ended the night angrily, each decamping to our separate rooms.

The next day, we had plans to join Alex and one of the Happy Hour Chicks, Kara, for a game of tennis doubles at the courts at Kara's apartment complex. Laura was still sulking as we walked to the nearby community. I kept my thoughts to myself.

"Who is this girl again?" she asked as we got close to the courts.

"She's one of Dee's friends. I met her at Chick Happy Hour and she's part of my doubles group. She's good—played in high school, I think."

"She's a lesbian then?"

"I think that's the idea."

Alex pulled up just as we reached the parking near the courts.

"Nice togs!" I said as she stepped out of the car in full tennis regalia.

"Wow," Laura said. "I never knew."

"Alex went to college on a tennis scholarship," I said.

"Oh my gosh, well, I know who my partner is today."

"That's Laura," I said. "Nothing more important than winning."

"Hey, sister, that's a little sharp," Alex said, giving me a stern look.

"Over here!" Kara called from inside the court fence. "Let's get started."

Fortunately for me, Kara was as good as Alex, and Laura and I were at about the same level. We had to play a tiebreaker to end the match, which went to Alex and Laura on an ace from Alex.

"That was a great match," Kara said as we all shook hands.

"Nice of you to let us win the first time out," Alex said to Kara. "I could tell you were holding back."

"Not at all! But I do demand a rematch."

As we stood around a cooler, downing sports drinks, Kara suddenly came up with an unfortunate memory, directed at Laura.

"Hey, I've been racking my brain as to where I remember you from. You were at the Triangle Ball. In Washington. Right?"

From the look on Laura's face, you would have thought she'd been accused of grand larceny.

"Uh, yes, were you there?"

"I wish! But no, I recognize you from *The Washington Post* photo they have in the bar at Sue Ellen's."

I could see Laura using every ounce of restraint she could summon in order not to melt down right then and there.

"Jen," she said, "I really need to get going."

"I thought we'd go grab something to eat," I said, glancing at Alex.

"Go ahead," she said, gathering her things and mumbling apologies.

"What's up with her?" Alex asked. "Is something going on between you two?"

"It's nothing," I lied. "You know, she's a workaholic. She gets the shakes when she's been away from the office too long."

As I approached our apartment door after lunch with Alex and Kara, I braced myself. My hand was actually shaking as I put the key in the door.

"What the fuck?" she yelled at me as I closed the door behind me. "Did you know about that article? The photo? Have you seen it?"

"Well, uh, I didn't know it was hanging in the bar."

"But you knew it existed?"

"Laura, I didn't see the point of telling you about it when there was nothing we could do at that point."

"What if people find out?"

She threw herself onto the couch, wailing and thrashing, melting down like I'd never seen her do.

"This will ruin me!"

"Laura, please. Stop. It's old news by now. I'll ask the bar to take it down. Don't worry."

"I can't believe I was so stupid. To let myself be photographed."

She pounded her fist into the couch cushions.

"Listen, I think it's…this is probably as good a time as any for me to move out. I can stay with Alex."

"How will that look?"

"No one has to know."

"Jen," she said, sitting up and straightening her hair. "It's not that I want you to go. I don't want to break up. But I don't know how to fix this right now. I know you're not happy. I'm miserable. Maybe it would help, a little, if we had some time apart."

"I just think it can't hurt."

"But you can't see anyone else," she said with a pout, pulling me over for a hug.

* * *

Two months later, our firm had its annual retreat at a resort property in Austin. Laura and I hadn't seen each other privately in those months, but had spoken on the phone a few times. We were both hurting, confused, and seemingly incapable of finding a way forward. The separation had made me realize that I was deeply in love with her, which had the effect of truly depressing me.

The first day of the retreat offered a choice of tennis or golf. We had decided ahead of time to choose the opposite sport so as not to end up in a cart or on a court together. She was to play golf, I was to play tennis. There were drinks, a lot of them, all day no matter where you were. And some other party favors for those who were more adventurous. And it was a sunny, warm, dehydrating day. At four, we were all back in our rooms, showering and dressing for the evening. I decided on a short black skirt and a V-necked white blouse, heels of course.

At cocktail hour, almost everyone was quite under the influence. We all gathered by the pool for some "official business" to satisfy the tax write-off. As we got seated for dinner, I caught sight of Laura across the room. She wore a tight-fitting, lavender silk dress that revealed every muscle and curve. My heart pounded and I felt nauseated. I gulped down a glass of water as fast as I could, but I really thought I might vomit. I got up and rushed to the bathroom.

After splashing cold water on my face, I started to calm down. I reapplied makeup and stood staring at myself in the mirror, trying to determine whether I looked normal enough to go back out there. Just then, I saw her come in, her reflection looking at mine, her lips slightly parted. I turned to face her.

Neither of us said anything. She moved toward me slowly at first, then quickly, placing her hands behind my head and pulling my face to hers, my lips to hers. She thrust her tongue into my mouth and moved her hands down my body. She lifted my skirt, her hand pulling at my underwear and finding my throbbing clit.

"Oh, god," I said. "I've missed you. Oh, god."

"I've never wanted you so much," she whispered hotly into my ear.

She penetrated me and I screamed into the nape of her neck, silencing my cry as much as possible. I unfastened her dress and pulled the braless bodice down to expose her breasts. I buried my face there, breathing her in, kissing and licking, pulling her against me with my hands on her ass.

I had just dropped to my knees and pressed my face against the triangle between her legs when a drunken Jonathan Barbour stumbled into the women's room.

"What the—hey, let me in there."

He stumbled in our direction and I froze, my head suddenly lighter than air, my vision fading as I fought the need to pass out. Laura took only a split second to make her decision. She pushed me away, screaming and grasping at her clothes, calling me names I cannot bear to remember. A performance worthy of an Oscar. Jonathan tried to calm her down, looking at me as though I were a rapist.

I tripped and cut my knee on a cracked tile as I sought an escape route, blood running down my leg as I ran blindly toward my hotel room, crying uncontrollably. Tears of humiliation, of anger, of disbelief. I threw my things into my suitcase and called for my car to be brought around. I knew I shouldn't be driving, but I couldn't stay here.

I drove recklessly and erratically back home to Dallas, the 180-mile trip done in less than three hours. I had driven to the apartment I had shared with Laura, feeling what I needed to do rather than thinking it. I took plastic trash bags and stuffed them full of the rest of the clothes and shoes I had left there, scouring the place for anything that belonged to me, doing my best to erase any evidence of myself. I drove to Alex's and collapsed into her arms.

"Oh, honey, I'm so sorry," she said. "I'm just so sorry."

I woke up the next morning with a fully formed plan. I wrote my resignation letter and put it in the mail to Brian. I would send for my office things. I called Christine in San Francisco and asked if I could crash on her couch for a while. And would she introduce me around Silicon Valley? I packed my most treasured belongings and took them to UPS, bound for California. The rest I donated to a woman's shelter—lots of suits and high heels. I wouldn't need those in California. I went to say goodbye to my parents.

"I don't understand, honey," Mom said. "What happened? You were doing so well."

"I need a change. I'll explain it some day. Please just have faith in me."

"Always," Dad said with a knowing smile. "You've always landed on your feet."

"Thanks, Dad."

I hugged them both and Dad walked me to my cab.

"Jen, does this have something to do with your, your girlfriend?"

"I can never get anything past you, can I?"

"Whatever happened, don't let it sour you on people. Don't even let it sour you on her. You're young. People change."

I kissed my dad goodbye while thinking there was no way in hell I would ever see or speak to Laura Peters again.

CHAPTER FORTY-SEVEN

Was it my sense of loyalty that made me consider going back to San Francisco? Some old-fashioned notion of being true to marital vows? My mother's admonition? An unwillingness to admit failure? Or did I truly hope to mend the broken relationship with the woman I had built my life around for the past twenty years? To start over. To begin again.

Whatever the reason, and perhaps it was all of these, I did go back. I didn't tell her I was coming, just in case I changed my mind before arriving on our doorstep. I was deeply conflicted.

Laura had made it clear what she wanted. Very clear. I believed her when she claimed she had thought about me, about us, every day since the day I left Dallas in 1997. She'd had that long to make up her mind.

Choosing Laura meant destroying my family. Or at least changing it so dramatically that none of us would recognize it. So I had to go back, try again, to see if Mary and I could make it work. More than work. Thrive. We deserved to be happy, both of us.

Even as I tried to relax in my seat on the flight to SFO, I found my mind buzzing so loudly I couldn't settle down. I tried the breathing exercises again. This time it helped. A little. The flight attendant handed me the glass of wine I requested the minute I sat down. That helped. The whirring of the airplane's engines soothed my rattled nerves a bit. The smell of chocolate chip cookies heating up in the first-class cabin kitchen roused my appetite and I couldn't refuse one when the attendant wafted it under my nose.

The woman next to me cuddled under her blanket and a sleeping mask covered her eyes. She breathed easily, obviously asleep. I, on the other hand, only managed to fall asleep with less than an hour left to go, then woke with the jolt of the wheels hitting the runway.

For a moment, I couldn't remember where I was or why. Then it flooded back, pulling me under like a giant wave crashing. I couldn't remember a time when I had felt less certain about what lay ahead. No end game stood out. No goal appeared. No conclusion felt imminent.

The car service I had ordered met me at baggage claim, though there was nothing to retrieve as I had packed everything I needed into a carry-on. I followed my driver to the parking garage and slid into the back of his Lincoln Town Car, my heart thumping harder as I anticipated my reunion with Mary.

More breathing exercises.

I asked the driver to stop at a wine shop a few blocks from our place so I could show up with something she and I had always enjoyed sharing for a special occasion. The proprietor of the shop welcomed me with a hug, noting that she had seen Mary earlier in the day and she had picked up the same wine, so maybe she had already planned to surprise me. I didn't bother to tell her that my visit was itself a surprise.

The wine conundrum bothered me. Why would Mary have purchased our special wine for no particular reason? She would not have, which meant she had a reason. Maybe Mom had tipped her off about my visit. It certainly was possible. Mom's memory was unpredictable and she was at times a meddler, for reasons that always made sense from her point of view. I decided to go with that as the explanation.

I asked my driver to let me out a block away from home and to wait for me just in case there was a change of plan. He popped the trunk and I took my carry-on out, more confident than not that my surprise would be met with enthusiasm.

My heart rate increased a bit as I trekked up our forty-five-degree angled street. When I reached our driveway, I looked up to the large bay window overlooking the street. What I saw brought me to my knees. Mary and the young intern, entwined in an embrace that suggested coupledom. Not just passion. Not just a tryst. A relationship.

I retreated to the shadows so I could continue to observe them without being noticed.

They were talking excitedly, as if engaged in a very important planning exercise. From my angle, I could see Mary's face clearly. She had a look of delight and intensity that I could not remember being directed at me in a very long time.

It hit me. I had lost her, not recently, but months or even years before. She had gradually stopped complaining about my workaholic tendencies and had been pulling away without my even noticing. I felt suddenly ashamed. Stupid. Boorish. She deserved her happiness and I could see she was beginning to find it. Tears spilled down my cheeks, but not because of what I had just seen and now knew. But for the loss of the unrealized potential of us. It had been there and somehow I had let it slip away.

I walked back down my street, turned the corner and waved at my driver. He put my case back in the trunk and opened the door for me.

"Back to SFO," I said, sliding back in.

I was shaking. The chill in the outside air now seemed to permeate my skin. I couldn't get warm. I asked the driver to turn up the heat.

"You okay?" he asked, looking at me in the rearview mirror.

"Yeah. Just feeling like an idiot."

"I been there. Maybe you shoulda brung flowers."

"Maybe I should have done a lot of things."

I took one of the bottles of water from the door pocket and tried to quench my thirst. My body seemed to be dehydrating in response to my shock. I opened a second bottle and glanced at my watch. It was just before five p.m. I had no idea what I would do next. I just knew I couldn't stay in San Francisco.

"What airline?" the driver asked as we entered the airport grounds.

"It doesn't matter," I said. "I don't actually have a ticket yet. You can let me out anywhere."

Once inside the terminal, I stood in front of the departure screen, mindlessly looking at flights as they rippled through the schedule. A flight to Vegas caught my eye.

"Why not," I said out loud to no one.

I bought the ticket and settled in at a bar near the gate. I had two hours to kill. I ordered tequila and soda and stared at the television, feigning interest in a football game.

"Is this seat taken?"

My heart skipped at the sound of that familiar voice. I turned to greet her.

"Wow," I said. "You have one helluva sense of timing."

She sat down and told the bartender she would have what I was having.

"How did you know?" I asked.

She smiled guiltily.

"You're going to be annoyed. Or worse."

"Tell me anyway."

She sipped her drink at first, then tipped it back and drained it.

"When I knew you were coming back here, I will admit, I was hoping against hope. Well, maybe I was also sticking pins into a voodoo doll. No, I'm joking. But I was rooting against it. Against her, the two of you."

I nodded. "I get that. It's not annoying."

"That's not the annoying part."

She gestured to the bartender for another round.

"I used one of my PIs."

I slammed my glass onto the bar.

"What?"

"Just to follow you. Just today."

I could feel my cheeks burning red, but I was confused. Not sure what to be angry about.

"I wanted to know. If I should come. If I should chase you. Or not. I'm sorry."

"How did you get here? It was only a couple of hours ago that I was standing in front of my house."

"I came last night. I chartered a private jet at the last minute. Just in case."

She stared at her drink, avoiding my eyes.

"Oh my god, girl. You are so fucking aggressive."

She bowed her head as I stared at her. Sitting there next to me. In the San Francisco Airport. I started to laugh. I laughed so hard I couldn't stay seated on the barstool. She started to laugh with me, and soon enough we were huddled together, our heads touching, our hands clutching.

"Is the jet still here?"

"What do you think?"

She kissed me. Hard. And hungrily. And when she brought that ring out again, applause erupted in the bar as someone ordered shots all around. I couldn't stop smiling as we strode, arm in arm, down the hall toward the private jet lounge and into the future. And I couldn't stop thinking about Dad, winking at me from the distant past.

Bella Books, Inc.

Women. Books. Even Better Together.

P.O. Box 10543

Tallahassee, FL 32302

Phone: (800) 729-4992

www.BellaBooks.com

More Titles from Bella Books

Mabel and Everything After – Hannah Safren

978-1-64247-390-2 | 274 pgs | paperback: $17.95 | eBook: $9.99

A law student and a wannabe brewery owner find that the path to a fairy tale happily-ever-after is often the long and scenic route.

To Be With You – TJ O'Shea

978-1-64247-419-0 | 348 pgs | paperback: $19.95 | eBook: $9.99

Sometimes the choice is between loving safely or loving bravely.

I Dare You to Love Me – Lori G. Matthews

978-1-64247-389-6 | 292 pgs | paperback: $18.95 | eBook: $9.99

An enemy-to-lovers romance about daring to follow your heart, even when it's the hardest thing to do.

The Lady Adventurers Club - Karen Frost

978-1-64247-414-5 | 300 pgs | paperback: $18.95 | eBook: $9.99

Four women. One undiscovered Egyptian tomb. One (maybe) angry Egyptian goddess. What could possibly go wrong?

Golden Hour - Kat Jackson

978-1-64247-397-1 | 250 pgs | paperback: $17.95 | eBook: $9.99

Life would be so much easier if Lina were afraid of something basic—like spiders—instead of something significant. Something like real, true, healthy love.

Schuss – E. J. Noyes

978-1-64247-430-5 | 276 pgs | paperback: $17.95 | eBook: $9.99

They're best friends who both want something more, but what if admitting it ruins the best friendship either of them have had?